C000296146

Amadou Sidibe

THE DESPAIR OF LIFE

Limited Special Edition. No. 24 of 25 Paperbacks

Amadou Sidibe is a Guinean-British born in Conakry, Republic of Guinea, the youngest of seven children of the best parents on Earth. Amadou Sidibe's love of writing began several years ago as an educated young adult back in his native-Guinea. Ever since then, he has relied on writing to voice his opinion in a creative way that spread out fresh hope to those in despair. To chase after his dreams, Amadou moved to the United Kingdom and settled in London.

He studied Global Business Management at the School of Management at the University of Central Lancashire (UCLan) in Preston.

After his graduation, Amadou Sidibe worked at the Research Office as an Information Support Officer for Funding, Development, and Support at the University of Central Lancashire. He also worked as a Medical Administrator and Data Analyst at IntraHealth/NHS. Despite spending a few years in a rewarding career, he still held on to his love of writing books.

Amadou Sidibe

THE DESPAIR OF LIFE

AUSTIN MACAULEY PUBLISHERS™

LONDON · CAMBRIDGE · NEW YORK · SHARJAH

A CIP catalogue record for this title is available from the British Library.

ISBN 9781788486620 (Paperback)
ISBN 9781528955843 (ePub e-book)

www.austinmacauley.com

First Published (2019)
Austin Macauley Publishers Ltd
25 Canada Square
Canary Wharf
London
E14 5LQ

Dedication

This book is dedicated in memory of my late parents.

I could never have done this without your faith, support and encouragement.

Oh, Mother Hadja Fatoumata! Oh, Father Thierno Elhadj Boubacar!

It's impossible to thank you adequately for everything you have done since my day one, from loving me unconditionally, to raising me in a stable and respectable household, where you instilled traditional and cultural values and taught me to celebrate and embrace life.

Oh, dear parents!

Oh, Mother! Oh, Father!

I owe you endless gratitude and appreciation for being there when I needed you by telling me what I'm capable of achieving in my life. You gave me the support that I needed to pursue my studies and to build a dream to chase after. You made me believe that I have the talent to reach my goals, no matter what.

Oh, dear parents!

Oh, Mother! Oh, Father!

After a long day of hard work, you spent a countless hour each night on teaching me how to do my homework when I struggled to do it on my own, in which I became an independent learner. You shared the way to overcome difficulties and find solutions. You taught me to take courage and look at the fear directly in the face until it backs down. That kept me challenged and motivated to do my best.

Oh, dear parents!

Oh, Mother! Oh, Father!

You guided me through a difficult situation when I found myself lost in a void, not knowing what to do. You directed me and by your example, showed me how to bring my life back on track from despair to hope. You made me realise that I am worth everything that is combined with dignity and integrity in this world. I never had an outstanding experience until you told me that I am a humble and generous son.

Oh, dear parents!

Oh, Mother! Oh, Father!

You got involved when I was wrong and yelled at me when I refused to recognise it. You made me realise that I can change my character by developing good habits so that I could be better understood by people who live around me and be judged by the contents of my knowledge, and not my background.

Oh, dear parents!

Oh, Mother! Oh, Father!

You were so strict with your rules which some people called very harsh. You got to know my friends and choose wisely who to play with, where to go, and even introduced me to specific games to play, and for that, if I had missed one point at that time, it could have led me on the wrong path today. You stood firm when I brought a ton of arguments to let me do what I please in life, and that could have led me to things that would jeopardise my future.

Oh, dear parents!

Oh, Mother! Oh, Father!

You understood when I attempted some new challenges. You supported me on the journey even if it didn't seem realistic and recognised, that's what I wanted to do, and listened to me. You taught me to surround myself with good, respectful and responsible people throughout my everyday life.

Oh, dear parents!

Oh, mother! Oh, Father!

You showed me that nothing comes as easy as we could imagine in life, only hard work could really pay off, and that doesn't matter who you are. You left home early and came back late at night to support our every living need and want. You gave me the strength to stand up for myself and expect nothing less than the very best from people.

Oh, dear parents!

Oh, Mother! Oh, Father!

I owe you endless gratitude for showing me the true love that I deserve. Without both of you, I wouldn't be the person I am today. You may not be amongst us to celebrate my achievements and the releasing of this book, but your memories will never be erased.

I love you and miss you in every step of my life. Years may come and go, but your legacy will never be forgotten.

May your souls rest in Peace.

Ameen!

Your proud son.

Acknowledgements

First and foremost, I would like to thank my friends, to the Guineans and to many other African communities living in the UK, and organisations who shared my passion and enthusiasm and encouraged me to start writing this book and finally to get it published.

A huge thank you to Enock K. Kimbowa, Mahamoud Abidine Ade, Celestin Wa Mbiola Musakai, Saikou Diallo, Mohamed Conde, Tahirou Diallo, Nadège Ndjoli, Rasna Jagdev for reading my manuscript and making constructive comments and their constant support through my research. I also thank the publishing team at Austin Macauley Publishers Ltd for showing confidence in my work and for their help in bringing my story to the broad audience.

Finally, I would like to express my endless gratitude to my family, cousins and parents for their continuing love and support they have shown me throughout my life. My father Thierno Elhadj Boubacar and my mother Hadja Fatoumata, thank you both for giving me the strength to reach for the stars and pursuing my dreams. I must also acknowledge and thank my brothers Mamadou Sidibe, Ousmane Barry, Alpha Oumar Barry, Oumar Sidibe, Ibrahima Wann; my sisters Djenaba Sidibe, Mariama Sidibe, Kade Sidibe, Aïcha Bah and their families; my lovely wife, Hadiatou Barry and my beautiful children, Mohamed, Fatoumata, Hassatou, and Raihanatou Sidibe. They all kept me going, and this book would not have been possible without them.

Table of Contents

Abdul's Family Roots

It was the hottest day of the dry season; the sun's rays gleamed and blinded the villagers. The bodies of the men who ploughed the fields to prepare for the planting season, flooded with a significant drop of blackish sweat that dyed the colour of their working clothes, their skins were wet as if they just pulled themselves from a swimming pool. Drinking enough water was almost a full-time occupation so that their bodies could be hydrated to maintain the balance. Children who were playing in the street sought refuge under the shadows of the giant Baobab trees, breathed with strength and haste, while the women who remained in the village hastened to do their domestic work. Not far from these women, a man had arrived in the village from the savannah region in the north of the country, tired and thirsty. He was a fetish priest, a hunter, armed with an old rusty shotgun and a machete, and he was scary looking. His bushy eyebrows and wide nose gave him a very stern look. His long hair braided with cowrie shells, and the abandoned beard made him look even more horrible. He did not speak to the natives; all eyes turned on him as he walked through to the centre of the village, and people roared with laughter. He went to seek refuge with the customary village chief.

As he approached the chief's compound, the drumbeat to inform every man and woman that a stranger had arrived to invade their land, so that they could get ready to face the intruder. The customary chief had just started a conversation with the village elders who gathered to discuss the impact of the dry season. The first rains were late, and when it came, it lasted only a short duration. Afterwards, the blazing sun returned, fiercer than it had ever been before, and burned all the green grass that had appeared with the rains, and that prevented the grazing animals from feeding. While explaining the situation, they heard the voice of the town-messenger named Maladho, piercing the air and the beat of his drum saying. 'We have an unexpected visitor in our town, be prepared,' he beat the drum again. The council of elders and the chief wondered what it was all about. Then Maladho informed the chief, and at the end of it, he beat the drum, and this was the message he pronounced. 'All warriors of the village are asked to gather at the chief's compound before dusk.' People tried to figure out the nature of the emergency - who was this stranger? Where did he come from? And why was he here? Before sunset, the compound was full of men and women; some came from the neighbouring villages who heard the message.

All were talking in low voices. At last, the customary chief stood up and thanked the crowd for coming. Then there was perfect silence. The chief designated Maladho, who was a powerful orator and was always chosen to speak on different occasions, such as this one. He stood up and adjusted his long boubou, which passed under his arms and lifted it above his shoulders. He thanked the chief and then thanked everyone for responding to the message. And then suddenly, like he was possessed with excitement, he pointed his finger to the unknown stranger to come forward and explain himself to the chief and the crowd the reason for his presence in their peaceful village.

The stranger stood before the chief and began to narrate his story. 'My name is Donso Soba, from the clan of hunters. We were celebrating our annual traditional ceremony. The whole village turned out, men, women, elders, and children. They stood around and formed a huge circle, leaving the centre free for the griots and dancers. The elders sat on their stools already reserved for them at the front, and all others, including the young men and women, stood at the back, raising a song and clapping their hands. In the middle, the griots stood up and went around singing each hunter's praise as we came before them in the circle. The music and the dancing began; soon, all hunters joined the dance floor and followed the move rhythmically of Dundunba music, the dance of strong men. The drums beat and flute blown; women and men clapped their hands in glee. We, the hunters, leapt up and down in elation. The brandishing and the firing of guns in the air increased. The air was filled with dust and the smell of gunpowder. In the middle of firing came a cry of agony and shouts of horror. A sudden silence took over the crowd. Among the people stood up in the circle, a young woman lay in a pool of blood; no one knew how she had been shot in the head and who did it.

'I, Donso Soba, was the last hunter to fire my gun. I was therefore accused of accidentally killing a young woman. I was arrested and jailed, then released later because of lack of evidence. When the family of the young woman heard I was about to be released from jail, they took the matter into their hands and stormed my compound. They demolished my walls, set fire to my house, and destroyed all my belongings, threatening me with death.

'I was informed about the situation before the day of my release. The only option left for me was to flee from the village, for my own safety, and seek refuge in a village where I could feel safe and free. That was many years ago, maybe five or ten years,' said Donso Soba.

The crowd whispered together with compassion and sadness. Suddenly, everybody in the crowd spoke at the top of their voice. The village chief stood up, and the order was immediately restored, and the silence swallowed the noise. He sat down and conversed a few words with the village messenger. The council of elders listened silently to the end and said. 'We have heard your story, and we need a moment on our own to decide if we could allow you to stay or to expel you from our land.'

The council of elders then went away to consult together in the chief's house. They were silent for a while. Then the drum started to beat again. The elders came back from their consultation. They thanked the crowd for their patience. The village chief began to speak, and all the while he spoke, everyone was silent. 'We have heard your story and have now reached a decision to let you stay as long as you wish,' said the chief.

The latter granted him hospitality as the custom required when a foreigner arrives desperately in need and seeking refuge in your land; you should accept to protect and shelter the refugee as long as he does not cause harm to others.

Donso Soba was nicknamed Alpha Bhõnoh, because he ate eagerly, and ate almost anything he could get without ever getting satiated.

A plot of land on which to build a house and two plots of land to cultivate during the upcoming planting season were given to him at the exit of the village. He constructed a hut made with brown clay bricks, the colour of the earth. It had small windows and a closed fitting door. It stood at the top of the hill at the western end of the village with a splendid view so he could see the daily activities of the villagers. At the opposite end of the compound, Alpha Bhõnoh built a shrine where he installed the wooden symbols of his personal gods. He worshipped them day and night and made sacrifices with animal blood. He lived there alone, before converting to Islam and got married to the younger sister of the customary chief named Hadiatu. He followed and practised the Muslim religion daily before his wife, and the villagers testified it before the council of elders.

Alpha Bhõnoh and Hadiatu had a son, whom they named Boubacar. This child was raised like a prince, but the union of the two parents did not last long, Alpha Bhõnoh died in the long run from a short illness, leaving behind his wife and his only son. When Boubacar reached the age of eighteen, he began trading and became one of the largest importers and exporters of goods in the village. Boubacar's prosperity was noticeable in his household. He had a large courtyard enclosed by a thick wall of white bricks and a gate made of iron. His four-bedroom-house stood immediately in the centre, surrounded by three huts to accommodate guests.

A dignified and respectful man, he married three women of different ethnicities, and they all lived under the same roof. His determination to succeed, his courage to face challenges, and his destiny earned him the honour of being chosen as the indisputable leader of the village. His first two wives died successively after a short period of illness and left children behind them. The third wife, Fatima, had not been lucky earlier to have children, but after several attempts, she finally conceived a baby boy. She was Abdul's mother in childbirth. Being her first delivery, she was assisted by her mother, who served as the midwife and some neighbourhood matrons who brought their assistance to the operation. As the custom required, no man had the right to participate except the husband in some cases. At the presence of his mother-in-law, Boubacar tried hard not to attend the childbirth. The delivery took place in one of the huts which had been prepared for this occasion. The process of delivering Abdul was long and painful; there was no medication to lower the pain. The anti-inflammatory drug and the anaesthesia were rarely found in the village. Her mother and the matrons felt Fatima's screams and occasionally knocked them off with her head and twisted her arm gently.

Fatima encountered enormous difficulties and sorrows, and her mother saw her in this unbearable state without help. The only remedy was to offer her hot boiled Kenkelibah leaves mixed with honey and lemon to drink. She comforted her with hope and encouraged her to push hard while she received in return, punches from her daughter.

'Push hard! Push hard!' shouted her mother.

A scream of joy came from the delivery room, and cries of a new-born that announced the birth of baby Abdul in this world filled with happiness, pain, and sorrow. Boubacar's mother-in-law came out from the chamber transformed into the maternity ward her face dripping with blackish sweat. She headed to her son-in-law, who waited impatiently in anxiety under the shade of a mango tree planted in the middle of the courtyard next to the family house and brought him the good news. Boubacar's warm tears flowed from his eyes, and a sudden joy overlooked him. Then he stood up and thanked the Almighty God for giving him another son. Shortly after that, the news quickly spread all over the villages like a handful of powder blown by the wind. His mother-in-law returned into the delivery room and started to bath the new-born with lukewarm water.

She made baby Abdul drink some water and fresh cow's milk, then she covered the new-born with a towel, traditionally made with pure cotton, and handed him over to his mother for breastfeeding. The new-born and his mother remained in the house for seven days, during which the child should not see the daylight, nor be shaved, nor be called by any name. After the mother-in-law and the matrons had left, Boubacar went to join his wife and the new-born to spend the night together. They waited for the celebration day that would begin early in the morning and will continue for the next seven days and will end after the naming ceremony.

At dawn, the last brightness of the moon that filtered through the foliage gradually gave way to the daylight. The sun rose slowly to the centre of the sky with dazzling beauty, and the humid, yellowish-brown sandy alleyway covered by the fallen dried leaves, began to reflect the heat that lay underneath into space. A cold and dry harmattan wind from the north of Africa blew down gently, causing a movement of oscillation between branches of every tree. The birds chirruped and flew perpetually from one branch to another. All else was silent, no human activities around. Then from the centre of the village came the faint beating of folk melody mixed with musical instruments; Djembe, Kora, Balafon, Flute, Shekeret, and Kalimba each played the dance of Dundunba, Tumbucesse, Yankady and Makuru representing the cultural heritage of the country. The sound rose and faded with the wind. It was the beginning of the birthday celebration.

The whole village gathered at Boubacar's courtyard to congratulate him and brought their help in this challenging but happy task of preparing the ceremonial celebration. Every man, whose arms were strong, was tasked to decorate the courtyard, the place where the ceremony and dance would take place. They then painted the wall all around in white, the colour of peace. Some women swept and scrubbed inside and outside of the house floor, fetched water from the well and filled up a gigantic pot left under the shade of a tree in the middle of the courtyard. Others were busy doing the make-up and plaited Fatima's hair coiled at the back of her head. The griots walked around and sang to praise Boubacar and the new-born. The seven days passed quickly, and the ceremony was now only a few days away.

The following day, Boubacar went to consult the clairvoyant to find out the destiny of his son, as he did in the past for all of his other children. The clairvoyant was called Barkidji, and many people came far and near to consult about what the future held for them or when misfortune dogged their steps. He was the trustee of the elders in the village. Many years ago, when Fatima was newly married, Boubacar had gone to consult the clairvoyant Barkidji for his wife's infertility, he predicted that Fatima would conceive a boy very soon after all these years of her struggle. He then informed Boubacar that for the pregnancy to happen, he must sacrifice a goat and some kola-nuts. So, he trusted every single word coming from Barkidji. The clairvoyant Barkidji said to him: 'Before sunrise, go to the hill, bring your son with you and pray to God for giving you another son, a miracle will soon happen.'

At dawn, before the cockcrow, Boubacar came out of his house, holding in his arms his son, Abdul. The baby's head was covered with a kind of white hat, and the rest of his body was also covered from the neck down to the toes with a fabric blanket made of white cotton, very light and soft. He walked up to the hill that overhung the village. He knelt, laid the child on the ground and raised his hands above upward, looking at the sky, and began to murmur in a low voice. Suddenly, he shouted in a loud voice. 'Hoy! Hoy! Hoy! He was born, my son, the youngest, and my successor.' He straightened up and walked back to the village. Down the slope of the hill, he met with the medicine-men who made many incantations followed by benedictions and predicted the future of the baby by following the norms of ancestral custom and then let him continue his way. He stood there, remaining speechless for a while. Suddenly, a cloud appeared above his head that covered the sky partially and followed him slowly as he moved. This cloud resembled a thick solid mass of darkened shadow, and the sun seemed hidden behind it. Boubacar looked around this magnificent event and wondered if it was going to rain partially at such an unbelievable time in the middle of the dry season. While he stood under the cloud with this unfamiliar sight thinking about what will happen next, then he heard an echoing voice coming from the darkened cloud. A strange and sudden fear descended on him as he stood gazing in the direction of the sound.

'This child has been chosen and will be named Abdul! Yes, Abdul! The guardian of our custom, upon him, rests the destiny of this village. I order you to go at the edge of the river called Djan Djan, which is almost non-existent, a river that has never been visited by a human without being authorised by the great Djinn spirit which holds the ancestral forces. This river took its source at the top of the mountain and flowed down to move steadily and continuously in the stream,' the voice said.

'Who are you?' asked Boubacar.

'Oh, human being with limited knowledge, you still do not know who I am,' the voice replied.

'No, I do not know you!' said Boubacar.

'I am beyond the knowledge, the past, the present, and the future. I am the Djinn spirit that watches over the village. Now do what I said!'

'What can I do to get to this unknown place?' he asked.

'Oh, human beings, you are so ignorant! You'll go straight ahead to the north and follow the market road right behind the community prison. You'll find a shiny wall, pale blue, and transparent ocean-like colour similar to the reflected mirror glass. A door will be in the middle, push and enter, and then you will find yourself at the river,' the voice said and kept a moment of silence before it continued its instructions.

'At dawn before the cockcrow, you will go to the edge of the river. Once you've arrived, you will find at the threshold of the mountain, a big aquamarine stone adorned with a unique decoration of its kind. Do not be afraid, because you will encounter enormous difficulties on the way, such as roaring, grunts of ferocious beasts and growls of the wild animals which shall torment your head, and these voices will stun your ears. Continue straight ahead, do not divert your way, or turn your back - follow your path. If you run because of fear, you will become crazy, and you will be locked away for many years to come, and if you close your eyes, you will be blinded for the rest of your life, because those voices are there to welcome you,' the voice from the cloud said.

'Once you get to the point indicated just behind this ornate sparkling aquamarine stone, you will find a calabash containing liquids, and protected by amulets richly and curiously encircled with white bird feathers and cowries. You will then take one handful of sand that surrounds the sparkling stone and pour it into the calabash but beware to avoid that the water coming from the top of the mountain touches your body. This mysterious liquid contained in that calabash will remove any evil spell and protect your child. Remember, before his bedtime, to never fail to wash his body with the liquid, as this will make him invulnerable to the evil spells - yes, to the evil spells!'

Another moment of silence, then the advice continued.

'After you have done all your tasks, you will remain at the same place until the river, the mountain, the stone, and all else that surrounds you disappear. At that moment, you'll find yourself in a familiar place and not far from your home. But beware, you'll stay all day long without eating or drinking,' the voice concluded. Then the solid darkened mass in the sky broke up in a tiny bubble of a shining diamond. Soon, it disappeared as if nothing had happened; it was a huge unexpected event, bearing the full power of both darkness and beauty. Boubacar nodded his head slowly and headed to the village.

The next day, as soon the first cock had crowed, Boubacar went to the indicated place, and carried out all the instructions given to him by the voice he had heard under the darkened cloud. The calabash which contained this mysterious liquid, according to belief, should protect the child from an evil spell that could cause harm. The invocation of the Djinn spirit, which often appeared to some people in the village, was very serene. Then in the evening, he brought the calabash safely and deposited it in a safe place inside the house, out of sight, especially that of his wife. The same night before baby Abdul went to bed, as usual, Boubacar washed his body with the liquid while pronouncing incantations in a low voice, and the baby slept peacefully in his cradle.

The day of the naming ceremony approached, and Boubacar mobilised his family and neighbourhood to begin the festivities.

The enjoyment that had reigned in the village for the last seven days, during which a grand traditional celebration that was organised, had come to an end. Boubacar sent one of his relatives to the market to buy cow meat and fish in which the variety of meals would be prepared. A fat sheep was purchased, which would be slaughtered for the sacrifice during the naming ceremony. There was no shortage of willing helpers. The tasks were shared with neighbours who brought their help to make the event a success. These tasks were divided amongst the groups, depending on their cultures and regions of origin, as well as on their cooking skills: The neighbours who originally came from the coastal areas took care of cooking jollof rice with fish; the helpers who came from the Fouta Djallon, Boubacar's own family, were engaged in preparing the sweetest foods such as couscous made with fonio and a delicious okra sauce, and couscous made with maize corn and natural fat yoghurt called (latchiri eh khossan) in Fulani language; the remainders of the helpers who originated from both the North of the wooded savannah and the forest regions of the country were in charge of grilling plantains, tubers such as yam - sweet potatoes with palm oil and maize corn porridge.

The instructions and orders were implemented in such a way that no one felt neglected in the crowd. Boubacar's courtyard was busy and crowded in a way that could only be compared to an anthill. Cooking tripods were set up on every available space by putting together three blocks of stones and making a fire in their midst using firewood. Heavy cooking pots went up and down the tripods, helped by few strong men, and the cooked foods were put in different plates and bowls and kept in a safe place, waiting to be distributed to the various guests. Shortly after that, the in-laws and the guests began to arrive. They brought with them gifts consisting of sheep, chickens, cattle, goats. The most meaningful gift was a white bird with a black patch encircled on the neck that was brought to Boubacar's attention, but he did not see the donor to express his gratitude. He asked himself. 'Who could this unknown person be?' Suddenly, he remembered the voice he had heard under the cloud. He soliloquised in a low voice and then shouted. 'Praised be to God! Praised be to God!'

All relatives and friends were present, some having come from nearly half a day's journey away were seated in a big circle on the chairs and benches made of bamboo. The griots went around singing each man's praise as they came before them and would not stop praising until they got money from them.

Boubacar and Fatima emerged from the house and went around the crowd, shaking hands with all of the guests to thank them for coming. It was clear from the way the crowd sat that the baby was about to receive his name. Boubacar and the village elder who lead the prayers in the mosque called Imam, went to consult together with Fatima in their private room. As the parents already knew the baby's name, now it was the time to tell the Imam that the baby will be named Abdul. Boubacar wrote Abdul's name on a paper and handed it to him to pronounce it publicly.

Fatima's mother emerged from the house with a calabash, leaving behind two other older women preparing to shave baby Abdul's head before the announcement of his name by the Imam. She fetched water and went back to the house, then dampened baby Abdul's hair with the water and started to remove his hair painlessly with a sharpened razor blade. The Imam went to join the curious crowd who waited with impatience to know the name of the baby. He then stood up in the midst of the massive circle of guests, facing the elders, and took out from his pocket the written piece of paper given to him by Boubacar. He glanced at it, then at the crowd, awaiting authorisation. When all cleared, he read a few words from the Qur'an. At the same time, the sheep were slaughtered, and the baby's name was pronounced in his loud voice:

'Abdul! Abdul! Abdul!'

Then the Imam offered a prayer and said. 'In the name of Allah, the compassionate, the merciful. We have named this child Abdul today. May he zealously learn the faith of Allah as he grows up. Throughout his life, may nothing separate him from that faith. May he be charitable in all his doings and be just and true towards his fellowmen. Amen!'

The griots of the village rose and went to Boubacar and Fatima, singing and praising as they stood before them until Boubacar gave them money, then went around singing each man's praise and continued asking for money in return. At the guest huts, there was another group of griots led by Baba Galley. Due to his reputation and his loyalty, Baba Galley never went to any ceremonies but that of the dignitaries with his famous comic voice; nevertheless, he was a veritable singer. As usual, in naming ceremonies, there should be a namesake, but for this case, the namesake did not exist for this child, because the given name (Abdul) was chosen, therefore, the griots could not get the opportunity to earn enough money through the namesake.

The sheep meat was divided in two. One part had stayed at Boubacar's and shared with his neighbours, and the other side had been given to his in-laws who had also participated in this communion. Soon after everyone had received their share of meat, Baba Galley and his group of griots stood before the guests, who were waiting to be served, and began to sing for the foods to be served and eaten. He sang, in a harmonious tone:

'Come quickly! Come quickly! There's a salad! There's jollof rice! There's a couscous! Come and eat them! Come and eat them.'

His group stood behind him in tune with the song and replied by whispering in a hushed voice, *'Eat, I'm not eating! Eat, I'm not eating! Eat, I'm not eating.'*

'Everybody now knows the baby's name. His name is Abdul, the son of Boubacar, the village chief.' They continued dancing through the cheering crowd.

The song spread through the crowd until everyone was clapping their hands, singing and laughing in a vibrant atmosphere. This call for food to be eaten animated the ceremony. Soon after they had finished singing, Boubacar's children and those who came to help them with the cooking began to bring out the food, and all griots present whistled in surprise. Bowls of water with which to wash their hands were set before the guests. No matter how heavily they ate, there was always a large quantity of food leftover at the end of the ceremony. When all was laid out, Boubacar rose and thanked everyone for their patience. The order was given, foods and drinks were distributed to all the guests, and everyone got satiated and enjoyed the delicious meals. It was during this naming ceremony called 'Dénnabõ' a Mandingo expression which means to take the new-born out after a resting time, generally seven days that Abdul's mother resumed her freedom and Abdul received his name. The ceremony ended peacefully and with the utmost respect given to the village chief, Boubacar.

Five years of happiness in the family, after Abdul was born, he was raised like a little prince and looked after by his siblings but also by the rest of the community. He was the hope of his father and mother, but that hope did not last long as his mother passed away.

A dark and saddened night, only God knew what had happened in the house. The night was impenetrably dark. Such darkness always held a vague terror for the villagers; no one was allowed to walk after midnight for fear of evil spirits unless absolutely necessary, but the risk to be killed was higher. Boubacar went to check all rooms to make sure his children were in their beds. He re-joined his room and blew out the oil lamp and stretched himself on his bed. Suddenly, he heard a noise from one of the rooms in the house; he knew there was something sinister about that noise. He stood up and went to check in every single room in his house to make sure that the entire family were still in their beds and sleeping safely. When he went back to sleep, he heard a cry from Abdul, which pierced the quiet night air and awakened the whole neighbourhood.

Boubacar woke up and lit his oil lamp to see what had happened. He walked over to the bed where Fatima and Abdul were sleeping and took Abdul to his room to calm him down. He sang for him till Abdul slept, he laid him in his bed; then went back to Fatima. He found her laid inert in the same position facing the wall; he jumped up in fright and tried to figure out if she was dead or alive. A cold shiver ran down his back, he shook Fatima gently and noticed that his wife was not breathing at all. Her eyes widely opened, and thick white saliva poured out from her mouth - he quickly tried to resuscitate her. After several unsuccessful attempts, he realised that his wife had fallen asleep for eternity, leaving behind her five-year-old child. The first cock had not crow yet, and the whole village was still deeply darkened when Boubacar took his gun and shot three times in the air – a sound that devastatingly shattered the silence of the night. The villagers listened anxiously and peered curiously through their house windows in the direction of the gunshot. The sound gave a clear message that a family member from the council of elders was dead.

At dawn, the darkness had slowly begun to give way to the rising sun. Soon after the Fajr prayer, all villagers left the mosque and headed to Boubacar's house to offer their condolences and brought their support to the family. In the morning, Boubacar's courtyard was full of crowds - the women and children wailed endlessly with sorrow, and even men could not hold back their tears. They rolled on the ground in all sorts of contortions and gesticulations; they wept incessantly and ran into every corner of the courtyard; moreover, they lamented, more others joined them on the ground. The burial was scheduled in the afternoon at two o'clock, which would be after the midday prayer called Dhuhr. Fatima was raised on bamboo stretchers and carried away by four strong men.

Boubacar stood up in front of a long procession and sauntered slowly down the road towards the cemetery for her final resting place. As they passed, the crowd lined the street to give their farewell to the deceased by waving their hand with sorrow.

After his wife's death, Boubacar was expected to get remarried to another woman as soon as possible according to their tradition but decided to focus on raising his children with a religious upbringing, especially Abdul, the youngest of the family.

At the age of seven, Abdul's initiation began with circumcision. He was admitted to the society of the wise elders of the village, where he learned the customs and the religion. He attended his first primary school in the nearby village of Kimbelly, the homeland of his late mother, Fatima, whom he had almost no memory of except what his father had told him. This young man was gifted with extraordinary intelligence and lived his life between the schools, the Madrassah and home. He did not have enough time to play with his friends, he gave himself to learn new things, and his father taught him certain secrets of village life. As he grew older, his father revealed to him some secrets, such as the voice heard under the darkened cloud and the origin of the choice of his name.

At the age of fourteen, Abdul completed his primary school studies and the Madrassah; now he wanted to leave his native village to pursue his secondary school in the capital city Conakry.

Previously, Abdul's father had categorically objected that he leaves the village for his studies, because Abdul meant everything to him, even though he had twelve children of whom Abdul was the youngest of the family. He did not pay them much attention, as all his hopes and thoughts were on Abdul because, for him, this child would bring a fortune. Boubacar went to consult his clairvoyant, Barkidji, to find out what the future held for Abdul and his intention to pursue his secondary school studies in the capital, Conakry. The clairvoyant Barkidji said to him. 'Your son, Abdul, will have a bright future if he follows our custom. Let him prepare for that bright future, he will finish his studies and travel abroad, but later will come back and die here.' After these consultations, he agreed that Abdul could leave under one condition and that he had to stay with his maternal uncle, Bobo.

Over time, the village chief decided to remarry for the fourth time after the death of Fatima, with one of the most beautiful and intelligent maidens of her generation. Her ambitions to succeed, her determination and her courage attracted her to most men in the village. She was called Amina, the daughter of an influential, wealthy businessman and politician named Osman, who had never struggled and had never sought financial assistance or solicited an audience at the level of government officials. He was very arrogant and proud.

Boubacar was the village chief and head of a large family; he governed not only the entire village but also controlled the taxes which, moreover, were the foundation of social development of his village. Trade and farming were the focal points of all activities, so he was better positioned to ask for Amina's hand to her father.

Considering the opportunity he had over other candidates, Boubacar contacted his loyal companion and tireless friend, Maoudho Saliou, the renowned emissary and the powerful orator of the village, and spoke to him about his desire to marry Amina. They both agreed to begin the first steps. To cover the deal of the negotiations, Boubacar went early to the market to be the first customer so that he could choose the ten best Kola nuts. He entrusted the task to Maoudho Saliou to go with them to Amina's parents and asked if she was engaged or intended to any family member such as her cousins.

Before the sunset, Maoudho Saliou took his way to pass on the message to the future in-law's family. As emissary and regulator of wedding ceremonies, he knew that by going at that time, he would find the whole family at home. Upon his arrival at the in-laws of Boubacar, he discovered that the entire family was gathered around a dining table waiting to be served, except Amina's father, who had just arrived from work and deposited his work bag at the backdoor. He was ready to join the rest of his family for dinner.

'Salaam Alaykum!' Maoudho Saliou greeted.

'Alaykum Salaam!' replied the father.

'What news has you bring to me so late at my home?' asked the father.

'Oh, I am the bearer of good news for you and to the whole family,' he said with a smile.

He waited for permission to sit down so that he could convey the message with respect and presents the Kola nuts as the tradition demanded. When authorised, Maoudho Saliou sat down and transmitted the message. The future father-in-law accepted the Kola nuts and reassured him that Amina was neither engaged nor proposed to a third person, (cousins and others). In return, the in-laws told him that Boubacar was welcome to the family, which meant that the door was opened for him to begin the negotiations.

'Wonu Seneh! Wonu Seneh! (Welcome! Welcome!)' said Amina's father in Sussu language.

'Well, I almost lost words to express my gratitude to you, but let me give you my blessing, and thank you for accepting Boubacar's marriage proposal to your daughter,' replied Maoudho Saliou.

Maoudho Saliou was well known in his role as a facilitator in wedding ceremonies and also by the two families as one of the noblest mediators in the region. So, Amina's father entrusted him to facilitate the communication between him and his in-laws, Boubacar.

Upon his return to Boubacar's home, Maoudho Saliou found a good meal cooked with couscous and a flavoured peanut sauce kept for him to soothe his breath. After satisfying his appetite, he transmitted the good news from the in-laws, Boubacar stood up happily and went into his room. On his return, he gave Maoudho Saliou an envelope containing a lump sum of money. Surprised with the gesture, Maoudho Saliou did not long delay to take his leave in haste but forgot behind him his rosary and his scarf, which he used to cover his neck. Moved by the good news, Boubacar contacted his family and the rest of his community to inform them of the situation in which he was involved, and his desire to marry a new woman. A delegation was formed, including himself, to go and greet the family of his future wife so that he could obtain their consent and blessings.

At first, the greetings began at Amina's aunties, then at the uncles. As in most traditional families, there would always be someone who would oppose the union regardless of the positive or the negative situation that the family faced. Yaya was one of Amina's uncles who had categorically opposed that Boubacar married his niece Amina because he was very concerned for her safety and thought that:

There is the age gap that differentiated them and the fear that she will be the next victim, after a series of deaths recorded at Boubacar's home, whose three of his wives mysteriously died to unknown causes when they were all young. Perhaps, something with sinister forces and power of darkness was hidden behind their death, but nobody could see or even allude to it.

To defend his decision, Yaya went to meet Maoudho Saliou to get more information about Boubacar's private life, so that he could find tangible evidence against his refusal to let his niece marry the 'would-be' groom Boubacar. Upon his arrival at the emissary, Yaya presented a Kola nut to Maoudho Saliou. He broke it in the middle and threw one part in his mouth and chewed.

'Thank you, and welcome to my house, which is also yours! How can I help?' asked Maoudho Saliou.

'I have come to pay you respects and also to ask you a favour. But let us have a seat, then I can explain,' replied Yaya. Maoudho Saliou brought two goatskins, one for him and one for Yaya. They sat, and Yaya asked him to know everything about Boubacar against a substantial lump sum of money and a traditionally well-embroidered robe. After a brief conversation, Maoudho Saliou reassured him that he would provide all the information he would like to hear.

'You came to the right place. I share your concerns, but it would be necessary to come back early tomorrow morning and bring the promise with you. Then, I shall tell everything you need to know about Boubacar's private life,' he reassured him.

Satisfied with the conversations, he rushed to go back home and prepared for the promises held for the next day. Maoudho Saliou was very poor; his only way to have money was through ceremonies and conveyed messages on behalf of the elders of the village. And he needed money to feed his family. A sudden idea crossed his mind to swindle both Yaya and Boubacar in the hope of gaining money and goods, but with precaution.

He knew that by defaming Boubacar, he would lose the confidence of his friend and that of Amina's father (who also held too much on this marriage for the sake of his political career ambition). By choosing to say nothing to Yaya, Amina's uncle, he would not get the promises kept from this one. The best way for Maoudho Saliou to win over the confidence of his friend, Boubacar, was to show him how important he was in dealing with this unbearable situation and that without him, he would never get married to Amina. He must inform him of the conspiracy formulated against him by Yaya, who was a crucial member of his in-law's family. So, all these corrupt behaviours in a position of trust were orchestrated to deceive both without their knowledge that they were being betrayed by their trusted man to earn money without providing the slightest effort.

Soon after Yaya had left Maoudho Saliou's house, he got up and went slowly to glance at the window to ensure that Yaya had gone and was far away from his compound. Then, he jumped through the small window from his hut to reach the other end of the alley; then crawled on his belly behind some shrubs so that no one could see him.

When he arrived at Boubacar's courtyard, he straightened up as if nothing had happened and headed straight towards the veranda of the house and knocked at his door.

Tuc! Tuc! 'Salaam Alaykum!' Saluted Maoudho Saliou.

'Wa Alaykum Salaam!' Answered Boubacar.

'What a surprise to see you at my home so early! Is there a problem I can solve for you?' Asked Boubacar.

'Oh, my friend! Your friendship is dearer than anything to me, never in this world, regardless of the nature of the problem, a plot or whatever fomented against you that I'm aware of and stay without telling you,' he said, sighed and then continued.

'The reason for my visit is straightforward and short. I had received a visit to my house - I reserved to tell you the name of the person, who wanted to know everything about you so that he could prevent you from having what you hold too much in your heart,' said Maoudho Saliou.

'May I know the name of the conspirator?' Asked Boubacar.

Maoudho Saliou nodded his head; he moved his right hand over his head and stroked his white beard, then fixed his eyes on the lips of his interlocutor while waiting for an offer from him.

'Oh, I see, if you can tell the name of my enemy, I will give you a lump sum of money and a fat cow!' Promised Boubacar.

'I accept this offer. Tomorrow early in the morning comes to my house; you will find the person I am talking about; I mean the culprit. But before we close the deal, I'd like you to give me the promises held now before I leave your place,' insisted Maoudho Saliou to which Boubacar agreed.

As agreed, early in the morning, Boubacar went to Maoudho Saliou's house to feed his curiosity, and to his surprise, found the uncle of his future wife. Yaya was quietly seated on a wooden chair, traditionally made of varnished bamboo, and smartly dressed in a white robe with a velvet hat on his head. Yaya raised his head then saw Boubacar coming through the half-opened door. Suddenly, he panicked but tried to keep his coolness behind his scarf that he held in his hand. Disappointed, a cold shiver ran down his body as he saw Boubacar entering the hut. Yaya's hands were no longer responding to his command; he trembled as if he had seen a lion ready to devour him in one bite.

'Salaam Alaykum!' saluted Boubacar.

Maoudho Saliou rushed to open the door. Soon after, Boubacar was shocked to see the person who wanted to spoil his chance to get married to Amina. He stood quietly at the front of the door and refused to exchange a handshake with Yaya. Having no choice, the uncle of his future wife immediately stood up and went to greet him, then went back to re-join his seat. Boubacar was astonished to the extent that he no longer wants to know more than what he saw, he apologised and then said to them,

'I was on my way to the town and decided to say hello to you, I shall come back later,' said Boubacar, then he slammed the door behind him as he left.

Knowing the person who wanted to know everything about him, Boubacar waited until the evening and went back to see Maoudho Saliou and learnt more about the content of their conversation. He found out that Maoudho Saliou did not know much about him, and had told Yaya, a good and prosperous life story of him.

Yaya did not get what he wanted to hear, and soon he returned home, he abandoned his quest and tried to resolve the situation amicably with Boubacar so that the conspiracy was not known or heard by a third person in the shame of being disclosed. Yaya, who found himself opposed to this union, felt betrayed by Maoudho Saliou; he eventually agreed to participate in the marriage for fear of being excluded from all future activities of his family.

After both families gave their consent and their blessings, Boubacar went to consult the clairvoyant Barkidji to choose the beneficial day for his wedding and fixed the date for the wedding celebration.

The wedding day approached, Boubacar's courtyard was stormed by men and women, and each brought their support the way they could. Maoudho Saliou, as Boubacar's best man, ran all sides, up and down, and valued himself in front of the guests. He tried to mobilise all the necessary resources, livestock, and clothes for the bride-wealth and a lump sum of money to be distributed to individual members of the in-law's family and to the griots who came to praise them. It was a costly ceremony. Boubacar's courtyard was busy with helpers. All cooking pots, calabashes, and bowls were thoroughly washed. Temporary cooking tripods were installed in four designated places, and three blocks of stones were brought together to make a fire in their midst using firewood. Some of the women cooked jollof rice, and the others prepared meat and fish sauces. The children fetched water from the well and filled the pails. So much of it was prepared that, no matter how many people from the in-law family to the neighbouring village who attended the wedding ceremony ate, there would always be a large quantity of food leftover at the end of the ceremony so that it will be taken home by some guests.

Early in the afternoon, when the heat of the sun began to soften, Boubacar's family and guests departed to his bride's family home and brought with them all the resources, foods, and bride price. Soon after they arrived, they presented the Kola nuts to Amina's father, who welcomed them to the family. Boubacar and the elders of his village sat with their hosts in the circle. A calabash containing ninety-nine Kola nuts artistically tied in white paper with another bride price attached to it and stood in their midst. Amina, her mother, and her aunties emerged from the opposite room and went around the circle, greeting all the guests. Soon after the presentation, both families left immediately and went to the mosque. The bride price was given and accepted by both families in front of the witnesses; the wedding was sealed and followed by the benedictions. The newly married couple left the mosque to the reception.

When Boubacar and Amina appeared holding hands, a loud cheer rose from the guests. The griots with their musical instruments went from song to song, and all dancers made their way to the newlywed couple and began to dance to its beat. In the evening, the enjoyment was from all activities, meals, dances, and congratulations, which continued to the rhythm of the music. The griots sang and praised each guest as they came before them. The Drums, Balafon, Tambourine, and Flute resonated throughout the village; the party went on until late at night. When the time was far spent, a group of people from both families took Amina away to spend the night with her husband. They sang and walked to its beat all the way to Boubacar's temporary accommodation where they stayed for the night. Early in the morning, the families and friends who slept under the weight of fatigue were awakened by the sound of a gunshot, which meant that Amina had just lost her virginity, which was an honour for her family and tremendous respect for herself. A procession was organised to accompany the new bride to her husband before the guests left for their village.

The Day of Departure

Now a young man at the age of fourteen, the day of Abdul's departure fast approached; the whole village was invited to the feast. It was an occasion to give their blessings to Abdul for his future endeavours. He was considered as a rising star by his father and sunshine by his community because he was the only child who had decided to leave the village to continue his secondary school studies in the capital city. As soon as day broke, the elders began to gather at Boubacar's courtyard and sat in the circle as they arrived. It was clear from the way the elders sat that this was not only for the feast but also a blessing ceremony. After exchanging handshakes with guests, Boubacar went to sit on his hammock and stared at the readers of the Qur'an called 'Karamoko' who had begun to read the Qur'an, which was part of the blessing ceremony. Abdul walked slowly and quietly to his father without distracting the readers. With a smile on his face and told him: 'Dad, I know it bothers you to let me go for my studies, but rest assured that if everything goes well, soon after my studies, I'll come back to rebuild your house and make you the happiest father on earth,' as often said by children to make their parents proud of them.

His father patted his head with his right hand and replied with a smile.

'Son, I know who you are! And I trust you; I will let you go without fear. My blessings and that of your mother will follow you wherever you go in the world and whatever you do.'

His father left him and went to join the guests. A few minutes later, Abdul, overexcited to hear the meaningful blessings from his father, also went to re-join them in turn. After the elders and the Karamoko had finished reading the Qur'an, the Kola nuts were passed around. Boubacar's wife, Amina, and Abdul's siblings began to bring out the food. When all were out, Boubacar rose and spoke before the feast:

'Thank you all for accepting my invitation for the blessing of my son, Abdul, who is about to leave us soon to pursue his studies in the capital city, Conakry.'

Food was served. The oldest of the elders said. 'We all know your generosity, but this feast is bigger than we expected, and we all will take out some of the food to our families. Thank you. May Allah bless your son Abdul and brighten his future. May he succeed in his studies and become president of our country.'

Abdul was overwhelmed with joy. Suddenly his mood changed, his eyes filled with tears, and his thought went back in days when his father told him many stories and secrets in which only a few he could remember. However, Abdul took the opportunity to ask his father about the secrets that he had revealed to him, such as the mystics and the world of Djinns which for so long, had never escaped from his mind. Yet, it exists according to the details and palpable evidence that his father had shown him in the village. His curiosity led him to know a little more about the culture, and especially about the spiritual and supernatural power that his father possessed.

As soon as the Qur'an reading session and the sacrifice were over, Abdul's father left the guests and went to take rest under the mango tree planted right outside the family house not far from the little square room where Abdul used to play.

Sitting quietly on his hammock, Abdul went to his father and began to ask him a lot of very pertinent questions, as do many children. He tackled the most important subjects that he held over his heart, such as the secrets, the Djinns, the voice heard under the darkened cloud and all that ensued afterwards.

That evening, Abdul was determined to know everything before his departure for Conakry. And suddenly, he could not hold his breath for any longer and wanted to know it now; He began to ask: 'Dad, how was my name chosen, and why?'

'You had told me about the Djinns, who are they?'

'Can you clarify whose voice was heard under the cloud?'

'About our customs, what are my sacred totems in everyday life?'

His father slowly raised his head and pointed his eyes straight at him; he seemed hesitant to answer Abdul. He was unsure whether to detail everything to him, as for Boubacar, Abdul was too childish, just fourteen years to know more than what he had previously disclosed to him. After careful thought, he decided to explain everything to him.

'We live in this world with Djinns spirits. These Djinns are intelligent spirits of lower rank than the angels, capable of appearing in human and animal forms and influencing humankind for either good or evil. They see us, but we don't see them, and they are impervious to human weapons. They have the powers and the abilities to transform themselves into almost everything. However, we, as human beings, don't have these powers. Among these spirits, there are good ones who could bring us fortunes, and there are evil ones who could bring us misfortunes,' explained his father.

Abdul was astonished and remained silent; then his father continued:

'These Djinns spirits and the darkened cloud often appear to me at least once a year; it is an inheritance from my father. Initially, I didn't want to associate myself with these kinds of things. Many years ago, your grandfather had explained to me how your great grandfather, who was a warrior, had come to the Djinns of the forest and made a lot of sacrifices so that they could protect him during the war against the foreign aggression when defending our land. It was something that I had never accepted, but being the only child in the family, I inherited it.' He sighed for a moment, then he continued:

'Before you were born, these Djinns came to me in the form of a dream. They told me about your birth, because your mother had tried several times to conceive but in vain, and each attempt resulted in a miscarriage. They are the ones who instructed me to go to the tiger bushes in the hills to find and harvest a shrub species called Kinkelibah leaves, then boil them with lemon and give to your mother to drink so that in seven days, she would conceive a baby boy. And that happened the night after I went to consult the clairvoyant Barkidji, who also predicted that you would be born in the near future. That's how you came into this world,' he told Abdul reluctantly.

He sighed sadly, as the weight of many years of memory borne down upon him. Abdul thought that his father had a heavy heart and was full of emotion. Boubacar's voice interrupted for a while, then he went on. 'That is why, soon after you were born, your name was ordered to me by the voice heard under this immense cloud.' His father kept silent, then he continued:

'As you can see, there is a large amount of respect that has been given to me in this community, while I am no better than the others. Since I was chosen to be the head of this village, so far, I have not had an opponent; the power has been left to me. It's up to me to do whatever I want in this village. My name is everywhere and on every villager's lips. I am the one who rules over all these neighbouring villages of the locality. If this destiny has been possible, it is by the grace of the strength of these spirits called Djinns.' He went on.

'And besides all these, let me provide you with sound advice - the advice of a wise father to his son.'

'Oh, son, listen to me carefully.'

Abdul replied intently. 'Yes, Father, I'm listening.'

'You see, this life.' Boubacar continued. 'The one that we live on today, it's full of circumstances which will bring immense joy and uncontrollable disappointments and would be difficult sometimes for you to face, but everything will come with learning experiences. So, try to find what is necessary for you to learn in life once acquired, you should practise them.

'Oh, son, I believe that you are very intelligent to follow these pieces of advice because they will bring you a lot of benefits in every step in your daily life. Son, I gave you all this information because you're my child, the beloved among my children. I have nothing to hide from you. So, let me tell you the truth: To be successful and prosperous in life, you have to change your bad behaviour and replace it with a good character so that you could develop good habits in your everyday living. And that will lead you to a long-lasting, peaceful, and respectful life. Never get involved in drinking alcohol and use any drugs to please yourself, avoid taking them, these are self-destructive behaviours. You should never commit to an uncharacteristic error such as having sexual intercourse with a woman other than your wife, these are taboo, and you should avoid them at all costs so that one day when I am no longer alive, these divine powers could come to you. You will inherit them as part of your spiritual guide,' said the father, and after a pause, he continued.

'I had met all these behaviours and honoured my commitments, that's why I regularly received these appearances at least once a year and all the benefits that followed, one after the other. But, of course, if you want to inherit one day, which is not far away from now, before my final day, you must have to follow my advice.' Boubacar thought that once his son left for the capital, he would not be able to see him again, as he saw his death coming soon, and Boubacar already knew that he would die in cold blood, it has been revealed to him but not having known exactly the moment: When? How? Where?

Abdul, overwhelmed by the sound advice and information detailed to him, he did not know what to do, because his dad meant everything to him. His father sighed once and kept silent; then an absolute silence reigned all over for a few minutes

Abdul exclaimed in sadness. 'Dad! Dad!'

His father replied calmly. 'Yes, son, I am here,' in a low voice. 'Go now and have a rest, it's already night, you should be preparing your luggage by now,' insisted his father.

Abdul got up and walked over to the family house where his room was located just in the opposite of that of his stepmother, Amina, the wife and beloved of his dad. His stepmother glanced at him, fiercely with her red eyes like the eyes of a lion when about to kill prey its size and lost it. Amina was never fond of Abdul. She stood still and gave him the evil eye as he walked past her. Abdul turned back his head and went to his room. For Amina, the departure of Abdul was to be celebrated because she could do as she pleases to manipulate her husband to reach her objectives, and to boost her father's political career ambitions.

Abdul entered his bedroom and laid down immediately in his bed, his eyes vaguely opened throughout the night. He was sleep-deprived and not in a good mood; the night was long and quiet. With nothing else to do, Abdul turned his back and faced his small rectangular window, which allowed him to have a splendid view of nature.

He dived into deep thought; the sky shone with sparkling stars adorned with the diamond colour of the dark night, beneath the howling of the bat hanging on the branches of the mango tree, rejoicing in its ripe fruits. Abdul tried to close his eyes, but in vain, his body resisted sleep. He was hopeless, and the sadness had become his best friend and was not leaving him alone. Not having known that much of his late mother to embrace him, he fell in the void as he missed her warmth and comfort; there was no one to whom he could share his emotions. He sought to sleep, he closed his eyes and pretended that he was falling asleep, but the image of his father was there in his head. He saw him sitting on his hammock; the memories stunned him in the head. Abdul began to cry silently until he fell asleep with anguish in his heart.

Early in the morning, he was awakened by the sounds of wooden mortar in which a lady called Saran pounded the corn and pestled them to powder to prepare porridge for the early breakfast. Saran was well-known for her early and late cooking by all the villagers. Abdul got up abruptly and threw a glance from his small rectangular window and saw a glowing brightness of the day that erased the stars of the night. The rising sun returned the nature of its true colour; he then went back to his bed again.

He heard a noise at his door. Someone was knocking on it. *Tuc! Tuc! Tuc!* 'The breakfast is ready, son!' shouted the stepmother. Abdul got up abruptly and walked over to the porch where the excellent breakfast was left and went to sit in his usual place next to his father's bamboo chair and waited to be served first as always. His eyes moved curiously at each corner of the table where the variety of dishes were deposited; two bowls containing steaming corn porridge and millet, where he was served when it was still warm. After he had finished eating, he turned to the roasted cassava tubers, which had been cooked under the hot ashes from a traditional wood-burning stove used for cooking; he drank one cup of fresh cow milk. He rested for a while and got up, then returned to his room to pack his suitcase.

On the eve of the night before Abdul's departure, another big party was organised at Boubacar's courtyard. The village elders, the marabouts, the fetish priests, and all those who had time to cross the threshold of the gate were welcome, as no one should be ignored or stopped from coming in and participate on this precious day of celebration. Sharing this great feast was an important moment of meeting with all the community so that their blessings accompany Abdul in the future. After everyone was satiated with the food, they blessed him by shaking his hand and pronounced a few words.

'May God protect you and facilitate your pathway towards your studies! May the luck smile at you! Be blessed! May God guide you in the right direction!'

Others recited the Qur'an adapted to the circumstance. After they had blessed him, one by one, they then resumed their way. Abdul went and sat next to his father on a locally manufactured mat without saying a word; he looked sad and shy. After all the guests had returned home, Abdul went back to his room and remained there until the following day, as the anguish he felt was nearly unbearable, then he fell asleep quietly.

The day of departure had finally arrived, and early in the morning, right after the first cockcrow, his father knocked on his door. Abdul woke up and opened the door.

'Keep this little bag. Everything is inside, never separate yourself with this bag; it's a lucky charm. It was a gift that I inherited from my father,' Boubacar said to Abdul.

'Thank you, Dad, I will keep it safe and take good care of it,' he replied to his father.

'Come and say farewell to your stepmother and then say goodbye to all those who live in the courtyard and to the neighbours,' added the father.

Upon seeing his father holding his baggage in hand, he collapsed into tears. 'Why are you crying, son?' asked Boubacar. Abdul wiped his tears, and his father held his hand and took him to the bus station. Abdul remained silent all along the way. He knew it was time to take his responsibilities in his own hands and face his future. The more they advanced towards the bus station; the more Abdul became discouraged.

'Let's go quickly; we're a bit late. I know how you greatly feel sorry to leave us and me too, I feel the same way, but be a man and arm yourself with courage. You will be all right and will succeed in life, your uncle Bobo will take good care of you!' his father reassured him.

'Don't be afraid of anything; the sacrifices already made for you will never remain without positive results. Do you hear me? Did I make myself understood?' insisted his father.

'Yes, Dad!' answered Abdul.

'All I ask you is to honour me, no more than that!' reiterated his father.

'I kept it in my heart and promise I will make you proud of me,' Abdul replied to his father.

'Very well then, now I am filled with joy. My son be brave, you can go now in peace!' he said to Abdul.

His father hugged him tightly and patted him consolingly on his shoulder and said. 'Go! My boy, go now.' Abdul walked away slowly with his luggage in hand and got into the taxi. He rolled down the car window and gazed at those who came to say goodbye to their travellers. He then turned his head back and stared at his father and waved to him from the car window. Abdul quickly glanced around him for the last goodbye. The car driver started the engine, and it roared to life, and then sped off. The car disappeared, leaving behind a cloud of reddish dust, both suffocating and blinding the travellers stranded at the station and under the watchful eye of his father.

The Big City

Conakry is the capital city of the Republic of Guinea, where all political and economic decisions were made and the most densely populated place in the country. The hectic, noisy sprawl of both Madina market and the taxi station were an absolute madness for those who attempted to get to work or to reach the downtown Kalum city. As usual, the long traffic jam on the Fidel Castro main road had left the vulnerable drivers in the hands of corrupt police officers whose duties were to ease the traffic and maintain safety on the road. But instead, they tried all their means and technical skills to rob them, as a result of staying in the long traffic queue. The passengers on-board, who had their journey affected, also found themselves robbed by the street traders turned thieves. They would come in pairs to the stranded commuters and proposed genuine products at the low price, as they made the offer the second thief used the magic tricks to exchange their products with a fake. Sometimes with nothing in the box but rags and handed to the poor commuters, then disappeared without a trace.

Inside the commercial centre close to the bus station, where almost all the activities were centred, was also overcrowded. There were so many people that if you drop a coin, it will not find a way to fall to the ground.

Abdul found himself for the first time in this busy Madina bus station, crowded with people, and even the largest shopping mall in the square repulsed customers. Street vendors jostling each other, peddlers, carters with their wagons were on both sides carrying merchandises. Abdul felt a bit astray in the crowd but determined to find his uncle, whom he had never known. Under an untimely rain, he took shelter at the shopkeeper's front door so that his Uncle Bobo could easily spot him.

Around half-past noon, beggars all over the place took the passer-by hostage, forcing them to give money. Abdul stood calmly in front of that door; he observed everything that was going on around him. He heard along the Fidel Castro highway, the noise of cars engines that blared in his mind, he only half paid attention to the men and women who followed one after the other under the pouring rain. The traders seemed to care less for themselves, but to cover their goods to preserve and sell them gradually to the first customers who showed up. On the other side of the market, women ran up and down, from left to right, looking for a carter to transport their luggage. He watched other women shipping out their merchandise to different sale places; he observed the symbiosis that existed between peoples who were going quietly to their various activities without any frustration. On the top and under the bridge at Madina market, he observed some people in a hurry looking for any means of transport. A lady named Bintu approached him and asked. 'Are you from here?'

He replied, 'No,' and limited himself there. He saw the woman with curiosity and absolute courage. Then he asked her. 'Are you a saleswoman in this market?'

'Yes!' answered the woman with a strained face. She then began to explain her miserable life as if she had been asked. 'I am a married woman with four children and have no reason to stay at home or sit without doing anything.' She continued to speak. 'We merchants, who have small commodities with which we manage every day to sell, we have to be here to sell our products so that we can feed our family. We cannot afford to stay at home even under heavy rain; we must get out of the house and sell at least something. Personally, I have a family of six; if I don't get out to sell my products, then it's the six heads who would sleep that day with an empty stomach,' she explained.

Gradually the rain became lighter and less frequent. People no longer stayed sheltered but got back to their business. Suddenly, it stopped raining; the sky resumed its blue colour under the appearance of the rainbow with its majestic colours, red, orange, yellow, green, blue, indigo and violet. A sign of relief for Abdul, he thanked the lady Bintu for spending her time with him. The constant horn and the rattling sounds of cars impressed him, the sun had now reached the middle of the sky, and it was sweltering. Some of the travellers took shelter under the hangar used for car parking, and others ran to look for cold water to relieve their throat. Abdul's face drenched with sweat. Under a suspicious glance, he saw a handsome and eloquent gentleman dressed in a navy coloured suit with a white shirt and a red tie coming towards him; he was holding a picture in his hand. It was his Uncle Bobo, without hesitation, his uncle clasped him in his arms, his eyes filled with tears; he took out a handkerchief in his pocket and wiped his tears while smiling. Uncle Bobo said. 'You look exactly like your mother, I do not even need to look at the photo to get the confirmation, and the certainty led me to find you, welcome Abdul!'

Abdul was thrilled to meet his uncle, whom he had never seen or known. He perceived the image of his late mother in his uncle Bobo's face, a similarity with the picture of his mother that his father had kept after her death. Without delay, his Uncle Bobo took his hand to show him a few shops and bought him some clothes. Immediately, he began to familiarise himself with his uncle, who kept telling him funny and comical stories. He then made mockeries and laughed at the vendors whose business was to sell expired products at the place called Avaria Market and the so-called pharmacists who stood proudly behind their counters without any medical qualification. And they could not even read their own names, let alone write a letter, were trying to convince their customers to buy their medical products and provided them with sound advice on how to administer a dose of the medications.

September was the beginning of the school year; Abdul was enrolled at Donka High School. Upon his arrival inside the campus, wearing his brand-new blue and white uniform, almost all eyes turned to him. He then walked towards the school director's office, and from there he was led by the head-teacher into his new classroom. He was happy to meet new people and to make new friends because he had never had this opportunity when he was in the village. Shortly after the start of the classes, all teachers noticed his intelligence, courage, and determination. Being too young and very disciplined with the support of his uncle, made him stronger and brilliant amongst his fellow students. He had not delayed obtaining his baccalaureate certificates and the admission exam to Gamal Abdel Naser University.

His progress was remarkable, and his results were passed on to his father, the village chief. Boubacar was inwardly pleased with his son's achievement, and he knew it was due to his uncle Bobo. He wanted Abdul to grow into an educated man capable of becoming a strong leader and take over his household when he would go to join his mother in heaven. He wanted him to be a prosperous man, get married, and have a lot of children, but he was not surprised at all about his son's development as he knew that his child was not ordinary like the others. Boubacar believed that Abdul is destined to be a great man. Being overwhelmed with the news of Abdul's achievements, Boubacar went to take a rest under the baobab tree. Suddenly, his thought went back in days when he fell in love and got married to Amina, the village beauty and how that led him to forget his beloved son, Abdul, he began to meditate and said: 'Him who loved endlessly his son, Abdul, was manipulated and distracted by his wife, Amina.' He came out of his thought and began to wonder what was amiss as he did not know what to do. The complications of his married life were getting worse; his wife's thirst for power compelled him to get involved in politics.

As being the daughter of an influential, wealthy businessman and politician, Amina wanted at all costs that her husband gets involved in politics, which he did not want to do. Her only objective was to use the popularity and wisdom of her husband to achieve her father's goals and hoped to gain endorsement and protection from the customary chiefs of the neighbouring villages. To attain her ends, she often made inappropriate declarations in favour of the actual government.

She had developed a magnitude of madness, hungered for a sense of self-worth, selfishness, and pushed her husband up to the extreme and gave him an ultimatum to choose between her and Abdul. Boubacar became her prey, and her wicked act of cruelty weakened him.

He realised that he had made a big mistake of marrying Amina. He was overwhelmed with sadness and sorrow, fearing that he would never see his son again and the loss of his loved ones and popularity among the villagers, but it was too late to act as the damage had been done. Therefore, his life was now in danger, and he started to receive threats from both sides, his antagonists had increasingly become stronger than ever before.

To challenge his wife, he decided to do something substantial to make her unhappy. To do so, he chose to join the opposition party and wrote a letter to Abdul, detailing his intentions to do politics as a career as well as the harassment and the threats he faced daily.

The letter arrived early in the morning, and it was handed to his uncle. Shortly after that, Abdul came back from the University, as usual sitting on the dining table, his uncle Bobo came to him holding an envelope with a smile on his face. His kindness made Abdul forgets all his stress; uncle Bobo said. 'Hello, Abdul! How are you?'

Abdul rose his head slowly and looked at his uncle and answered him. 'A hectic day, uncle, but thank God I'm at home!'

His uncle sat beside him on the same table and asked if he wanted to eat. Abdul replied. 'I had eaten in the canteen at the University.'

'Oh, right!' answered his uncle, enthusiastically.

Suddenly, Abdul began to tell him a funny story that had happened during a rally at the campus which was followed by an election; he won it and was appointed as student union president. His uncle nodded his head and said. 'Congratulations, and well done, Abdul! Like father, like son. It's your courage and the determination that had led you to this position, with confidence; you must assume your responsibility by defending it with integrity.' His uncle still held the envelope in his hand; then said. 'I have received a letter from your father this morning!'

To feed his curiosity, he hurried to open it, as he missed his father a lot. He took his time to read it carefully and understood the contents of the letter; he then crumpled it. He lowered his head down, his eyes filled with tears that flowed down his face and said to his uncle in a trembling voice.

'Dad is in danger!'

Sweat trickled down his face. He got up abruptly, holding the crumpled letter in his hand and went out of the house, and slammed the door behind him without saying anything to his uncle.

His uncle Bobo remained silent without saying anything; in turn, a cold sweat flooded his body as Abdul had never behaved in such a way in the past but understood his reaction.

It had been six years since Abdul had left his father in the village and came to live with his uncle in the capital city; he had grown rapidly to become a man like mushrooms in the autumn season and was endowed with tremendous physical and mental strength. So, his Uncle Bobo encouraged him to do more for his future.

Abdul's pride to be among the most intelligent and respected students at his University led him to seduce and flirt with beautiful girls he met along his way. He continued his habits until the day he met the love of his life, a girl called Hadja, standing at the very end of the corridor that separated his classroom to her computer room. The two eyes fixed like magnetic, he then approached this beautiful creature.

'Hello, beauty!' Abdul bowed,

'Hello, sir!' replied Hadja.

He felt entirely in the void when he heard that voice, so soft and so attractive. She looked tanned and fit, her teeth thin and white like ivory, no man could ever look at her without swallowing their saliva. That day was the beginning of their romance. Hadja came from a very large religious family; she respected her customs very much, which consisted of marriage before sex. The same as Abdul, who also came from a privileged family and had received the advice from his father not to have sexual intercourse with a woman before marriage, nor drinking alcohol or use any kind of drugs. All these counsels remained in Abdul's head, they both agreed to abstain until marriage, but this agreement did not stay long before being crumpled up and thrown away and put in the trash. The two lovers continued dating and strengthened their friendship to the extent that only the bed could separate them. Abdul was in his final year of studies at University, and Hadja was in her second year. The two lovers complemented each other, Abdul wanted to be loved, and Hadja wanted help in her studies as well as to have a serious relationship that could lead them to a good future.

A year after they had met, Abdul completed his studies and obtained his master's degree in finance in which he achieved a merit. On the day of graduation, a small farewell gathering was organised by the students. Abdul took the lead and stood up before the students and expressed his gratitude to his family, more precisely to his father and his uncle, who had never ceased to bring him their support during all these years of endurance and anxiety in which he completed his studies with honour. Then he said to his fellow graduates. 'To be able to reach this stage in our life is a great achievement. Therefore, we need to celebrate and enjoy every bit of it.'

At the gathering, his classmates decided to organise a dance party dedicated to all the students who had completed their studies in that year.

The same day in the evening, Abdul boarded a taxi. He went to meet Hadja, who was eagerly waiting for him at a safe public place near the taxi station in Hamdallaye roundabout, which was half-covered by the smoke that came from people who were doing a late open-air barbecue and from the exhaust pipe of poorly maintained cars. She managed to get a seat in front of a shop and faced the road; her eyes were fixed on all passengers who were getting in and off the taxis that shuttled along the main road between Bambeto and Hamdallaye. The rendezvous time had nearly passed, Abdul did not turn up. Hadja nervously glanced at her watch and thought that Abdul might not make it and said to herself. *'There's no point getting agitated.'* She then stood up and walked around, then came back to her place.

A minute later, Abdul got off the taxi. He was holding in his hand a bouquet of burgundy roses and red flowers and strolled towards the indicated place. Surprisingly, he found her very disappointed, he thought there was no chance to talk to her at that time, but it's worth a try. He then said. 'There you are!'

'Good evening, honey, my beautiful rose!' bowed Abdul, a thrill of joy invaded Hadja.

'Oh, thank you, love, for your compliment. I was waiting for you in anxiety,' she answered very calmly as usual.

They embarked on-board the taxi and headed to the nightclub where the party was organised. Each guest came in coupled and cleanly dressed flamboyantly like princes and princesses and went straight-ahead to the counter to buy drinks according to their choice of drink. After being served, they left and sat with the members of their group. Upon their arrival,

Abdul and Hadja went to the counter; they were served soft drinks and then went to join a group of friends where Paul, Abdul's best friend, was seated and drinking his liquor. Paul was originally from the forest region, and as Christian, he saw no obstacle to the consumption of alcohol. The ambience was on the menu, alcoholic beverages, food of all kinds, soft drinks, and the disco club was filled to burst. Only the strongest people could survive the stifling heat, even the ventilation system and air conditioning installed in these sweltering premises could not give enough air to breathe. That night was a special moment for Hadja because she had never been out on her own clubbing at night, let alone participating in such a dancing event, considering the strictness of her parents and the respect for her tradition and religion.

After spending a few hours on the dance floor, both felt tired and thirsty. Abdul went to bring their drink that they had left on the table before joining the dance floor. But, before he arrived at the table, Paul had consumed their drinks mistakenly without realising that those drinks did not belong to him and left his own large cocktail in the same spot. Paul then went to use the toilet. Abdul brought back the glass he found on the table and handed it to Hadja.

'It's too hot in here!' murmured Hadja,

She walked up to him and accepted the glass from Abdul, she then drank one sip and then two sips, and deposited the glass on the table, she resumed drinking and dancing at the same time. Whilst Abdul was concentrated on watching his friends who were breakdancing on the dance floor. She went to make Abdul taste the alcohol, and then both started to drink endlessly.

'Oh! A good taste, it seemed that these drinks were mixed with mint, lemon and Cola-Cola,' said Hadja.

Both carried on drinking steadily and hugged, then kissed; they then smiled lovingly at each other. While both were having fun, a fellow student called George, who was a spoiled son of a minister in the government, and he was well known by all students for his big spending when he went out clubbing. He took the microphone and spoke loudly to everybody to stay calm and that he was going to buy them drinks and ordered the bartender to begin serving his friends. She filled the cups and gave it to everyone according to their order and way they were seated; they continued their habits of drinking, talking, and dancing.

At last, one student emptied his glass and shouted out. 'Can you add more drink, please? My glass is empty!' the others replied. 'We have seen it.' They roared with laughter. The bartender came back and filled his glass, then poured out for others. Paul had finished using the toilet and finally went back downstairs to meet his friends. Unfortunately, he found them so drunk and lurching from table to table. Their speech was slurred as to be almost incomprehensible. He decided to take them to his flat to rest, as he lived alone and the place he lived was not far from the town where the party was held. A few minutes of walking, they arrived at his flat, Paul left them to rest and then went back to continue partying. When left alone in the room, under the influence of alcohol, Abdul sat beside her and kissed her then pushed her gently backward until she laid down on her back, she was shivering with fear, but with pleasure too. He gently unbuttoned her colourful blouse from the back and with steady hands, removed her bra. Using his cold fingers, Abdul caressed her skin and started to kiss her neck gently, and as the kisses progressed, he moved lower towards her breast, and soon, she stopped shaking. His hand went to the straps of her skirt, and he pulled it down over her knees.

'No!' she said.

'Please, Hadja let me do it?' begged Abdul.

'No! Please stop it,' she insisted.

Abdul looked at her and thought. *This might be a good idea.*

She pushed him away and stood up as her pleading was ignored. Still, at the same time she felt guilty as she had already developed an infatuation with Abdul, she gently took off her clothes, they began kissing again, again and again. A sudden thought crossed Abdul's head and rejected Hadja against his body. She fell back on the bed, and then she stood up and threw herself on him again. While kissing, Abdul sank in deep thought *If I slept with Hadja in this condition, what would be the consequence? Would this be abuse or rape? Her parents, would they take me to justice?* He murmured. However, these ideas, which buzzed his head, were diverted by his sexual desire. He let himself be dominated by his stupidity and slept with her clumsily. She had never known a man in her life, and as a result, she lost her virginity painlessly and too quickly. A few minutes later, Abdul got up with a stain of blood on him and realised the severity and the consequences of his act. He rushed to clean all traces of blood and let Hadja sleep.

The sense of guilt made their memories more pleasant, and if they had planned this seduction, then they had been willing but not to say eager and regretted at the end.

Abdul got dressed and sat on the chair while waiting for Paul to arrive so that they would wait till dawn to set off, and that would be safer for Hadja.

He sat down for long and did not sleep at all, he tried not to think about his actions, but the more he tried, the more he thought about it and thought about what he had done was wrong. There was no doubt that he had made a mistake, if Hadja could cover their act without telling her parent, then he would be totally safe, and no one would ever discover their secret or to be accused of rape. When Paul came, he explained to him what had happened, and being a loyal friend and confidant, Paul comforted him and then decided to take the responsibility in his hand and destroyed the pieces of evidence so that they could finally make an end to the matter.

At dawn, it was still dark. Hadja awoke and found these two young men seated on the chairs.

'You were not sleeping?' she asked.

The two friends looked at each other. 'No, we did not feel sleepy at all,' they replied.

She had regained consciousness and remembered what had happened between Abdul and her during the night. She felt uncomfortable, violated, and disappointed. She was clearly in a bad mood and had a face like thunder when she looked at them sitting on the chairs. She was disgusted and began to react by blaming herself for what had happened. Her worries turned to her parents to what they might think about her, she remembered her family value and reflected that to her action, and her thought went back. *Losing her virginity is losing the honour of the family, and Abdul could never marry her again according to her tradition.* She hid her face between her hands and began to cry; then she went back to bed again. A few hours later, after she had a good rest, she decided to go home to face her parents. When she got up from the bed, she was so weak that her legs could hardly carry her but tried her best to walk to the door. She felt the pain between her legs and began to cry incessantly.

In the village, a popular uprising was organised by the opposition party to denounce corruption, injustice, favouritism. It was during this peaceful march that the village chief, Boubacar, who was actively engaged in this movement, was quickly spotted by individuals that supported the government. He immediately became the target of the group, as his opponents saw in him an obstacle for the incoming presidential election. They decided to get rid of him at all costs after he had survived lies, blackmail, and several attempts to destabilise him. They finally used a new strategy which consisted of assassinating him. But to reach that point, they took advantage of a lack of knowledge among the village elders and distributed a dose of falsehoods blended skilfully with calumny to destroy Boubacar's image and tarnished his honour. The village chief was furious after being informed of these conspiracies against him; he went home angry and made a verbal attack on his wife. He had never called his wife by her name, but that day he called her Amina and said. 'The opponent was opposed, and the fight will continue until my last breath!' he stopped there.

Amina could not believe what he was talking about. She laughed and said. 'What on earth are you talking about?'

Boubacar bit his lips as anger welled up within him, he stared and shouted at her again and made her understood that he knew all the plot manipulated by her and her father against him. She denied the accusation and began to cry while claiming her innocence. Boubacar knew she was not speaking the truth and told her that he would lose his temper and beat her up if she continued to deny it.

Amina panicked and began to cry; she knew that her objectives were over, and her goals would never be achieved. A desperate fear enveloped her, she knelt and begged God to come to her rescue, her husband had never shouted at her before, and this action had driven her crazy. She was not aware of all that her husband had changed position and had joined the opposition party; she was still in her naivety. She then began to ask herself a series of questions, *How, why, and when my husband had changed his decision without keeping me informed?* She turned her anger to her father, who had recently disagreed with the village chief about the current political situation in the country but never wondered why her father wanted to kill her husband. She knew what her father was capable of, whereas, in her marriage, it was the interest that bounds her father and her husband. If her husband succeeded in changing his political opinion, then her father would be disappointed with him because her husband had testified to her father endless support and unwavering fidelity.

Boubacar's neighbours heard his wife crying and sent their voices over the courtyard walls to ask what was going on; some by curiosity came over to see for themselves. He tried to explain and emphasised his points to them what his wife had done, but none of them seemed to pay attention as there was not a single evidence to present.

Two weeks had passed since Boubacar argued with his wife and threatened to beat her. Everything seemed to get back to normal; Boubacar invited the council of elders and some farmers for an urgent meeting to discuss the difficulties that the villagers are facing in their daily activities. After the difficulties had been exposed before Boubacar, a young farmer spoke. 'I have come to you for help; perhaps, you already know our actual situation. The first rains were late, and I need to borrow money to feed my family.' Another farmer introduced himself and explained his problems. Most of the farmers were indebted, and they owed every neighbour some money.

After everyone had spoken, Boubacar cleared his throat and said: 'It pleases me that you have come to explain your difficulties. I don't have enough savings. But I can lend you some money to make a fresh start, and you can only repay me after the weather situation has changed.'

In the middle of lending money to those in need came a sudden interruption from a distance that created a panic amongst those present in the meeting. It was a cry of agony from the neighbourhood, every man, including the council of elders, immediately abandoned whatever they were doing and rushed out in the direction of the cry. One of the peasant farmers shouted out. 'We cannot all rush out like that in the middle of the negotiation, leaving us with nothing, but misery.'

'It is true,' said another.

Suddenly all other borrowers shouted at the same time. 'We will like the village chief to stay behind and continue the negotiation; Maoudho Saliou will report the matter back to Boubacar.'

Boubacar stayed behind to continue negotiation, and all the rest went to see what had happened. They found out; a family man had accused his neighbour of having an affair with his wife and set fire to his compound when the suspected man was sleeping in his hut. Luckily, the man survived but lost everything. The bad news was reported to Boubacar, frustrated, he entered in his bedroom and wore his white robe embroidered in multi-coloured silks, and a light blue hat on his head. This hat was made traditionally and ingeniously weaved by a process known to the Fulani craftsmen of Fouta Djallon and enviously garnished by them. He took his Qur'an and held his inseparable walking stick in hand. He then went to the scene of the tragedy. Upon his arrival, he investigated the damage caused and realised that it was enormous; he then addressed the two angry peasants facing him. The family man, who had accused the neighbour, stepped forward and presented his case and said. 'My wife, you see over there, is having an affair with my neighbour for many months. A lot of friends and neighbours can be my witnesses. They saw my wife getting in and out of his hut many times, and when I confronted my wife, she said all stories were false, and people were jealous of her beauty. When I was told on the street that my wife was at her lover's hut, I struggled to keep my composure and left to check my farm, when I came back, she was not at home. I checked every corner and asked my neighbours and even went to knock on her lover's door and made a lot of noises like a pig; no one answered my call. At that point, I was convinced they were doing something behind that door, my only option was to burn down the hut on them, and I did it now my case is finished. Thank you.'

The accused neighbour also stepped forward and said. 'That man is crazy and a liar; he came to my hut months ago and asked me about his wife. I told him my hut is not a police station, and I am not a police officer to ask for a missing person and never to come back again; otherwise, he will meet with my anger, and my reaction will be deadly. I can swear on the Qur'an his wife has never been my lover, I am sick and stayed at home all day, and I had not seen the daylight for the last couple of days until he burnt my entire compound when I was sleeping, and now my case is finished.'

There was a loud murmur of surprise and disagreement from the crowd; Boubacar asked for silence, and order was immediately restored. He asked for witnesses that were present, but none of them had a witness. Then he said. 'I have heard both of you; my duty is not to blame one person and praise another but to find the truth for this attempted murder and to arrest the culprit.' Boubacar and the council of elders went away to consult. They murmured for a long time; then, they came back for the final verdict. Therefore, the family man was found guilty of an attempt to murder his neighbour with premeditation. He was later arrested and sent to prison. When Boubacar was making his way home, he was spotted by a group of individuals who were marching peacefully in mass demonstrations against the government hostility and social injustice. He was called to join the street protest. Happy to do so, he joined the rally and made his voice heard. They sang slogans and shook cardboards on the street. When they were interrupted by security forces who had responded with tear gas that led to an outbreak of violence on the street, shops were attacked and looted by criminals on the loose. The police launched a search to crackdown the group leaders as the authority had prohibited the demonstration, several protesters were arrested, and those involved were subjected to beatings, and others suffered injuries. The local people were ordered to stay home, shops and weekly markets were all closed, traffic hermetically blocked.

Boubacar escaped from being arrested and went to hide in a safe place in the forest; a group of men who saw him running for his life followed his footprint to find him with all their means so that he could be humiliated. They kept searching all surrounding areas and dug a deep hole on the ground to all the footways that led to his home and covered with weak, dead branches and leaves so that he could be trapped on his way out. The sun had set, and dusk settled over the ocean. Sudden darkness fell to the sky, and the sun seemed hidden behind a thick cloud. At that point, they knew it would not take too long to find his hideout. Gradually, the daylight gave way to the darkness, and silence returned to the world. They searched every corner, caves, and trees in silence.

All of a sudden, they started talking; one of the group's members felt tired and asked others to abandon pursuing Boubacar for another day. 'Hold your laziness!' screamed the rest of the group. Their voices echoed through the dark void. 'You are crazy to let him escape after all we had done; we've received money to do our job, which is to discourage him from doing politics, and how can you explain that to the assembly?'

Boubacar heard the echoed voices coming and disappear from the thick darkness. A strange cold shiver ran down his body as he stood to gaze in the direction of the voices and thought that his enemy is not far from his hideout. He hurried to the main footpath that led to his courtyard; he turned left in the opposite of the voices. His eyes were useless in the darkness, but he made his way effortlessly in the middle of the sandy footpath covered with dead leaves and branches. The group of men spotted a strange shape like humans moving towards the village, and then they followed it closely. Boubacar broke into a run, and he immediately stopped, the enemy ran behind him and stopped, their footsteps on the fallen branches and leaves echoed back. At that point, Boubacar knew that they had seen him. He began to run, holding his Qur'an and the walking stick with his hand to defend himself against the enemy. He hit his right foot against a stone and fell, an extreme fear seized him. He stood up and realised the enemy had stopped running behind him, and he thought they had gone towards the exit of the forest and waited for him to come out. He changed his direction and ran to the trapped area. When he reached the place, he tripped up and fell inside the trapped hole. He was captured and subjected to torture and injuries, which led to his death. They dragged the dead body near the crocodile-infested river and left it there so that the body could be eaten and thought they must go before being caught. As they roamed around, they had time to think, what will they say when they got to the assembly? They would not dare to say Boubacar had been killed and eaten by crocodiles; they panicked and ran madly in the forest.

At dawn, Maoudho Saliou's wife and other women were returning from the stream where they had fetched water; then, they saw an unidentifiable dead body laid on the edge of the river infested by crocodiles. They screamed and threw their water pots and fled the scene. They went straight ahead to the village chief

Boubacar's house, he was not there, and let his wife informed him the situation when he's back. They went to Maoudho Saliou's compound and found other village elders were already concerned about Boubacar's whereabouts. The news spread very quickly through the villages like a wildfire blew by the cold, dry wind from the Sahara Desert called 'harmattan' and the stories were distorted as it was passed from one person to another. Some said the dead man in the river was half-eaten by crocodiles and others said his head was missing that's why the body cannot be identified.

A large delegation of elders went to the scene of the tragedy, already invaded by curiosity. Soon the elders arrived, they led the way to the body. Maoudho Saliou was astonished as he last saw Boubacar when the tragedy had taken place in the village, where the family man was found guilty of attempting to murder his neighbour and sent to prison. And that was the day before he was killed, he recognised his friend Boubacar from his robe, the Qur'an and the walking stick that was left next to the body by his killers. Everyone was astounded and asked themselves why he had been killed and who could be the perpetrator of this horrific crime?

The villagers were informed of Boubacar's death, a panic widespread all over, screams of sorrow and broken hearts. The way he died, even his enemies, hid their tears of joy to grief for his death. Maoudho Saliou adjusted his robe and tight behind his back, then spoke. 'The enemies of my friend have dared to murder our village chief; we will find those animals, and we will bring them to the justice, and if they refused, then we will kill them all.' The crowd shouted with anger and wanted justice to be done now. Many others expressed their anger, and in the end, it was decided to follow the normal course of justice. They took the body and went back to the village to prepare his funeral. It was the custom requirement that Boubacar should be buried the next day in his native village.

A letter was written and sent to Abdul, informing him of the death of his father. Abdul had become an adult looking for work to fulfil the promises kept to his father, such as: rebuilding his courtyard and the family house. His Uncle Bobo was so sick that he was no longer capable of helping him find a good job; the unemployment rate had become increasingly worrying. But he was always optimistic that one day he would find his dream job because he believed in two things in life, wisdom and destiny.

Early in the morning around seven o'clock, a cold breeze wind blew gently. Abdul sat beneath the mango tree not far from the veranda. He was immersed in deep thought. A car parked outside the fences surrounded by barbed wire, he jumped up and raised his head with a frightening look. A gentleman opened the car door and walked up to the house.

'May I help you, sir?' asked Abdul.

The gentleman replied. 'I am carrying a message.'

'What kind of message?' he asked.

'It's a message from the village,' he replied.

The gentleman asked him. 'Are you Abdul?'

He replied. 'Yes, indeed.'

The gentleman slipped his hand into his carry bag and pulled out an envelope and a white handkerchief that his father always held in his hand. He allowed his intuition to guide him; he began to meditate and asked himself a series of questions in a sorrowful voice.

'*What happened to my father?'*

'*To the village?'*

'*To those peaceful villagers?'*

Abdul rushed to open the letter and read through it, line by line, and understood what had happened to his father before and until his death. A cold shiver ran down his body as he remembered the last time his father embraced him warmly at the bus station when he was leaving the village for Conakry. Then suddenly a thought came upon him, his mother had died many years ago and now his father. He tried in vain to force the thought out of his mind and then decided to settle the matter the way he did when his mother had died. He cried the whole day incessantly and refused to taste any food; he did not sleep at night. He tried not to think about the way his father died, but the harder he tried, the more he thought about it. He was so weak that his legs could hardly carry him, and that greatly saddened his uncle to see him suffering this way.

He had not been lucky enough to have a father who could look after him for many years to come like other children have in their life, at his early age, he had become an orphan, and he was going to make his decision all alone which would not be easy as he thought. Fortunately, his uncle Bobo was there by his side, and he could count on him. *But for how long?* He asked himself this question. He continued meditating. *I am already known by many of my school friends and others and even beyond. My success is based on solid personal and academic achievements.* At a young age, Abdul had already completed his study, and it won't take him long to find the key to his happiness and to build his future. Apart from that, he is already alone because he had grown up in his mother's absence, his father did not have enough time for him like other children, but instead, he was much more involved in social affairs than family matters. As a result, they barely exchanged a few words that bound them but granted him the little time he could to teach him some secret in the village. He was enormously grateful to have him. After all, Boubacar is his father, his biological father.

After a lengthy consultation with his uncle, he decided to go to the village to attend his father's funeral. Upon their arrival at the bus station, his uncle handed him an envelope containing a lump sum of money to facilitate his journey and brought his share of contribution to support the grieving family. In the middle of laughter, the peddlers who were advertising and selling their goods around the station during the departure tried all their means to interrupt passengers and draw customers' attention to their products. He glanced at the taxi drivers who competed among themselves to find one single person to complete the number of passengers in their cars, which were already overloaded and had exceeded their weight recommended by the manufacturers. It was time to embark; his uncle shook his hand for so long, he thought that the taxi was about to leave him. He rushed to release his uncle's hand to avoid missing his departure. He ran and climbed into the taxi and sped off.

Before noon, the taxi reached the village. At the station, Abdul was welcomed by his father's friend named Saiku, who was informed of his arrival and accompanied him to the family house.

'Oh, there you are! What a long and tiring journey?' asked Saiku.

'I'm tired and exhausted,' replied Abdul.

They stared at each other, and the tears ran down to their eyes. 'Don't cry, Abdul. Such death was destiny as our ancestors said, people of good faith don't live long; they are considered as servants of God their place is in heaven. Don't cry we're here to support you,' Saiku comforted him, he sighed and continued.

'We should go faster because everyone is waiting for you to make the final decision.'

The burial should take place on the same day after Dhuhr (midday) prayer. The town was half-deserted; all activities were decreased in the village. The day after Boubacar's death, all villagers seemed to be in a depressed mood. They were sullen and silent, the weekly markets, shops, and stores; all were closed. Some police officers were visible in some crowded places trying to reassure the safety of the villagers and promised to arrest the culprit. The entire village looked like a battlefield of a war zone; only a few domestic animals were showing their presence on the streets.

After a long walk, Abdul and Saiku finally arrived at the late Boubacar's house. They found Abdul's uncle, the big brother to his stepmother Amina, had already taken the matters in his own hands and had ordered that the corpse to be sent to the morgue to proceed with the rituals baths, and the procedure should take a few minutes. Meanwhile, Abdul huddled with his family, and everyone explained what they saw and knew about the facts. After all the explanations were given, the last word was left to him, and he was convinced that his father was murdered in cold blood because of his political affiliation.

At noon, silence reigned in the courtyard, only a few women continued to lament, shrieking and yelling their affection and compassion before the deceased. As for men, they consulted in small groups to organise the duawu (blessing) before and after the burial.

The funeral time was set at two o'clock at the cemetery, not far from the mosque in the town. When all preparations were completed, and everything was ready, they put the corpse at the disposal of the family to make their final farewell before the prayers. Boubacar's corpse was lying on a stretcher; his body was enrolled in a white sheet traditionally called white 'percale.' All the orifices were clogged with white cotton and all scented with the 'laboundheh' natural non-alcoholic perfume. Only his face was not covered, allowing family and friends to approach

60

and glanced at Boubacar's corpse. He looked very restful; a beautiful smile was drawn on his face.

In front of the grievers, Abdul left the family and relatives' gathering and went to join the widow (his stepmother). He exhorted her to calm down, but he could not control her emotions, and even other extended members of the family kept begging her to retain her tears to avoid making the deceased suffer. According to the tradition, any drop of tear shed for the dead is truly as if you had poured a drop of acid on his soul. After she had received a counsel, of course, she stopped crying and left it to God.

The family members and other relatives paraded to offer their condolences. Others thanked Abdul for attending his dad's funeral, and each brought him their words of support.

Being the youngest of the family, Abdul did all the necessary things he could to make his dad's funeral ceremony a success. So, he was trapped in an anthill movement of up and down from left to right, sorting out the needs and wants of the mourners. Still, Abdul, who had lost his beloved father, showed an example of optimism and dignity. He concealed his grief to offer support to the crowds who were greatly saddened by the death of his father. He was endowed with indomitable courage to exhort everyone to calm down and begged people not to shed tears. He fully invested himself so that his father's corpse was buried in the utmost respect.

After the funeral, the Imams and the village elders appeal to everyone to act in good faith and listen to the reading of the Holy Qur'an for the blessing before closing the ceremony with a feast. Abdul had fulfilled his duty as a responsible man, and that was his father's wishes: to act and take responsibility in the event of his absence.

When Abdul returned to the capital city Conakry, he was spiritually well awakened with a calm mind. Abdul changed his desire to be a financial expert. He intended to do politics as a career, he then joined the opposition party and entered into a battlefield not only to know the culprits of his father's assassination but also to fight against corruption, unemployment, poverty, insecurity, bad governance and to defend the interest of the younger generation, which represented a large proportion of the population, mainly graduates without proper jobs in a country that is vaguely rich in natural resources and yet only a minority who could easily claim to be self-sufficient not even rich. And the rest of the population predominantly malnourished, fetched water in the wells, and lived mainly in shantytowns below the poverty line where one hour of electricity made the population happy for the whole night. The political and ethnic tensions in the country had risen steadily and had reached a truly precarious level, and that many people hoped to have the first-ever democratically elected leader to put an end to years of intolerable levels of hardship, dictatorship, coups, and violence in the country. At the beginning of Abdul's involvement in politics, the opposition had suspended its street demonstrations to dialogue with the authorities. However, the lack of political will of the government to engage with the opposition party left them with no choice but to organise a new strike called 'Dead city' in the capital, Conakry, with the slogan. 'Freedom, poverty and no to corruption.' Abdul had become a powerful orator and was chosen to speak during the rally to motivate more youth to get involved in politics to support and vote for his party if the election took place.

He then contacted his best friend, Paul, who immediately responded to the call and brought his supporters to organise the march, he then assigned him to find a convenient location for the gathering and asked to share all responsibilities and tasks.

Paul was a faithful and loyal friend to Abdul; their friendship was welded like a magnet, and he was candid and sincere. He immediately agreed to what his friend Abdul had requested earlier on the phone. Back in the days, when they were at university, Paul had never called Abdul by his name when it came to students' gathering, he always called him 'Emperor' because of his courage to mobilise and invade whatever he found in his way. Paul was also an excellent orator as his friend; Paul presence motivated Abdul. Together, they went to their party headquarter to finalise their plan with their political leader and drew up conclusions.

The march began, thousands turned up for the demonstration to demand their rights; the roads were blocked on both sides, residents panicked and ran for shelter behind their doors and glanced at the protestors on the street, and the shopkeepers rushed to close their stalls. Abdul began his ambiguous and nauseating speech against the ruling party. He denounced the intolerable levels of hardship and lashed out in anger and spoke. 'The government had promised to strengthen democracy and fight corruption, but the same government has been implicated in corruption scandals, election irregularities and cracking down on freedom of expression. Which kind of country are we living in?'

The crowds then shouted with anger and thirst for violence. 'As we gather here, some poor people cannot attend the demonstration to claim their rights because fighting for survival is part of their daily routine in which half of the population live in misery in this wealthy country. And the natural resources are being taken away from us and sold to other rich countries around the world. The money is diverted to different banks account for the benefit of the greedy members of the government and left the population with nothing but misery.'

The crowds roared once again with anger, he then continued. 'Despite being a major exporter of bauxite and hold the largest reserves in the planet earth. Our dear country, Guinea, remains among the poorest nations in the world.' He made that speech with courage and determination by facing huge crowded opposition supporters and the undecided people. He argued the reason why his political party had organised this peaceful march and that only his party could help to reduce poverty, provide excellent education, and improve their lifestyle. Paul took out an envelope filled with money in banknotes, the party t-shirts, and began to distribute them to motivate the supporters and undecided voters to join their political party. They sang and shouted slogans under the watchful eyes of the uniformed officers and military police that were stationed at different key points looking for any violence caused by the protesters so that the troubled makers would be arrested and beaten with their truncheons.

A moment later, the peaceful demonstrations turned to violence. Some of the opposition demonstrators attacked the people wearing the ruling party's t-shirts and those they believed to support the government. The two groups clashed against each other, which resulted in severe damage to valuable properties. The security forces responded with tear gas, tanks, and other means to disperse opposition supporters who had burned tires, erected barricades in flashpoints across the streets, and to those who threw stones on heavily armed police officers. Some members of the security forces, particularly the police, demonstrated a partisan response to the protests using the ethnic slur and engaged in criminal conduct against perceived opposition supporters, resulting in several injuries. Many other people were admitted to hospitals with gunshot wounds, and others were arrested and detained. When the political leader was asked to intervene for those arrested and jailed during the rally led by the opposition party, the party assembly, including the leader, responded negatively to the demands and said that those involved in street violence were not part of their movement. However, the party assembly had appeared to take inadequate steps to ensure discipline by their supporters.

Abdul and his illustrious companion escaped unharmed, but an arrest warrant was issued against the protesters' leaders, including Abdul and Paul, who was the culprit sought by the police. Abdul took refuge at an imam's house; the next day, he received the terrible news that his friend Paul was arrested. A cold shiver ran down Abdul's body as he remembers the last time they ran for their lives, and each found a hideout for their own safety. A strange weakness descended on him as he stood staring at the messenger; he then lost control and fell on the floor. He got up abruptly and went to find his uncle Bobo, then told him all the vicissitudes and the situation in which he was involved, such as the arrest warrant brought against him and his guilt in the clashes. After the brief explanation, he went to rest in his room, while quietly awaiting the decision of the authority over his arrest as he had no place to hide without being found by the police.

At six o'clock in the morning, when the armed police officers arrived and knocked on his uncle's door to arrest him, they commanded Abdul to come outside, and he refused to obey the order. The inspector at the head of the police operation became angry; he warned Abdul that unless he opened the door peacefully, they would break the door. Abdul murmured and spoke. 'I will leave this house over my dead body.'

The officers stormed his uncle's door. They smashed it to the ground, they entered the house by force and said. 'You are under arrest on suspicion of inciting violence and damage to the government properties; now you are coming with us!' Abdul resisted not only to go with the agents but also refused to go despite the injunctions presented to him at the beginning. After a long argument, they finally used the physical force against him that resulted in his arrest, handcuffed, and led him straight to the police station. While on their way, the inspector warned him again and said. 'You have the right to remain silent. Anything you say can and will be used against you in the court of law.'

Three days after being arrested, he was transferred to the Central Prison of Coronthine in Kalum, commonly called 'Kampala' by the detainees and known under the official name 'The Urban Security of Conakry.' This notorious prison had small cells, suffocating with a heat accentuated by overcrowding, an infestation of cockroaches and nauseating smell of rotten food. In reality, it should not be built for humans to be locked up, not even for those who were guilty of worse crimes, let alone the innocent people who had claimed their right to a minimum living standard in a state that claimed to be ruled by a democratically elected government, where human dignity was placed at the mercy of the most corrupt officials.

Upon Abdul's incarceration, he sent a message to his uncle to inform him that he was imprisoned. Although he had already explained the reason why he was wanted by the police and would be arrested at any time, nevertheless he detailed all his mistreatment then he apologised for the damage caused to his door. During his period of imprisonment, he became acquainted with other political prisoners who were detained for a long-extended period, and were waiting for their fate to be decided, they eventually became his fellow fighters for the democracy. To get out of the ordeal, Abdul set up a plan with other prisoners, a tactic that could help them escape from this vast prison surrounded by fences of five metres high and overhanging by barbed wires. Each corner of the eight sides of the wall was installed with an infra-red surveillance camera. This huge prison had only two gates. The first was the main gate where the prison officers stood sentinel, twenty-four hours a day with their dogs, and the second, which was a small portal that helped evacuate the corpses of dead prisoners without drawing the attention of the densely populated neighbourhood. Sometimes they used the same gate to move the blindfolded and hooded detainees to different cells during the night interrogations where they end up sexually abusing them unless they agreed to cooperate with the inspectors. But his plan failed because, among his fellow prisoners, there were criminals who had killed and should be sentenced to death, drug dealers with whom the guards took advantage through their network to provide themselves cannabis and other narcotics. When the plan had failed, Abdul was transferred from his cell and added to another group of troublemakers in a cell already crowded. Abdul ate nothing throughout that day, and the next, he was not even given any water to drink, and the ten people in that cell could not go out to urinate or go to the toilet when they were pressed. During the night, they were closely watched by guards who often taunted them and knocked their heads with their batons. They were left to the mercy of all sorts of diseases; the physical and mental tortures were part of their daily lives; they were hungry and thin like a skeleton and left to die. Abdul had lost ten kilos after a few weeks in a cell which was overfilled with inmates to the verge of collapsing.

'Many of us are waiting for our last breath, and death is a pleasant relief,' said Abdul.

Besides, the sexual promiscuity amongst detainees there was a category of prisoners such as the minors, and the weak, of course, were sexually targeted by their fellow inmates as they had influence and were physically stronger than them. The correctional officers who are meant to protect them were accomplices of their actions because they took advantage of them too.

Abdul's family in the village was informed of his arbitrary arrest then his imprisonment, the story spread quickly through the villages and was distorted as it was passed on from one person to another. Some said that Abdul was killed the same way as his father; others said that he had already been taken to court and condemned to death and that the police officers were already on their way to arrest the rest of his family who remained in the village. His stepmother Amina, who at that time had disagreed with her father, Osman, regarding the death of her husband began contacting people of goodwill to help her find a way to get Abdul out of prison as she had since ceased all paternal relations with her father and had stopped all contact with the rest of her family except her uncle, who was a General in the army. Amina could also renew contact with her father and ask for help, but she preferred not to talk to him about Abdul's actual situation. For her, all these misfortunes were orchestrated by her father because before Boubacar's death; her father had taken a suspicious distance in respect of her late husband, who had joined the opposition party. Ever since then her father Osman, as a politician, had tried to reconcile with her and now he wanted to redeem himself to his family and had already apologised to Amina as he had poorly misbehaved in the past and he would like to offer his assistance to resolve the matter and share her anguish.

The relationship between Abdul and his stepmother Amina had deteriorated since the death of Boubacar. Despite the prevailing circumstances, Amina had tried to persuade Abdul to join them in the village to take over the businesses of his father and collect the money from the debtors. Still, Abdul wholly ignored her. Although age was respected among Abdul's brothers, but achievement was revered as he was the only educated adult who had achieved a degree in the family. So, he was in an excellent position to take over their father's businesses.

An emergency family gathering was organised by Amina's father, who directed this important meeting behind closed doors.

Amina spoke first and said. 'We are all gathered here to discuss the fate and the danger that Abdul faces daily while in prison. For my child and beloved son of my soulmate late husband, Boubacar case, there's no way that I shall lower my arms and let you decide a bad fate for our son.'

Her father, Osman replied with a smile. 'My daughter; there's no way that someone could betray you, especially in Abdul's case. Personally, I cannot betray you, as I had badly behaved in the past but not this time. Oh, daughter, if time could come back, I should have defended and protected my son-in-law when he was desperately in need. However, the time lost cannot be retrieved to correct my mistake, as I acted out of pure selfishness and foolishness in which my arrogance had dominated and controlled my life, I am now feeling ashamed and sorry about my actions in the past. I am here at your side to help you find a way to get Abdul out of prison.'

Amina felt a bit relieved by the statement of her father; she had finally won his support.

Omar, one of Abdul's siblings, raised his tone. 'All we have said here must be taken seriously and with action and let each of us leave this room with an idea in mind so that Abdul can avoid the judgement in this country. I am going to tell you clearly that first of all, Abdul was wrong in the first instance; he shouldn't have joined this opposition party, which was nothing but a group of corrupt individuals who defend their own interests. The dishonest government officials could give the opposition party a small amount of money to silence them, and Abdul would be left defenceless at the mercy of the court and the authority will do all their means to show the human right organisations that these political detainees are nothing but a bunch of criminals who deserved to be locked up for the safety of the population. This will make it even harder for these organisations to find the truth about the miscarriage of justice that people often protest about.'

After listening to everyone, Osman whispered. 'All that we had discussed here must not cross that door.'

Abdul's trial was approaching, and he would have to go before the judge to answer the charges against him, the situation became extremely difficult for both Abdul and Paul. Their indictment was not surprising, although they were not the instigators of the disturbances and the cause of materials damaged and loses during the demonstration, they were nevertheless charged, and they would be brought before the most reputable court of justice of the country.

Before their court date, Abdul's family met at Amina's maternal uncle, a General of the army, to help them find an escape plan. Amina was the only one who spoke to her uncle and pleaded. 'Uncle! I just want to ask for your help. I know that you don't sell your aid; your honour is worth a thousand. I would not allow myself to offer money because you have enough, and nevertheless, I appeal to your compassion. Our son Abdul was accused and imprisoned months ago during a peaceful march that turned violent and ended with arbitrary arrests, and now he faces justice, and he is defenceless on his own.'

Being a General in the army rank, Amina's uncle listened to her carefully without any appropriate reaction and then asked a simple question:

'Is he guilty of the alleged charges against him?'

'No,' she replied with a trembling voice for fear of being rejected by her uncle.

In the beginning, her uncle was unaware of the severity and the degree of the culpability, because he did not want to get involved in trivialities without knowing what had caused Abdul to get arrested in the first place so that he could avoid any possible problem which could stain his personality and his honour. *'Nevertheless, it is a family problem,'* he thought. He did not know that after their conversations, he would be in charge of helping Abdul to escape from prison, but being the hope of his family, he agreed to help her and at the same time, created an escaped door in case if the plan failed. He was a man of action and the only one who could resolve the challenges of the family. The General decided to use a tactic that could help Abdul disappear between the walls of justice without any trace. However, he could not do it all alone, therefore he needed another trusted person to carry out his plan together, and he also needed time and preparation. He saw in his niece face anxiety and despair; he knew without him, Abdul would risk being condemned for a long time to come. He stood up and embraced her warmly, then he said.

'Niece, I am against any abuse of power and all those who abuse their intelligence or take advantage of the poor people and use their property unfairly. I am also against the selfish, who often reject their wrongdoings on the back of innocent people or who refuse to support them,' he paused then continued. 'I know that Abdul must be in one of these particular cases, I feel his pain, and I will do my best to get him out of jail and help him to escape from that prison whatever the cost. But one more advice, you have to go and consult a marabout to predict the future of our plan, once the ground is fertile, we will cultivate together.'

Only Amina could understand what he meant. So, she left and went to find a marabout to consult the future of their plan, and the dangers involved before they start working on it.

Upon her arrival at the marabout, she implored him:

'Oh, dear marabout! As the proverb says. It is not the day of combat that you will start training to fight against your enemy.' She paused then continued: 'I am here today in the midst of an imminent need, which is why I have just asked for your spiritual help, your clairvoyance, and that of your blessings. I know that you have a reputation for telling the truth; your words are clear as the spring water from the source. I know that your word is worth millions, I cannot afford to offer you money because I do not have enough, but I appeal to your grace. My son, Abdul, is accused by the ruling power of organising a popular uprising that has caused enormous materials damage, lootings, beatings, and injuries against police officers while he is not guilty of the facts. He is currently in prison, awaiting trial on the facts that he did not recognise.'

'How do you want me to help?' asked the marabout.

'There is no secret between you and me, in fact: we have combined an escape plan for Abdul before the judgment day,' she said in trembling voice.

'Oh, I understand!' said the marabout.

The marabout spread out his prayer mat on the floor, called 'Djouldoukoun' in Fulani language or 'Salidhebeh' in Sussu language, and sat down in the middle of it. He opened a large book written in Arabic and caricatures that resembled the Egyptian pyramids with rectangular numbers, written in Greco-Latin, and held in his hand a very long rosary bead and asked.

'Remind me of your son's full name, his mother's name, and his date of birth, which is, in fact, the most important in this consultation.'

When all the information asked was given, he sank into deep taciturn prayer for a long moment. His eyes closed and held the rosaries in his right hand, which were making a chronological movement following a circle of writings in his book that was wide opened, while at the same time, he murmured some verses from the Qur'an in a low voice. After some minutes of ritual, he finally came out of his deep prayer and said.

'Oh, Amina, from my consultations, I saw no obstacle towards helping Abdul. He will come out from prison safely, and then all those who will fight for his cause to rescue him would have absolutely nothing to blame for, and besides that, other people will be blamed and will be jailed instead. By that time, Abdul would be gone far from here. However, take these two small bottles, keep them safe. On the day of his judgement, soon after the first cockcrow at dawn, before sunrise, you must leave your house and arrive at the first crossroads, pour the contents of the first bottle and turn around without drawing the attention of other people around you or any passer-by. Then, you will keep the second bottle until you see Abdul, then you will make him drink two drops of the contents of this second bottle. Once you've done this, the grace of Allah and his glory will help him out of this situation.'

Amina went back to meet her uncle and explained everything that the marabout had told her and the two bottles that had been given to her. The General got up and went to meet one of his best childhood friends, named Ibrahim, a great doctor based at Donka Hospital.

During break time, Ibrahim saw a man dressed in military uniform with three stars on his shoulders. He said to his colleague.

'What a surprise this afternoon to see a senior army officer's heading to our centre. If it is not a case of illness, it could be an investigation.'

His colleague replied. 'Perhaps, another arbitrary arrest as you already know what's going on in this country.' The two men began to laugh endlessly. The General approached slowly but surely because he did not want to be seen or to draw the attention of others while meeting with his friend.

'Hello, my friend, Ibrahim! How are you?' he greeted.

'I am absolutely fine, by the grace of God; I am still here safe and sound. Thanks for asking.'

'How about you and your service?' replied Ibrahim.

'I am fine, I was on my way to meet one of my colleagues; then I decided to have a look to see if you're still alive as it has been a while,' answered the general with a smile.

They two men laughed like little children. The General did not want to tell him the reason for his visit at that time, as he wanted to know first if his friend was still working at the hospital, then make an appointment with him in a discreet place to discuss his plan. The time was short; Ibrahim's break was at the end, so he should return to work at any time. Then, they set up a rendezvous to meet in the evening at a local cafeteria not far from Ibrahim's house.

That evening after a lengthy discussion, he detailed the whole situation to his friend, and the two interlocutors agreed to play each a crucial role in this affair. Ibrahim, as a doctor, knows well and how to combine drugs to create an overdose once swallowed; it will cause reactions in Abdul's body from that point; he would be sick physically or psychologically. He would not be able to appear before the judge, and mostly, as an accused of a crime, it would be necessary to require medical assistance. Once at the hospital, the General would play his strategic roles that would lead Abdul to escape from the medical centre.

The two collaborators agreed on the plan, but the General was initially reluctant to accept the risk of using overdose medication so that Abdul could escape from justice. He saw a negative side of taking an overdose and began to ask himself in case if he dies, he will be held accountable for his death. Given the fact that the General is a trusted member of Abdul's family, he would not have a choice but to assume the responsibility of acting immorally. However, looking into the positive side of it, Abdul will be free from the ordeal of being condemned to something he did not commit. So, he had no choice but to accept his friend's proposal to honour his words of helping Abdul; then he sank into deep thought for a while.

'General! General!' Ibrahim exclaimed in surprise.

The General jumped abruptly and glared at Ibrahim as if he was in a deep sleep and answered. 'Yes, Ibrahim, fatigue, and stress had prevailed me. Let's go back to the overdose that you had suggested. Do you have any idea about the medication that should be used for this overdose? If yes, so how will the drug be given to him while he's still held in a highly supervised prison? As I personally don't know anything about the overdoses and their effects,' the General asked hesitatingly.

'Oh, General, Abdul is ours. Don't worry too much, I will do my best not to harm or cause him a long-term health problem in the future,' said Ibrahim. Then he continued explaining.

'This overdose is just something that will prevent him from appearing before the court of justice, a drug that will cause him an allergic reaction such as pimples on the body, oedema, discomfort, and even sometimes diarrhoea. Once this has appeared all over his body, the authorities would have no choice but to call for medical assistance. From that point, you will use your knowledge to inquire about all the information and tactics that will be applied until we succeed in getting him out from this mess,' concluded Ibrahim.

However, Ibrahim's proposal was only simple ampicillin called 'Biogaran' that is often used in the treatment of various infectious diseases, including those of the lungs, bronchitis, nose, throat or ears, blood, the digestive or urinary tract, the genital tract, the gums, and the teeth. Heavy responsibility and decisions were now required to be made; the General found himself caught between a rock and a hard place; he must make a quick decision and act before the day of the judgement. Then he asked Ibrahim a question with a serious tone.

'So, Ibrahim, like all medicines sometimes have undesirable effects, then what will be the consequences of this product 'Biogaran' in case of an overdose as you have indicated recently?'

'My friend, in general cases, this 'Biogaran' does not cause enough acute toxic effects, even in case of taking accidentally strong doses. But bear in mind that the overdose may cause symptoms such as digestive disorders, kidney disorders, neuron-psychic disorders, and electrolyte disorders,' replied Ibrahim. Then he continued. 'And besides of all that, what has made my choice fall on this medical product, is the fact that there is no specific antidote in case of overdose. The treatment will rely primarily on swallowing activated charcoal usually a stomach pumping is necessary, and on symptomatic measures, Abdul's hydro-electrolyte balance would be carefully monitored. This overdose could also be eliminated by haemodialysis; particular attention would be paid to Abdul's hydro-electrolyte balance.'

He knew that it was an immoral and unprofessional act, a great danger and a huge risk to take and if it went wrong, they would be exposed and sent to prison. It would not only be limited to just on that, the problem could go beyond to tarnish their personalities and reputations, but as the saying goes:

'Who risked nothing to invest, will get nothing in return.'

Then he decided to take a risk in this case, which Ibrahim considered minimal risk. And that the General in his role of a senior officer in the army would do anything in his power so that this affair end in the most significant discretion and Abdul would obtain his freedom somewhere in the world far from Guinea because the police would hunt him down and chase after by the justice of the country. At eight o'clock that same evening, Abdul's fate was decided, their meeting was productive.

After explaining the risk and the complication that led to the overdose of this drug, they sought to find a way to introduce a pack of 'Biogaran' ampicillin tablets inside the prison without drawing the attention of the prison guards and inmates.

The General contacted a young woman who owned a convenience store opposite to the prison gates and mainly sold foods and household goods to prison officers. She had maintained a friendly relationship with most of the officers who worked day and night. She was well informed about what was happening behind the prison doors and could introduce anything inside the cells at will. The General took the opportunity to smuggle inside the prison a pack of capsules, and a piece of paper detailing the plan and how to swallow the pills through the convenience store owner. Abdul seized the envelope without delay, slipped it inside his underwear, and asked the guard to accompany him to the toilet. He took advantage of reading the contents of the letter, thinking that something terrible had happened to one of his family members, as he remembered many years ago receiving a similar envelope from his late father detailing the danger of life-threatening he was facing in the village. That message had brought him nothing but a lousy souvenir. But this time he was wrong because this envelope was a bearer of hope and freedom. After reading carefully, he folded and put it back inside his underwear, and he went out of the toilet very happy. He was then sent back to his cell by the penitentiary guard.

The judgement day approached; anxiety multiplied amongst Abdul's family members. Amina went to meet a clairvoyant named Karo who was also well known for predicting the future of those who came to consult him when misfortune dogged their steps, she asked for another consultation in this matter. Having not succeeded in what she was looking for, she relied on the decision taken by the General, who at that time had requested vacation to attend the funeral of one of his comrade in the army who had died in a road traffic accident. A coincidence just happened, the judgement of Abdul and the public funeral ceremony of his comrade in the army would begin at the same time, and the next day the deceased would be taken to his final resting place in its village called Telimele. The General wanted to be a part of a convoy that would carry the body of the deceased to its native village. He immediately contacted his friend Ibrahim so that he could arrange for an ambulance and made it available for him to use for the event. As planned, the ambulance would be used to evacuate Abdul out of the country; Ibrahim promptly executed the order and negotiated with the funeral service to procure an ambulance.

The next day early in the morning, Abdul should be brought to justice. He applied effectively the written advice that had been given to him and the capsules to swallow before he went to sleep. He took six capsules at once around seven o'clock that evening, just as the other inmates were discussing their fate, then he went to join the group. After two hours, he began to feel uncomfortable, which led him to withdraw from his inmates and sat in the corner, his back leaning against the wall. Afterwards, he felt an intense pain in his stomach, he collapsed to the ground in agony and remained crumpled to the floor in a dead faint for a while then gradually the pain eased off. He went back to his usual place. He sat on the corner; he stared at the inmates without saying anything to anyone, very worried he began to think about his fate. Nevertheless, he retained his coolness because, for him, what will happen to him that night would happen to him one day regardless of the situation he would face in the future.

He sat down, rubbing the sleep from his eyes. A sudden deep sleep caught him; he slept like a new-born. At six o'clock in the morning, he was awakened by the noises made by his inmates who were banging on the doors and shouting at each other. He got up quickly and swallowed eight capsules at once, meaning that he had taken fourteen capsules in the space of ten hours. He fainted and fell on the floor and went into a coma. He remained there under the watchful eye of the detainees and the prison officers who were supposed to bring him to the court to face justice. Although none of them knew what had happened and how to resuscitate Abdul, his body was covered all over by pimples, discomforts, and skin rashes.

Abdul stayed lying on that dirty smelling floor helplessly, his fellow inmates began to utter loud noises by knocking on the wall, and others screamed desperately and loudly. 'He is dead! He is dead! He is dead!" Which shrieked the attention of the commander in charge of the penitential guard.

When he heard the noises, he ran over to reach the cell. Surprisingly, he found a prisoner lying on the floor and asked the crowd.

'He's pretending, or he's dead?'

At that point he was wrong to ask such a question while a detainee was in a coma, by identification, he found that it's Abdul who should appear before the court of justice in three hours and was now in a coma and no one witnessed what had happened to him. Tormented, he informed the judicial police department before their arrival; he had tried to resuscitate him several times. Not having succeeded in his attempt, he ordered to transport him to the Central Hospital University (CHU) of Donka, a place where Ibrahim, the friend of the General, was based. He was escorted and stayed under the watchful eyes of the judicial police officer. The tribunal was informed, and his judgement was adjourned until his condition returned to normal. The General's first plan had succeeded, and now Abdul was no longer between the walls of the central prison.

Ibrahim knew that after he had taken the overdose, there would be a surprising reaction on Abdul's body and that any signs of intoxication caused by the ampicillin 'Biogaran' would impose a hospitalisation. Regardless of the dose ingested and any poisoning due to the absorption of a large quantity of these drugs into his body would also require pre-hospital emergency treatment by a specialist from the emergency department. Ibrahim was contacted as a chief surgeon who was also a cardiologist on duty at the CHU of Donka. Upon his arrival at Abdul's bed, he noticed the facts and the reactions on Abdul's body and transferred the patient to the recovery room, where Abdul regained consciousness. He gave him an antitoxin that counteracted the toxin and then followed a detoxification procedure. But being under the supervision of the judicial police, Ibrahim solicited the expertise of his friend, the General, so that they could implement their plans. Once they succeed, they could easily smuggle Abdul out of the building without being seen by the hospital's staff or being suspected by his fellow doctors and the police.

Once the ambulance keys were handed to the General. It would be driven by the clairvoyant named Karo, approached by Abdul's stepmother, who would take Abdul to a secure hiding place at his aunt's house who lived in the village called 'Balaki' near the exit border of the country.

The General responded to his friend Ibrahim's call for support to implement the escape strategy and then developed a plan to get the police officer to sleep quickly before midnight. In the hope of achieving their goal, Ibrahim appealed to the consumption of hypnotic drugs, a commonly called sleeping drug, and took the responsibility to watch over all the movements and drinks that the police officer liked more to consume. He went to see a saleswoman who had established a small restaurant right next to the hospital; she sold there almost everything starting from beer to water. It was through her that the police officer procured drinks and even sometimes snacks like fried plantain.

The surgeon and the general agreed to use sleeping drugs to make the police officer fall asleep. In the evening, Ibrahim ordered a morsel of food, including a bottle of Coca-Cola, a cold-water bottle from the nearby restaurant, which should be delivered at his office before seven o'clock in the evening. While he was mixing a strong dosage of hypnotics in the bottle with pure water, the maid knocked on his office door just before the requested delivery time.

'The meal is ready, doctor; you are my first customer this evening,' she said with a smile on her face.

He rushed to take the meal from the maid and paid the bill.

'You can keep the change,' Ibrahim said calmly.

He slammed the door quickly behind her without even waiting for her to appreciate his gesture; he opened the container and then poured the contents of the hypnotics into the bottle of Coca-Cola. He then closed the lid of the bottle tightly, he took the food and went to the restaurant where he handed the food including drinks back to the vendor, pretending that he had been called for an emergency.

By kindness, the saleswoman wanted to refund him the cost of the dish in return; he insisted that she keep the money. In the hope of gaining more money, she decided to resell the food to another customer for more profits. Ibrahim went back to see Abdul, who was laid on his sickbed, he greeted the police officer and suggested that he could go and find something to eat if he desired to have food as he had not eaten since breakfast and he seemed to be very hungry.

As the saying goes, an empty stomach is like a broken heart; we cannot rely on it for decision-making.

The police officer got up abruptly without thinking twice about the danger of leaving Abdul alone on his sickbed and went straight ahead to the restaurant to buy food. Upon his arrival, as usual, he sat down in his preferred place at the back corner and ordered the food.

'Do you have anything ready to eat, madam?' asked the agent.

'Yes, Mr Corporal,' replied the lady.

The police officer hated to be called corporal. He got angry; then asked to be served faster as he did not want to be marked absent by his superior while he's on duty. He stared at the vendor lady as fear gripped him and thought that if something unexpected happened to Abdul, he would be severely sanctioned for abandoning the post before his break time. The servant offered him the food returned by Ibrahim without telling him that the meal he was offered has well been served to someone else and was backed by the offeree, and now she's deciding to resell it at a low price to the police officer.

'Whenever you come to my restaurant, you are always in a hurry; it seemed like there's a fire on your stools, and you won't even have time to speak to me. So, I offer you a meal ready with a discount of twenty per cent including cold drinks, I do not often do promotions, and it is quite uncommon to find such discount for customers like you,' argued the saleswoman.

Surprised by the offer, the police officer asked to be reassured that she wasn't joking before committing to take the meal.

'A discount of twenty per cent is an opportunity not to be missed, and especially with a cold drink, that is a gift from God,' he whispered.

The police officer had fallen on his lucky day, which would allow him to save at least some money to use for his transport to facilitate his return home, but at which price? He then went on to ask for the food.

'How much is the total price?' asked the police officer.

'Oh, don't worry, you can eat first, then we'll discuss the price afterwards,' replied the lady.

Being starve to death, he emptied the plate and drank all the bottle of Coca-Cola in one go and took the bottle of water with him. The saleswoman handed him a piece of paper as a payment receipt for his meal, and he went back to his post. Ibrahim was still in the room where Abdul was resting; the officer knocked on the door and thanked Ibrahim for the time taken to stay with the patient during his absence.

'Thank you, doctor, for keeping the door safe,' said the officer.

'My friend, that's nothing; it's just an act of good faith,' replied Ibrahim.

After a few hours, Ibrahim glanced at the window and caught sight of the officer dozing off. He quickly dressed Abdul in a nurse's uniform and lined up cushions instead, which replaced him and covered all in the blanket so that nobody could imagine that it was not Abdul. He glued a note on the door, written: 'Keep calm, the patient is resting.'

They left the ward then walked towards the morgue. At that time, Abdul was getting better and held a large file of records kept in a clipboard as if he was returning from consulting patients. No one stared at him, not even the cleaner who often came to clean his room had recognised him.

The departure for the funeral time approached, the general had the control of the situation in hand, the convoy had been prepared, military trucks were available to all those who wanted to attend the funeral of the deceased in Telimele region. The departure was scheduled that night, and the arrival was expected in the morning.

The burial was scheduled for the next day after Dhuhr prayer at two o'clock, the General and the ambulance driver went to meet with a carpenter who they entrusted to make a perforated coffin that would allow air to enter and exit in both sides. They took it and went to the hospital where Abdul and Ibrahim were waiting for them to arrive impatiently.

Upon their arrival at the gate, the two men disguised themselves like an ambulance crew and pretended that they were taking a corpse from the morgue. Their access was authorised, then they drove slowly towards the morgue, Ibrahim had already given the plan details to Abdul, and he had memorised everything in this head. He followed exactly the way it was instructed to him, he got inside the ambulance and laid down in the coffin with food and water beside him, including a small storage tank of oxygen with a mask in case if he needed it. The engine started, and they drove off, Ibrahim stood up until the ambulance disappeared from his naked eye. He went back to review the situation in which he had left the police officer to eradicate any involvement by proving himself that he was unaware of Abdul's disappearance. He went to find two of his teammates who became witnesses of his action, and they went together to check on Abdul's condition so that he could be clear of any suspicion that could charge him with the patient's daring escape.

Upon their arrival at the door, they found the officer in a profound sleeping position and was heavily snoring as he could, and that snore was so loud it could wake the dead. A written notice glued at the door: 'Keep calm, the patient is resting.'

Ibrahim suggested to his teammates to come back later, as they were not allowed to enter into the ward without the presence of a judicial police officer except in emergency cases. His plan was well played, but his anxiety was far from over. He remained concerned until he reassured that Abdul had arrived safely to the hiding place indicated by Karo. He was worried that someone might have seen him with Abdul or have been aware of what he was doing when he smuggled Abdul out of the ward but tried to be busy to let the time pass quickly instead and did not leave his colleagues aside, he remained preoccupied all along the way. After four hours had passed, Ibrahim reassured himself that at this time, whatever the difficulties they might had during their journey on the road, they would have already reached their destination. He interrupted the discussions between his colleagues and asked that one of them should go and check on the patient again.

In the middle of having fun, another colleague volunteered to go and went to check on Abdul again; he found the agent in the same sleeping position. He rushed into the room and lifted the blanket, which covered the supposed Abdul's head; he found that the pillows were lined up in the exact position like a human being, and Abdul was missing. With a loud shout of astonishment, the officer jumped in his seat and stood up abruptly and went to join the doctor in the room. Then Ibrahim and other colleagues followed them to see what had happened. All senior doctors on duty that night were summoned, and an inquiry was triggered. An instruction was given that all doors were to be locked; the movement of people was restricted all over the place afterwards. The police officers were informed, shortly after their arrival, blockades were set up around every room, and each department of the hospital building was searched, not a single place was neglected; even the parked vehicles were not left out. The heavy presence of police officers was at the entry and exit of the hospital. After having spent more than three hours of consecutive searches without finding Abdul, an internal investigation was launched. Consequently, Abdul's family members were called by the police for questioning, and they were released without charge. Shortly after that, an arrest warrant was issued against Abdul.

At that precise moment, the trio had already arrived at the hiding place in Balaki near the border between Guinea and Senegal. Where they short-stayed to elaborate a plan on how to persuade the border control officers to believe they are carrying a corpse in their ambulance so that they could cross the border easily before dawn. 'At last, we have arrived safely,' said the General.

The clairvoyant Karo's aunty welcomed them with a hearty, hospitable reception. The General owes his gratitude to Karo for the long and tiring journey from the hospital to their destination in which they had never encountered difficulties, only a few checkpoints, but that did not prevent them from passing.

Meanwhile, another problem surfaced on how the General could make it to the funeral without any means of transport in the middle of the night. In the hope of getting to the region of Telimele, he tried to do his best to reach his friend's burial before two o'clock so that he could be among his colleagues during the funeral. If succeeded, he would be cleared off any suspicion involving him to Abdul disappearing, as many people already knew the family connection that bound him and Abdul. So, he decided to leave Abdul with Karo to continue the rest of the journey and preoccupied himself to find someone to drive him out of the village. In the meantime, Karo's aunty negotiated with a taxi driver who was travelling towards Telimele, where the funeral would be held. Before leaving the village of Bakali, the

General left instructions and paid a lot of money so that Abdul could cross the border in the utmost discretion, given the fact that the time they had arrived at the host house and they had found that all the borders were already closed.

The taxi driver accepted the demand to give the General a lift for free of charge. He took advantage of his presence to follow the direction indicated by the General as he did not have the car documents, nor insurance or tax. Some passengers on-board also did not have their identification documents, which would oblige them to pay a significant amount of money at each checkpoint to the corrupt traffic police officers before reaching their final destination. But with the General being on board the taxi, would not only secure their safety but would save them from paying an enormous sum of money before their arrival.

The General wore his military uniform with his starry rank on his shoulders, which showed his high ranking in the army.

They arrived in Telimele region before the time indicated. The General decided to get off half-way to the town centre. Then he walked and crossed the street to wait for the last convoy which should arrive at any moment. A few minutes after he had crossed the road, he saw a blue car with a slow speed; it was the car of his companion Djenaba, who also was heading towards the same direction to give her last farewell to the deceased. He took advantage of it and went all together to the burial ceremony.

The funeral was carried out in the best conditions according to their traditions. A moment after the burial, the General received a call regarding Abdul's disappearance from one of his army colleagues, informing him that they had received visitors from the police at their military camp and they were asking after him. But as things always worked in his favour, his colleague had explained to them that he had taken two days of annual leave to attend his comrade's funeral in Telimele region. Indeed, the burial took place that same day when the police officer called in. Shortly after their conversation, the General made a call to the national police headquarter and to the judicial police commissioner to let them know the overwhelming situation that involved Abdul's disappearance in which he was under the police surveillance. He warned them if any harm happened to him, there would be disastrous consequences.

'I'll be back tonight, I want to know what you did to this young man who was half-dead laying in the hospital under your control,' the General warned the police commissioner.

He knew that all the attention had turned to him as a member of Abdul's family. However, being a General in the army, there was absolutely nothing he could do to help Abdul to escape from prison except using the camouflage method in which he had succeeded with the help of his friend Ibrahim. He was willing to do everything to avoid drawing the attention of others and covered up so that no one will ever find out. Upon his arrival in Conakry, he went to the central police station to inquire about the outcome of the investigation, knowing that the wrongdoing was going to be based on the negligence and incompetence of the judicial police department and the way they had handled this case.

Back in Balaki, rain fell as it had never fallen before, it started shortly after the General had left for the funeral until now it poured down in violent torrents and washed away anything that stood on its way. Giant trees uprooted, and deep gorges appeared everywhere. The fierce storm left nothing in its way. Several houses were shattered as a result of the heavy storm. The trees all suffered from the harmful effects of its strength; floods recorded in certain parts of the localities. Gradually the rain and the wind became lighter and less frequent; villagers no longer stayed indoors but ran to check the damage caused by the force of nature. The departure time from Balaki to Dindefelo in Senegal had arrived; Abdul sat on the sofa next to a black coal stove that they used to heat the house. Karo's aunty poured the oil on the charcoal and went to look for a matchbox in her drawer made of clay. She cleaned the package and pulled a matchstick wood and struck it against the sandpaper box, the stick ignited, she then threw it into the pale pile of charcoal that flamed up immediately in the fireplace.

'The stove must be ventilated quickly to light up the charcoal, in that way, the smoke will be reduced,' she said to Abdul.

Abdul stood up and opened the window to allow the wind in, which in return took out the smoke. At that time, the driver was preparing the coffin and checked the storage tank of oxygen that could allow Abdul to breathe clean air.

'Your bed is ready, sir,' Karo said in a slightly more serious tone.

Abdul ran out towards the ambulance; then entered from the back door, Karo was still inside the vehicle to ensure that everything was fine and ready to be used.

'Sir, you can lay down in the coffin and straighten yourself, turn your head to the left to better allow yourself to observe the light,' said Karo.

'Let me check if the perforations will allow me to receive a bit of illumination,' said Abdul.

Abdul no longer had self-confidence as before when the General was with them, but he remained optimistic about his future and always saw the best in every situation. He wore the mask with a long rope, which was connected to the tank of oxygen to make it easier for him to breathe without difficulty. Next to his left-hand side, there were bananas, oranges, and a bottle of water. Karo carefully closed back the coffin and locked the ambulance door behind him.

He started the vehicle engine and headed towards the border of the country. They arrived at the first border control; the vehicle slowed down, then it advanced slowly up to the checkpoint. The driver came down from the vehicle with the paper certifying that it was a corpse inside the ambulance and that the family of the deceased are waiting impatiently for the corpse to arrive safely. A systematic check was carried out by the customs; they opened the back door then found a well-perfumed coffin with a strong scent of laboundheh (natural fragrance), they closed the door and lowered the barrier of the checkpoint. Karo drove the vehicle to the second border control; he then found another barrier. This one led to Senegal through Dindefelo. The customs officers at that place did not hold them long enough because a welcoming event was well prepared before their departure from Guinea.

When the ambulance approached, the driver used the ambulance sirens to alert the welcoming event organisers who had pretended to be in mourning after the death of a member of their family. At the control barrier, the vehicle was approached by two customs officers who were informed of their arrival but without being given more details and had not had the slightest information about what's going on.

'The vehicle documents, please, sir,' the officers asked the driver.

He took out the papers and handed them to the officers for checking. In the middle of answering the officer's questions, the mourners, including women and children from Dindefelo, headed towards the ambulance. They began to whine, shrieking and lament, pretending that they were crying for their lost one, a way to show the customs agents that they are saddened for the deceased, and they continued crying incessantly until the crowds gathered around and felt sorry for them. The border customs commander heard the cries, he left his office and walked to the ambulance, then asked the customs officers what had happened. Shortly after that, he opened the ambulance back door; then found a coffin with a strong scent of perfume, he felt breathless then stepped back. He quickly closed the door behind him and gave the order to let them cross the border. The driver got back to the vehicle and disappeared from the traffic towards the city of Kedougou, where they changed the ambulance to another car then continued to Tambacounda.

The Adventure

They arrived in the afternoon under the boiling heat. The market square was saturated with crowds; the merchants were selling everything, starting from foodstuffs to the pharmaceutical products. Itinerant merchants and street traders were almost everywhere doing the anthill movement, running from right to the left with their product in hand. The passer-by nudged at each other without any regards, the hangar built to shelter passengers was transformed into small restaurants all over the bus station. At the crossroads, the narrow street that led to the entrance of the market, a vehicle braked abruptly; the door opened gently. Abdul got out of the vehicle; he was greeted by a dried hot wind clouded by burnt dust.

'We have finally arrived at Tambacounda,' said Karo.

They were overcome by fatigue and starvation after the long journey, they both headed to the hangar that sheltered the food vendors to find something to eat, the choice of meals was immense on the menu. The vendors took advantage of the customers' views and offered them the most varied foods exposed in front of their counters, including meatballs, boiled or grilled corns, fried sweet potatoes, chicken soup, mango, fresh salad, and cassava tubers mix with taro and potato tubers. Apart from their potential customers, there were also subscribers of the market. The beggars of all ages showing their misery to all those whom they saw seated comfortably behind their dining tables and asked for some coins and foods leftover which had been kept in the kitchen ready to be thrown away. On the other side, the shrill cry of flies that wailed around made their presence felt by increasing their numbers, which interfered with the comfort and enjoyment of customers. After the insects had inspected each place and every customer, they finally landed on dirty food containers used by the customers and laid their white eggs one after the other. Soon after Abdul and the driver had satisfied their appetites, they resumed their journey towards Dakar, the Senegalese capital, to meet a businessman named Mustapha before midnight who should help Abdul to fulfil his European dream.

A long and tiring journey, the night was impenetrably dark and quiet except for the thrilling sound of insects and the roaring of wild animals. Abdul glanced through the car window and smiled when they approached the capital city Dakar. He saw from a distance a city lit by some small lamps that gave out yellowish light like a soft eye of a bright yellow object set in the solid darkness of the night. The closer they got to the city, the more he felt the unusual humid air that blew up onto his face as the car sped slowly, he wiped the sweat from his forehead and asked Karo, to switch on the air conditioning. When they reached the centre of the capital Dakar, the vehicle stopped. They alighted from the vehicle and took shelter in a cafeteria to wait for Mustapha, who had not delayed joining them. While waiting, Abdul seemed astonished and stared at young drunken partygoers chanting in the middle of the street and provoked the peaceful passers-by that caused a furious fight against each other. On the other side, the much-matured young men chatted with their lovers and calmly made their way to the most popular nightclub. Men and women queued in front of the club's main entrances, they valued themselves and bribed the security guards to jump the long queues and made their way in easily, all this eventful night went peacefully and smoothly under the watchful eye of security guards.

Shortly after midnight, a handsome man arrived at the cafeteria and stood at the main door. He wore a light blue suit that accentuated his dark complexion; he was tall and quite bulky around his neck and shoulders, he had an attractive face and dark brown eyes, he was not pretty like Hollywood stars but the kind of man that appeal to everyone. Abdul had never seen a man who looked so serious like this gentleman; he spoke little and listened a lot. Echoes crossed his mind, and he asked himself about Mustapha's behaviour towards him.

Is that my new guardian? Is that the one who will take care of me? No, I don't think so. If he's not the one, then who is going to direct me towards a better future! guessed Abdul.

'Are you Abdul?' asked Mustapha.

'Yes,' replied Abdul.

'As I promised yesterday, I did it today. Here is Mr Abdul, the one I spoke to you about on the phone,' said Karo; he then introduced Abdul to his new guardian, Mustapha.

The two gentlemen shook hands to seal their friendship. That night was the beginning of his adventure, and at that very moment, Abdul abandoned everything behind him and faced his destiny. Karo praised him for his courage and gently stroke his shoulder, then said goodbye to both before he resumed his journey back to Guinea. Mustapha was a very talented and courageous man, but a womaniser that Abdul had never seen before, he could flirt with any woman he crossed on his way and used all his means to get their phone numbers in the hope of dating. After he had used them, he will end their relationship and move on. He had that reputation, but he was also a well-known and respectful gentleman. After all, he was a businessman.

'You look very tired. Let's go home. I have prepared food for you,' said Mustapha.

The two new friends went home to eat, and for Abdul to rest. Upon their arrival at home, Abdul found his meal ready; he feasted and went to bed in the guest room, which was well prepared to receive him.

That was the very first time he spent a night in a large house where the comfort and warm welcome were part of the hospitable reception after several days of an ordeal journey. Abdul had now decided to turn the page on his past and focus on his future. After a long and tiring day, it was time for him to have a good sleep. He stretched himself on his soft mattress bed and slept deeply like a new-born baby, but his sleep did not last long. He woke up early in the middle of the night, then went and sat on the couch. All his thoughts turned to his family, and every time he closed his eyes, he remembered his father, his uncle, his friends, and especially the bad and the good things he had done to people who had lived around him. He was very sorry for his actions, and now he felt lonely to decide his fate. Apart from the warm welcome he had received on his arrival, he no longer wanted to stay at Mustapha's for another month. He wanted to leave Dakar as soon as possible for Europe at all costs. Echoes crossed his mind and sank into deep thought and started meditating.

How much will it cost me a trip to find a better life in Europe? Oh no, maybe I need to get a passport first, then a visa! Oh, not all that, perhaps it won't be possible for me to have a passport and why not follow the method that many illegal immigrants used to get into Europe, meaning to pay someone to smuggle me through the Mediterranean Sea by boat? Yes, indeed, an excellent idea, but at what price? Oh no, what a complication, then what should I do? Probably, I will leave it to God to decide what is best for me; he murmured while asking himself a series of questions and answered them instantly.

Mustapha had never had a deep sleep at night. He had that curiosity to know everything that happened around him when the night fell in silence, not only in his house but also in the surrounding neighbourhood. He had that constant habit of spying on his neighbours; he lived like a secret service agent and had adopted their lifestyles.

Early in the morning, Mustapha appeared before Abdul's room to make sure he had a good sleep as he had heard noises in the guest room, he knocked on the door.

'I felt that you hadn't had a good sleep last night,' he said to Abdul.

'No! Not at all, perhaps it might be the environment change that had affected me,' replied Abdul.

'All right, these changes will disappear in a short time, and you will get back to your normal sleep,' replied Mustapha.

'What do we intend to do today?' asked Abdul.

'Well, today, we will go around the city, and then I will introduce you to some of my friends,' replied Mustapha.

Mustapha was a quiet one, and that was the trouble. He didn't seem to have any vices. He didn't smoke; he never smelled alcohol on his breath and spent the most evening in his villa listening to the RFI and BBC news on his radio. He read a lot of newspapers and went on for long walks to look for women. Abdul suspected he was quite clever and could well introduce him to good people to find his way out of the country.

Dakar was too different from Conakry regarding climate and habitat. Nevertheless, they went for a walk under the overwhelmed heat that could not be measured to the weather in

Conakry unless you found yourself next to the sea or used the air conditioner to breathe fresh air. The extreme heat was unbearable; Abdul's whole body flooded with black sweat, which dyed the colour of his shirt. To mitigate the temperature, Mustapha took Abdul to the fashion store and bought him a shirt in which he got changed before they arrived at their destination.

'Here, I mean in Dakar, you have to get change several times a day if you're always on the move,' said Mustapha with a laugh. After a long and tiring walk to meet some of Mustapha's friends, unfortunately, most of them cancelled their meeting, and so Mustapha decided to postpone the rest of their visit and went back home before sunset.

'It's time to go home and have a rest,' said Mustapha.

Abdul was not at ease; he wanted to meet with Mustapha's friends to begin his visa process for Europe because, for him, any further delay could depress him, and he had already started feeling the anxiety. He became very anxious and suspicious of his guardian. Initially, he began to look at the situation and learned step by step what Mustapha could do for him, but then got to know him deep down before confiding his fears to him.

The following day in the afternoon was memorable for Mustapha, who had just fallen in love for the first time in his life after he had done several unsuccessful marathons behind girls. This beautiful creature was called Ramatu, a seductive girl. She had very fair skin, almost white, and undoubtedly one of the most beautiful girls he had ever met. She was lovely and admirable, and in addition to her quality, she had the most beautifully soft and silky long hair, which framed her elegant face.

He came back home running at high speed, and then, he slowed down. 'I finally found the love of my life,' he said to Abdul in a cheerful voice.

The news moved Abdul; he nodded his head and congratulated him on his new love life but worried much more about his future than Mustapha's romance, because, since the last few days, Mustapha had not had enough free time to discuss his fate.

He stood for a while, and then he left Mustapha and went to his room. His thought went back on days when his uncle was his guardian; he dropped everything and guided him towards his studies, unlike his new guardian Mustapha who's concerned about his love affair. If Mustapha did not change his attitude towards him, then he would be left with no choice but to take the matter into his own hands and decide his fate. After days and weeks of romance, Mustapha discovered that his beloved Ramatu was a professional prostitute and a well-known drug dealer. She dates and used businesspeople to sell her goods without the slightest suspicion from authorities. After she had finished exploiting them, she then will throw them into the gangster's hands to put an end to their lives. Mustapha had all this information from a reliable source, and he had now found himself trapped in a very alarming and disturbing situation. He loved Ramatu very much and did not want to lose her in any way, but the danger that followed his beloved was very imminent and frightening. Later that day, he called Abdul to his room and explained what he had discovered about his lover and then asked for his opinion on the matter and if he had to inform the authorities and the police?

'Is that necessary to inform the police or ending my relationship with her?' he asked for Abdul's opinion.

'Ending the relationship is not a solution,' replied Abdul.

Abdul had never been afraid of telling the truth, he pretty much like being confronted and especially put himself before the facts. He tried to persuade and remove the grief and fear that was hiding behind his guardian, Mustapha. He knew the relationship would not work between them as this kind of precarious love adventure would not predict a good future nor make his guardian happy; he had this intuition and had known for some time. Since the day Mustapha had blindly fallen into Ramatu's net and sealed his romance with her, Abdul's friendship with Mustapha had gradually changed over time. Still, he did not feel comfortable to see his unlucky-in-love guardian losing control of his life. Now it was time for him to show Mustapha how dearly he held to their friendship and shared his fear and sadness as the friendship belonged to someone who knows how to enhance, nurture and give value to it.

'Don't worry, Mustapha, we will find a solution to this problem,' he reassured him.

'For how long, my friend?' Mustapha replied with a firm tone.

'You truly need a moment on your own and a good rest. We'll discuss it early in the morning,' Abdul replied with a smile.

The following morning, after breakfast was hastily eaten, Mustapha left the dining table and went out. It seemed that he had not slept all night. Abdul sprang to his feet and went to re-join Mustapha on the veranda to reiterate his support and provided him with wise advice.

'Have you slept enough?' asked Abdul.

'Not at all,' replied Mustapha.

'Can we talk? Because I have something to say, you might like it,' said Abdul.

'A few friendship pieces of advice. You know Mustapha, my friend, life is full of positive and negative circumstances that will bring many joys and disappointments, and which sometimes will be too difficult to cope. But all these will come with experiences of learning what life means,' a moment of silence, then he continued. 'Surely, what had happened to you had given you an idea of life, now let's prepare for your future,' he advised.

Mustapha thanked him for this wise advice and then embraced him warmly and gave him a quick kiss on the cheek.

'My friend, I came to understand that the world can change people, and the same people can forget the evil things they had done to others and keep repeating the same mistakes all over their life. I have learned a lot and need to do more to repent myself of what I have done to people in the past. Probably not many people had appreciated my actions, but surely getting a faithful friend is worth more than the companionship of thousands of infidels,' said Mustapha.

Abdul was an intelligent and confident person, he knew what he wanted, and he knew, of course, that Mustapha's success would depend only on his effort. Later that day, after a long reflection, Abdul and Mustapha suggested that it would be necessary for them to go and consult his marabout protector, Samba Sarr, who was well known by several wealthy businessmen through his prayers. Especially his blessings which would not delay being granted by invoking God's name. As soon they made their decision, they hurried and went to see Samba Sarr and knocked on his door.

Tuc! Tuc! Tuc! 'Yes, come in!' said Samba Sarr, the two friends entered the house and sat next to each other.

'Oh, Samba Sarr, I come to you to ask for protection and blessings. In fact, I fell blindly in love with a beautiful woman whom I could not control myself. I found out that the same woman is a prostitute, and she's also involved in drug dealing. I am afraid, too afraid because I risked losing my life, my honour and everything that I owned,' his voice interrupted. 'I ask you to pray for me so that she could leave me without causing any harm. I know, and everybody knew your blessing is worth billions. For that reason, I don't know how to pay you for your work,' he pleaded his case before the marabout.

'I share your fear and your pain. I will pray for you tonight with the grace of God; we will find a solution to your problems. Can you come back to see me tomorrow morning?' said Samba Sarr.

The next morning, they went back to see the marabout Samba Sarr regarding their consultation result following their request. Upon their arrival, they knocked on his door and entered the house. Samba Sarr said to them. 'I am against lies and any other embezzlement. I don't like people who profit on the backs of others, but I will support those who want to stand up and make an honest living. During my prayer, I saw a lot of trouble rather than good coming to you, and that could happen to you soon. I have also foreseen the uncertainty and despair that will destroy most of your activities that include arrest, loss of property, imprisonment, and humiliation, none of you will get away from this situation. You have to be very careful because these things would happen within days to come, so it would be better for you to leave this country as soon as possible. Still, for now, I will do many prayers, sacrifices, and take necessary measures so that God might spare you from these problems,' the marabout provided him with the message. Then he continued.

'There is a proverb that said when they wash your back, you should wash the rest of your body. I'll do the best on my side, and you should play your part obviously in this case. By the grace of God and his helping power, you would leave this country safely without obstruction and arrests,' predicted Samba Sarr.

Mustapha and his companion, Abdul, decided to go and meet with Ramatu at her house next to the crossroad, which was not far from the alley that separated her house to Mustapha's villa. Abdul was curious and excited to see her in the middle of the day as he had not met her in the daylight, but only twice at night, and even then, he could not remember the exact time.

Upon their arrival, Mustapha knocked on her door. She took her time to open the door. Abdul thought the surprise visit to her house would make her scared. Still, the visit did not surprise Ramatu at all as she knew somehow, somebody would be visiting her soon and that could be either the police or Mustapha. She was very concerned about the situation in which she was involved, and that had become increasingly difficult and complicated for her to cope with. She wanted to leave Dakar and sought refuge somewhere away from the country. This willingness to leave the country was a bet won for Abdul since he had no money to make the journey. His hope turned to the goodwill of the two friends.

In the state of Ramatu's anxiety, Mustapha disclosed the prediction of Samba Sarr and said that they should leave the country as soon as possible.

'Darling, we should leave this country today or tomorrow the latest,' said Mustapha.

'But where shall we go?' she asked.

'Somewhere, far away from here,' replied Mustapha.

'Let's migrate illegally to Europe, as it is already too late to seek a visa!' added Abdul.

These ideas were very welcomed by both, without thinking of the risks and costs they would face during this long and dangerous journey before reaching Europe.

The Miserable

The day of departure had arrived. Abdul and his two companions left Dakar late at night to reach the city of Kayes early in the morning. They arrived at Kidira a few kilometres from the border that separated Senegal to Mali, the trio descended from the car, and they did the rest on foot to avoid Abdul being stopped by the customs officers in case if they fell into a systematic control. As they approached the border, more uniformed officers showed their presence and their hope of crossing diminished but determined to confront the situation at all costs. To help Abdul cross the border without being arrested, they decided to play false at the border. Mustapha ordered everyone to play their role and said.

'Ramatu, comb your hair, and do your makeup, stay in front of us! And for you, Abdul, pretend that you are ill! And I will be right behind you to look out for the easiest agent to negotiate with to make it easy for us to pass. That way, our journey will be easier.'

'Do I make myself understood?' he asked them.

'Yes, understood!' they replied.

They stood for a while to make everything look perfect, and then suddenly they made up their mind and went to the control office for the checking before crossing. The two presented their travel documents except for Abdul, who posed as a sick man.

'Sir, can you present your identity document, please?' asked the customs agent.

Ramatu rushed to speak on behalf of Abdul to avoid a possible mistake, then she replied to the agent in her mother tongue in (Wolof),

'*Samaa dieukeur laa, daffa febaar danio waarra demm settii faadj kaatt.*' A minute of silence, then she continued.

'*Samaa fautelaa, maa maa waaronn dieul passport raam. Nguirr yallah dimbaalee maa,*' pleaded in Wolof 'Senegalese language'.

'Oh! Sorry, he's my husband, he's suffering from an illness; we are going to see a traditional healer for his treatment. A minute of silence, then she continued.

'It is my fault to leave his passport at home, please let us pass,' she pleaded.

Facing that situation, the agent called his chief. 'Sir Lieutenant, we have a situation over here!'

Suddenly, Mustapha came to their rescue. 'There's no situation here, my sergeant!' said Mustapha.

He took an envelope out of his pocket and slipped a sum of one hundred-franc CFA banknotes in his hand; the agent quickly pocketed the money before being seen by his colleagues. To calm down the situation, he found an argument to dissuade his chief, who was on his way to inquire about the reality of the problem.

'Sir Lieutenant, the gentleman on the other side is seriously ill, the control is done, they are all clear, and they can pass,' he explained to his chief.

After a few minutes of walking, they found a second barrier on the Malian side of the border. But this time, Mustapha stood in front of his friends, as he now knew how to corrupt the customs officers whose duty was to secure the movements of people and goods in the borders. They approached very slowly and pretended to be local people who lived in the area. Surprisingly, they noticed that these customs agents were much more occupied bribing travellers than keeping the border secure.

Upon their arrival at the barrier crossing, everything went smoothly. No passport was asked neither identity card, only a sum of five hundred francs CFA was presented to an agent who let them cross openly and publicly in the sight of those who were present at the place. On the other side of the road, the taxi was waiting for them, ready to continue the journey towards the city of Kayes in the Republic of Mali.

They reached Kayes city before the cockcrow. The loud car's engine broke the silence of the night, and the wheels that crunched on gravel when the car stopped abruptly inside the compound, reverberated the popping sound distressingly. It was so terrible that the noises could weaken a strong man's heart. It was still dark, under the popping sound from the house that faces the car, somebody lit up the oil lamp. Shortly after that, the door opened abruptly and the woman who came to open it still had the heavy, sleepy face with a half-open eye, she walked directly to the veranda like a sleepwalker. The moonless night was still far from being illuminated; she lit her torch and leaned over to the left and the right; she remained standing a bit longer with a gaze lost in the darkness.

'Who are you?' No one answered; they sat in the car in dead silence. 'Who are you, for the last time before I call for help?' She asked.

The car doors slowly opened, the three silhouettes headed towards her, a cold shiver ran down her body as she stood gazing down at the direction of the dark silhouettes. She then heard a voice coming from a distance. 'Kadi, we are your visitors. Mustapha and his friends!'

'Oh, the foreign nomads, you came so late at night. You're welcome! Come in and rest,' she replied jokingly, then the door closed behind them.

The curious neighbours came out carrying their oil lamps in one hand. There was a light wind blowing, so they cupped their other hand to shelter the flame, they stood in the darkness outside their house watching the strange event as the visitors entered Kadi's house.

Kadi was a very welcoming business lady who always put the interests of others before her own. Apart from that, she also knew very well the circuit of the smugglers, the dangers and difficulties that ensued from the departure to the final destinations for those who fled persecution from their countries to chase for a better life in Europe as many illegal immigrants had come to her home in the past and had continued their perilous journey to get into Europe at any cost.

After a brief introduction and the reason that made them travelled to Kayes, then they sought her advice and explained their intentions to continue their journey through the desert to reach Europe. She provided friendly advice before letting them decide their fate.

'I had received immigrants who had come to see me before taking their journey to chase up for a better life in Europe, but many of them had never succeeded in their adventure. They came back to find me here, others had succeeded in crossing the Mediterranean Sea, and they had called me on my phone to update me about their situation. However, others were gone and never came back; some of them had died in the desert while others in the Mediterranean Sea.' she wiped her tears.

'The Mediterranean Sea has become the most accessible way to reach Europe but also the deadliest so far and the graveyards of many young people like you, who were in their middle life of having a family. So, it's a matter of winning or losing. In any case, I would not discourage you from continuing your journey,' said Kadi to his interlocutors.

The conversation ended with a long and deep sleep that eventually dominated them. After a long hour of rest, Mustapha received a phone call from a smuggler in Bamako, to go and meet with them immediately to begin negotiating their departure for Europe. At the same time, his other friends were still snoring as a result of the exhausting long journey they went through. Mustapha got up and went to inform Kadi of the good news.

'This call is very important to me and that we have to leave this evening,' said Mustapha.

'Good, as you wish, I will not hold you any longer,' replied Kadi.

'Dear Kadi, there's not words we can express our gratitude to you than to thank you for the welcoming and the hospitality you have given to us,' said Mustapha.

'It's my duty to help you, and I did it with pleasure,' replied Kadi.

After saying goodbye to her, they resumed their journey to Bamako, the Malian capital city, to meet the smuggler named Keita, who is the middleman and will guide them to Alfonso, the contractor, and then to the leader of the smugglers, John. The journey was long and arduous; the road was dusty and impracticable. The following day around seven o'clock in the morning, the group arrived in Bamako, and they went to meet with their smuggler, Keita, who was already at the Bamako Market and was waiting for them to arrive anxiously. A car approached and stopped, and the engine switched off, Keita lit a cigarette to signal his presence.

Mustapha and his friends got off from the car; then headed to meet Keita. After they had shaken hands, he cleared his throat and gave them a brief introduction of five minutes, then presented himself as a middleman and what he does in this business. They went and sat in a cafeteria and waited for another car to take them to Alfonso's to negotiate the contract, then to finalise the deal at John's house, located in one of the fourth district called Sebeninkoro in the city of Bamako. A cosmopolitan area that housed several ethnic groups which combined among others of Bambara, Fulani, Mandingo, Bozo and Bobo, all cohabited together in peace and harmony, and no one knew what other do for their daily activity to support their living in the neighbourhood. Nevertheless, it was a good hiding place for smugglers to live. While waiting for the car to arrive, Mustapha and Ramatu dozed off as a result of a long and tiring journey. Abdul stood at the corner facing the window and occasionally stared at Keita, who was using three mobile phones to send messages to unknown people. A few minutes later, he received a phone call; he looked on the screen then refused to answer. Abdul thought that Keita was planning to kidnap them; echoes crossed his mind and asked himself questions.

Why does Keita have three phones ringing without answering the calls? Perhaps, he had an idea behind his head to swindle us, he murmured, and then he openly decided to ask Mustapha. He gently strokes Mustapha's shoulder, who instantly turned his head and looked at him.

'Why does Keita use three mobile phones at the same time? Don't you think this is suspicious behaviour?' Asked Abdul.

'Well, this is the lifestyle of the businessmen and even me back in days when I was in Dakar, I had two mobile phones, I used one for the customers, and the other was for my personal calls,' Mustapha replied.

After a few hours of waiting, a car stopped right in front of the bar-restaurant. They went on-board, and the car disappeared from the traffic. When they arrived at their destination, Alfonso was seating in the cafeteria that faced the main road. He watched all the ant movements that peoples were doing on the street so that he could avoid any possible surprise from unknown customers whom he had never known nor met. Mistrust and caution were part of Alfonso's daily life because he did not know who these new customers are? He thought that they could be from the police or else.

'Prudence is the mother of safety,' said Alfonso

A few minutes later, the car's engine switched off, Alfonso walked over to the unknown customers and greeted them. Then took them to a house reserved for them to stay overnight, soon after they had entered, they signed the contract to take them to Europe while waiting for the leader John to finalise it the following day. After they had signed the paperwork, they will pay the full amount before they began for their journey to Europe.

It was almost dust when Alfonso had left; they went to bed so that they could wake up early to meet John and left their baggage in the living room. For the first time in twenty-four hours, Abdul and his two friends slept deeply. Ramatu woke up in the middle of the night and went to the toilet; she returned and went back to sleep. A mosquito wailed her ears; she slapped it and hoped she had killed it. She heard a bang on the door, followed by an unfamiliar movement in the living area. She gently strokes Mustapha then Abdul's shoulders, but both stretched themselves, and Abdul scratched his thigh where a mosquito had bitten him, he went back to sleep. Ramatu stood for a while, waiting for them to wake up, then she made up her mind and went to find out what was going on in the living room. She saw two silhouettes in the darkness; a cold shiver ran down her body. She shouted thieves and fainted then she fell down violently. The two robbers who had broken into the house fled with their belongings; the two sleepers heard something heavy falling on the floor. They jumped from their sleep and threw themselves against each other in the search for the lighter, anything that could lighten up the room. Shortly thereafter, Abdul found a box of matches.

'Here are the matches,' shouted Abdul.

As they ran to the living room, they found Ramatu unconscious laid on the floor, Mustapha asked Abdul to bring him water, then shouted.

'Ramatu! Ramatu! Abdul, bring me water quickly,' he broke down and sobbed like a child.

Abdul rushed and brought the water and then poured over Ramatu's head, while Mustapha was desperately trying to wake her up. A few minutes later, she coughed up and opened her eyes.

They carried her to the room; she stayed on her bed for a while, rubbing her eyes and stretching her small frame. Her mind went back in days when she was in Dakar, the problem she went through, and started to remember what had happened in the house that night. She got up and went to join them in the living room, in a very disturbed state; she then found both sullen and silent. Mustapha stood up and held her hand then he cried.

'Honey, they robbed us, everything is gone even my pants are gone, nothing left in the luggage,' said Mustapha.

The money they had kept for their trip to Europe was just a memory. Shocked, the three wretches sat around the dining table to discuss the future of their adventure. Abdul looked at them straight in the eyes and said.

'What I understand about this problem is that John and his rogue friend Keita burgled us.'

Each one spoke about their thoughts, and the anxiety grew among them, then Ramatu said.

'In fact, we do not have the money for the trip, and John will not be able to accept us of staying any longer in this house.' She wiped her tears and continued to sympathise. 'It will cost us dearly to survive without money, and besides that, we should manage to leave this house as quick as possible without being seen by the neighbours,' said Ramatu, her voice weakened but tried to continue. 'I remember seeing silhouettes of two or three people in the luggage area which seemed to have the normal shape that resembled Keita's but could not be John's for sure,' she said. 'So, it's Keita, let's go and arrest him, or let the police know about it,' said Mustapha.

'Leave the facts as they are and expect John to come and see the damage before making any decisions,' said Ramatu.

Each of them spoke the way they thought. Abdul spoke at last, which led them to a solution.

'I have an idea. If we applied it right now, it would help us overcome the challenges we are facing, and we will save some amount of money, too,' he said.

The two interlocutors were so desperate that they agreed on the word of an idea spoken by Abdul without even letting him finish what he was saying. Then, they let Abdul detail his idea and planned how to execute it.

'This idea is to create a scam network; I'll disguise myself as a marabout, you Mustapha and Ramatu will find and bring clients for spiritual consultation. In turn, I will use methods to extract money from them, and if we understood each other well, then we will use it to pay for our trip,' explained Abdul.

At dawn, they scattered on their own ways to find clients to scam. Abdul went to present himself to a man called Doumbia, a very honest and sincere family man who always put himself at the service of others. He asked him for shelter and said.

'Destiny led me straight to you. Indeed, I am a foreigner who is heading to the north of the country and, therefore, soliciting a place to rest for a few days.'

Doumbia accepted Abdul's request and offered him hospitality for some time.

'It's a duty to all Muslims to come to the aid of those in need. Here is the guest room, and you can rest as long as you want,' said Doumbia.

After Abdul's friends spent the whole day in vain with no customers and no rest, Mustapha decided to meet Ramatu, who was already tired and discouraged. She wanted to go back home to deal with the problems she had left behind her but had a lack of courage as she no longer wanted to meet her drug dealer friends. Therefore, she strove to do everything she could to find the means to continue her journey to Europe; she thought that the easiest way to make money is to break up her romance with Mustapha. Then she went to tell Mustapha that she no longer felt any affection for him. Upon her arrival, she found Mustapha in a terrible mood. He asked her to come to his rescue, when she saw his state of mind, instead of telling him the decision to break up, she decided to be supportive towards Mustapha and comforted him.

'It's only you who could get us out of this misery,' said Mustapha

She felt it was her obligation to sell her body to get them out of the situation; she became a prostitute to provide money for the group's need in the hope of continuing their journey to the West. During her new profession, any money obtained was controlled and saved into Mustapha's account. One day, the two squabbled about how the money she earned would be spent. By dishonesty, Mustapha took advantage of this fall-out and ran away with her economy. But Ramatu was determined more than ever before to continue her journey to build her future; she would not back down. She met several clients; among them was Keita, the suspect who had broken into their house.

Her first encounter with Keita automatically reminded her what had happened the night the burglary took place inside their house. Ramatu set up an excellent plan to trap Keita so that she could get back her personal belongings, she decided to approach him, but as it has been several months since they were robbed and they had only met once, Keita did not recognise her. Meanwhile, he became obsessed with Ramatu, and the two decided to go to Keita's for intimacy and made an appointment to meet in John's villa, where he stayed as a guest.

At the agreed time, Ramatu went to meet with Keita to fulfil her promises to give him pleasure during which she slipped the spare key into her bra and then left the place to meet Abdul and explained to him the whole story. Initially, Abdul was saddened to see her selling her body for money and totally refused to accept to hear that his guardian, Mustapha, had emptied all her economy and fled to an unknown destination. Still, despite the heart-breaking news, Abdul maintained his calm not to let himself be dominated by anger. He listened to her a lot and spoke less. This story of the break-up between Ramatu and his friend Mustapha made him weaker, and to what he did to Ramatu made him hate Mustapha for life. Still, Mustapha's action pushed him to take control of his own life and became stronger to face his destiny.

After all, he felt alone in his adventure but determined to pursue the journey to find a better in Europe. While they had fallen apart, Ramatu was making lots of money working morning and night in the bars and nightclubs in the capital and accumulated money for her future. And Mustapha, who's supposed to protect them and guide Abdul's steps towards the promised land, had fled with all the economy of Ramatu without leaving any trace behind him.

To fight for survival, Abdul asked Ramatu to give him all the information regarding Keita. After she had provided him with relevant information, he then said.

'Tonight, you have to get in touch with Keita and ask if he needs help, then you will tell him that you know a reputable, well-known marabout who could help him get rich quicker and become richer more than his boss, John, and if he agrees with that, then tell him to contact me immediately.'

In the evening, Ramatu applied what Abdul had said to her. Indeed, Keita wanted to be a reputable smuggler and have his own business like his boss, John. He also wanted to be independent, but due to lack of means, there was absolutely nothing he could do. So, he was willing to sell his soul to the devil to meet his needs.

'You know the foreign businessmen operating in Mali have money and besides that, they help each other. I feel like a foreigner among them in my own country, if you can help me find this marabout you told me about recently. Frankly, I'll be grateful,' Keita confided in Ramatu.

As agreed, the two made an appointment for a spiritual consultation with Abdul the marabout. On the day of the visit, Abdul spent the whole day transforming his room and preparing the robe, which he would wear for the spiritual consultation of that day. He went to borrow a goatskin prayer mat, long rosary, and long half white and red turban, which he would use to veil his face like those Tuaregs who lived in the north of Mali. Having the habit and experience to consult himself the marabouts to find out about his future, he had a perfect knowledge of how they do their spiritual consultations. He decided to use a few words extracted from the Qur'an to convince Keita more and to play him false so that they could get back what he had stolen from them.

The Robbers Robbed

At ten o'clock in the morning, Abdul disguised himself like a Tuareg, he wore a combination of the turban with a veil and seated quietly on a goatskin mat spread out in the middle of the room, as do the marabouts of his native country, Guinea. To his left-hand side, there were two black bottles containing saltwater, a darkened ink in a pot, and sand mixed with a white chalk powder wrapped up in a white paper. On his right-hand side, there was a cup filled with ashes picked from woods burning stove made locally with clay, which the women used to cook food. In front of him, there was the Qur'an and papers filled with illegible hieroglyphics characters, a formal writing system used in ancient Egypt. Two long powerful horns decorated with a red cloth, all surrounded by cowries and suspended at the top of the door so that it could be viewed soon after the client entered the room.

When you are in the adventure, if you cannot make money to survive, at least, you must learn a new skill combined with experience to make it happen, he murmured while making sure everything was done correctly.

The consultation appointment time approached, Ramatu and Keita headed to Abdul's room.

'Salam Alaykum,' said Ramatu.

'Wa Alaykum Salaam, please come in,' replied Abdul.

The two visitors took off their shoes, then entered and sat down on the well-prepared sofa for the appointment. While waiting for Keita to be introduced by Ramatu, Abdul put his hand into his right pocket and then pulled out a red Kola nut; he split it in two. He began to chew one part; then put the other part in his left pocket, after he had swallowed it, he then cleared his throat and pronounced. 'Waa Salaam! Waa Salaam!' to allow them to start the conversation.

'Grand marabout, I know that your word never lies, I have witnessed, and so has many, based on this trustworthy, it has made me come to you with my friend to help him in his projects,' she explained to Abdul the marabout.

'How can I help you, Keita?' Abdul asked Keita.

'I come to discover what the future holds for me; I also want to be rich and independent so that I can be able to create my own business, also chase away misfortune and bring back a lot of fortunes in my life afterwards. After you have done all, I will need your blessing…'

Abdul interrupted him and said to him. 'Before confirming if I could help you, I first have to consult my Djinns who hold my power.'

He opened his book and pulled out a sheet that contained the illegible hieroglyphics characters, then laid it on the mat in front of him, he took a piece of chalk, drew some square lines on the floor and put one cowrie in each square. He broke the half Kola that he kept in his pocket and threw it in his mouth and began to chew, shortly thereafter, he spat on the cowries.

'During my prayers, you must pronounce amen until I stop,' he told Keita.

He took the rosary and began to count the prayers as they are recited out loud. Suddenly, he murmured quietly and closed his eyes and meditated while he relied on the rosary beads to keep track of how many times he had pronounced the same words. A few minutes after the ritual, he stopped and opened his eyes and glanced up. 'You are going through a difficult time. I can help you. Your friend with whom you live in the house poses a huge obstacle to you, and he does not want your success. But don't be afraid because you have fallen into the right hand. If you do what I ask you today, in three days from tonight, your desire and wills would be exalted and will be fulfilled in seven days.'

He promised and then continued, he pointed his finger and said. 'Keita look at these short perpendicular lines drawn in order of magnitude on this paper. There are seven groups, and the smallest groups have fewer lines than the biggest ones, and each represents fortunes and misfortunes. You see, your misfortune is bigger than your fortune.

'You will take this bottle and rub your body with the liquid that is contained in it for three days, during which you must not be in contact with a woman. Then, I will give you this powder; it must be poured in the courtyard during the night, then you will leave and never return until the following day. Beware, when pouring the powder; make sure your friend is not at home. Otherwise, all the fortunes and good lucks will go to him, and you will have nothing but misfortunes and bad luck. In reality, none of you should return home until the next day.

'Now you can go, may the grace of God shine upon you! Remember, the work is guaranteed for seven days, so it would be better that you start doing what I have told you and apply them tonight,' insisted Abdul.

Keita slipped his hand in his pocket and then pulled out a lump sum of three hundred CFA and handed it to him. Abdul took the money and reminded him that this amount was not the price of his work and that he would be paid only after seeing the results of the job done.

'You will only pay me when you see the result, that's how I used to work with my clients,' he said.

Nevertheless, he thanked Keita for the gesture of goodwill; then, they went their way. A few hours later, Ramatu returned to Abdul's room and brought him the good news.

'Tonight, John will travel to Gao and shall only come back tomorrow night, so Keita should start using what you had given to him tonight,' she reported.

Soon after John had departed for Goa, Keita waited for a while to make sure that he had left Bamako entirely. Shortly after, he returned to John's courtyard and applied the instruction given to him and spent most of his time with his friends and never returned until the next day when he found out that his boss was on his way back from his trip, then he went to welcome him at home. Ramatu, who had remained in Abdul's room since she had reported the news, reminded Abdul about their plans. She then called Keita to make sure that he had applied the instruction given to him by Abdul. Soon after she had received the affirmative answer, she transmitted to Abdul the outcome.

'Tonight is our last chance to get back what had been stolen from us, only the moon and the stars will witness what will happen in the thieves' house,' murmured Abdul.

The two dressed in black that night from the heads to toes; they would be almost invisible in the darkness, and the place they were going was blackened out too; no electricity, only a few generators were making noises in different locations.

They boarded a taxi and went to John's villa. Halfway to the location, they got off and crossed the road and followed the path which led to the villa where Keita and John lived.

'Be careful and don't panic, look straight at where you are going, pretend that you're coming home,' she encouraged Abdul.

'Okay, but how do we get in as the gate is locked and the house too?' Abdul asked.

'Don't worry, I have the house key, but not the gate key,' replied Ramatu.

'Well, how did you manage to get that key?'

'This is not the time to ask these stupid questions,' she replied vigorously.

They carried on walking through the quiet streets with dimmed lights from oil lamps that kept some bars and restaurants illuminated. It was midnight, and they saw no one wandering around. Then they kept walking slowly, instead of heading straight to Keita's villa, they went to an abandoned semi-constructed building which had its fences wall close to John's villa. They made their way carefully across the rubble in the front garden, using the gap in the doorway to enter the abandoned semi constructed house to the wall that separated the two buildings. It was evidently dark; a thick low cloud hid the moon and the stars, they had to walk using a stick to guide them.

Soon, they reached the end of the wall; they climbed and jumped over the fence wall and fell into John's garden. A neighbour's dog barked for a few minutes they then stood up quietly and made their way to the main door of the villa. Ramatu took the key from her pocket and unlocked the door, then went to open the back door for an emergency escape. She shone a torch through the living room to make sure that they were going in the right direction, the darkened house smelled of newly cooked food then they realised that Keita had just left the building.

Both began to look at every corner of the house. During the search, they found some of the stolen items that belonged to them. Ramatu bent and glanced under the bed; she found a small bag that contained a lump sum of money around fifty thousand francs CFA.

'But fifty thousand would not be enough for the transport of two of us to Gao, let alone to introduce us to the smugglers,' said Abdul.

'Don't be discouraged; let us continue to search and check everywhere; we should not neglect any place; it's at the end of the effort that we will succeed.'

After they had carried out a thorough search and did not recover all their belongings, Ramatu handed all the money found to Abdul.

'Well, that's my way of helping you financially, you have been too kind to me,' she said with a smile on her face.

Abdul was overwhelmed with the humble gesture from Ramatu; he could not hold back his tears for any longer and began to cry incessantly.

'Hey, be a strong man, we shall meet in Gao tomorrow night,' she added. Abdul was impressed by the tactic used by Ramatu, which consisted in bringing the thief and then neutralised him and stole his belongings and recovered back some of their belongings.

'We have to leave this place now! Let's go quickly,' Abdul said.

She closed the doors gently behind them as if nothing had happened and ran away. When Abdul arrived at home, he went straight to Doumbia and thanked him for his hospitality, then returned the key and gave him an amount of three hundred francs CFA as a goodwill gesture. From there, he made his way to Goa, hoping to meet Ramatu the next day.

This gigantic city was situated at the gates of the desert and was one of the highlighted passages of illegal immigrants to Europe. The bus station was overcrowded by passengers coming from Niger, Burkina Faso, and other Malian cities. The door of the minibus opened, the passengers went down and headed for the exit. Abdul stood behind, looking for Ramatu, who should be there too. Approximately twelve metres away from the station, he saw a dark-skinned man; he was tall and robust, dignified and extremely powerful with a bald forehead and short hair on the side and short moustache. He was talking to a group of illegal immigrant candidates in the open air. Abdul introduced himself as an independent candidate who wanted to join the group for the conquest of Europe. A few minutes later, two other candidates joined them; the intermediate smuggler decided that they would sit in a restaurant to discuss clearly which procedure to follow. Abdul was calmed and listened attentively to the information that the intermediary detailed to its clients.

'It's a large and well-structured network. We have correspondents everywhere from here to Europe, they will take care of you until you reach the European land,' said the first smuggler, before being interrupted by his assistant who was also part of the smugglers' network and warned the candidates.

'Look, here in Gao, there are crooks among us who pretend to be smugglers, be very careful, they can easily take your money and disappear for good,' added the second smuggler.

Among the interlocutors, there were two key members of networks specialising in the organisation of illegal immigration to Europe, who had received terrible news from the suppliers of the Malian passport. The debate began. George was in charge of the network in Mali, especially in the city of Gao, and Pascal was in charge of controlling the finance. The phone rang. It was panic; their correspondent, who was in Nigeria, came to tell them that there was a lack of blank Malian passport for new customers, which would double the price to 250 Euros for a passport. A big concern arose not only at the level of the smugglers based in Mali but also at the candidates who had already paid the money to obtain their new passports. In the discussions, George decided.

'All candidates who do not want to pay double of what they had paid in advance, should wait until we are supplied the new blank passports before serving them to you,' he said loudly.

One of the candidates named Saidu burst out and shouted, 'Then how long will it take us before we leave here?'

Someone else shouted loudly behind the crowd. It was Aliou, another candidate who, in turn, continued to speak out. 'We have no more money to pay for food, no more for the shelter. What are we going to do now to pay you extra money, as you have asked to pay double to which we cannot afford?'

'I understand your frustration; it's not your fault. We'll take care of you,' said George.

The good news had just fallen to the ears of the desperate immigrants, not only for those who had paid in advance but also for Abdul, who had only fifty thousand francs CFA, a lump sum equivalent to 100 Euros in his pocket. So, he had time to look around very quickly to complete the amount asked by George. Abdul had not had any idea that any individual holding this famous Malian passport would enter into Algerian and Moroccan territory without a visa. He never thought that people would come to Gao to supply themselves with such passports to continue their journey to Europe at a very exorbitant price.

In the evening, Abdul and the rest of the candidates were taken to a house where they would remain until their departure day for the conquest of Europe. At the nightfall, Abdul mobilised all the candidates and tried to convince them not to pay 250 Euros for a passport.

'My dear friends, we have to join hands together to succeed in this adventure, but under no circumstances shall we have to pay 250 Euros for a single passport, while we have other expenses to pay all along our way to Europe,' Abdul explained to the crowd of candidates.

By protest, the members of the group argued among themselves. Those who had enough money did not care to pay whatever the amount to reach Europe. However, those who were struggling to buy the basic necessities such as food before their departure lashed out in anger.

During this misunderstanding, they finally agreed to help each other to complete the deficits as they shared all the same worries in this adventure. Abdul felt welcome in the group while hiding his secrets. Aliou, the youngest of the group who had confided to Saidu as his protector, saw himself being used financially by Saidu. Since then, he had decided to leave him and went to join Abdul as his new guardian. No one knows what had happened between Saidu and Aliou at the time when they were really in need of money to leave Gao. Aliou was very discreet and never spoke if he had not been asked, and he only answered when he liked, he was the kind of person Abdul had been looking for since his arrival in Gao, a person of trust to whom he could share his plans with discretion.

Their first night together under the same roof, Abdul tied his money in the black plastic, then coated it in a dirty cloth, and then threw it under his bed. Early in the morning, Abdul went out to try his chance to find some money to add on top of what he had already saved. Upon his arrival later in the evening, very tired, he discovered that his hidden money had been stolen. He was heartbroken to the extent that he could not do anything to get back his stolen money but thought to make his own investigation.

To catch the culprit, he kept his composure and conducted his investigations discreetly. Only Aliou who had seen Saidu taking Abdul's money under the bed, but Saidu threatened to kill him if, by chance, he tried to report him.

For so long, Aliou was afraid of his ex-guardian for fear that one day, he would take all his pocket money and leave him with nothing but to beg on the street. Abdul approached Aliou and whispered in his ears that his money had been stolen and that he would need his help.

'My small amount of money has been stolen this morning, but I confess that if I did not get it back before sunset, I assure you, Aliou, I will burn this house when everybody falls asleep tonight,' he growled.

Aliou found himself between a rock and a hard place, wanting to tell him the truth would not spare him to confront Saidu and stay silent, Abdul will burn the house. Even though he wouldn't act as he said, but then, he will feel betrayed by his conscience and the confidence that Abdul had given him.

'I read in your eyes that you want to tell me something about my stolen money, tell me before it is too late,' said Abdul.

'No, Abdul, you know I'm afraid that something bad will happen to me,' said Aliou, trembling.

'If you tell me, I promise nothing would happen to you unless you're involved in stealing!' Abdul replied with a firm tone.

'I hate the accusation, only God knows who had stolen your money,' he paused then continued. 'If you promise to defend me, I'll tell you who took your money,' said Aliou

'I promise not only to defend you but also to travel with you and go far away with you,' reassured Abdul.

'Very well, when you went out early in the morning, I saw Saidu under your bed taking your money, he even threatened me with death if I ever told you,' reported Aliou.

When all information was gathered, Abdul decided to get his money back without Saidu knowing the source of the information. After a long thought without a solution, Abdul developed a plan to take revenge in his own way, but to get there, he tried to know everything about Saidu. He went back to see Aliou.

'You know Saidu more than all of us here. Can you tell me what he loves doing most in life?' he asked.

'Like what, for example?' Aliou asked the question.

'For instance, if Saidu likes to drink alcohol or smoke drugs, and so on,' Abdul added.

'Okay, regarding smoking drugs, I don't know about that, but what I do know is he likes to get drunk, if he found the opportunity, and also, he loves prostitutes. Sometimes, he keeps his money at his girlfriend's room, who is also a candidate for Europe like us, and then he took advantage of robbing all weakest people like me and others whom he met on his way during a night out,' explained Aliou.

'Thank you for the effort you made to provide me with this vital piece of information, once again, thank you so much,' he said.

Abdul had received the necessary information; now, everything will depend on him to get back his money. The next day, he went to contact George so that he could have two passports for Aliou and himself for 500 Euros and insisted that they could be among the next convoy for Algeria. Upon his return, he went to find Saidu sitting in the bar, chatting with two young women.

'Hello, my friend, Saidu! Hello, beautiful ladies!' Abdul bowed to them.

Saidu introduced him to the two young women.

'My friend, they are called Safia and Mainouna,' said Saidu.

'Pleased to meet you,' said Abdul to the girls.

They stayed in the bar and began drinking until late at night. Abdul counted at the end of his fingers the bottles consumed by Saidu and his guests. From time to time, he sniffed and cast a look of disgust at Saidu, whose dirty feet, covered with wounds, emit a nauseating odour. He watched them to the point of reassuring himself that Saidu was completely drunk and could not even stand up for himself. So, he offered to walk him home to rest. Saidu suddenly stood up and lost his balance and fell back; his legs were no longer responding to his command; he began to sing and insulting the bartender. At that point, Abdul offered him his shoulder and helped him to stand, then walked him to their shelter.

'Lie down on the bed, stupid drunken thief,' said Abdul.

When he laid him on the bed, he took off Saidu's shoes and put them aside and began to search him. After ten minutes of searching in vain, he straightened upright, held his hands on the hips, and wondered. 'Where have I not yet searched?' he whispered.

'Oh, maybe inside his pairs of shoes!' Saidu was very smart. He had a lump sum of 1500 Euros; which he hid in his pairs of shoes that he wore all day long.

Abdul lifted the first shoe; a nauseating smell invaded his nose. 'Oh no, it smells awful,' he murmured.

Then he pushed forward his hand into the shoe, he touched a hard object inside, then took it out. Surprisingly, he found money inside the shoe. He quickly looked at the second shoe; he also found the money. He put the shoes back in its place next to Saidu's bed then went out quietly without being seen by anyone.

He walked straight to Aliou's room and woke him up. 'Come on, boy! Come quickly, take your bag, we'll leave here today! Come with me,' he said in a hurry.

The two adventurers disappeared in the darkness and went to meet George. Abdul had nothing to fear since he had come to Gao on his own and had nothing to lose as he got the money back and had stolen another extra to add on top of what he got back. George saw them coming in the dark at dawn. He rubbed his hand.

'What a happy morning!' said George. Then he continued. 'Don't worry; your life is in my hands.' He shook their hands to seal the deal.

Abdul paid him the sum requested for their passports, and the affair was resolved. George put them in the next convoy, which would leave Gao the same day to Algeria.

The Painful Journey

After having a Malian passport in hand, Abdul and his companion had enough to present to the Algerian, then to the Moroccan border. They were thirty passengers of all ages, including three girls, packed in a minibus for a long and tiring journey of nine to ten hours driving in the desert. After two hours of travel, the driver received bad news following a phone call, a double blow for illegal immigrants on board. The smuggler in charge of driving the group was speaking to a member of the smuggling network based in Algeria. After a brief exchange of words, the driver decided to disclose this unexpected message to the passengers on board and said.

'When we arrive in Kidal, only fifteen people among you will be able to continue their way to Algeria; the others will have to wait in Kidal for two weeks before continuing,' said the driver, then he continued detailing. 'I repeat, only half of the thirty on the board of this minibus will continue to the border,' he reiterates.

'The choice of fifteen people will be made by order of merit,' said the smuggler named Abedine of Ivorian origin. A silence descended from the sky and swallowed the noise, and then he continued.

'Don't be afraid, that's how we work here,' he said.

The smugglers left them in a total uneasiness that swept their hope away. After a few kilometres of the journey, the vehicle broke down. The engine overheated had caused the radiator coolant to leak. So, it would take a few hours for the temperature level to cool down; then they will fix the leak before continuing the journey. Another uneasiness was added on top of the first one.

'Don't panic; pray to God so that we can have a safe journey to Kidal,' said Abdul.

A minute later, another candidate spoke out.

'Discouragement does not have a place in an immigrant's life, especially when you know that your means are limited,' said the Togolese Firou. And then he continued. 'Two months ago, I took the most dangerous route toward the western Sahara to try to make my way to Europe. I was arrested by the police and then sent back to my country of origin, and I am here today among you, what are you worried about?' Firou hammered.

The engine cooled down, the illegal immigrants went back on-board, and the vehicle resumed its journey. After a few hours on the road, the group arrived in the Malian town of Kidal, thirsty and exhausted. They rested for a while and waited for another long road to Algeria. The city of Kidal was the most crucial gathering point for these smugglers and the most frequented area by illegal immigrants to reach the European Eldorado. After three hours of waiting, another problem was added to the two others. Still, this time, it was the candidates transported from Gao who would join other candidates who had already waited impatiently for their departure with other smugglers. To calm the situation, the smugglers immediately found a solution to their radical decision. They subdivided the group into two; those who had negotiated to have the Malian passport will go down the south to reach Tinzaoutine, and the ones without passports will pass northwards through Tessalit and then Bodj. Abdul and other candidates embarked on board of another pick-up vehicle to the Algerian border. Then they would make the rest of the journey on foot to cross the border, which was heavily monitored by the Algerian security forces who were already informed of their movements along the border. And they were prepared to arrest any illegal immigrants who tried to cross as the border of the two countries was closed. The smuggler instructed the group to be attentive and more vigilant, as the soldiers on duty in these places during the night were equipped with night vision cameras, and they were more feared than those on duty during the day.

The illegal immigrants found themselves trapped in a disturbing situation. Rahim, the Malian smuggler, made brief telephone calls to his counterpart based on the other side of the Algeria border. Then he went to meet a police officer standing alone beside a ditch to negotiate their crossing.

'You want to cross alone or with a group?' asked the border officer.

Rahim responded politely. 'Yes, sir! I want to cross the border with my group of people.'

A few minutes later, a second silhouette emerged. The situation worsened; they began to ask Rahim many questions until he ran out of words. When they realised that he could not answer any more questions, then the agents asked him for money to let his group of immigrants enter illegally into Algerian territory. After they had spent times negotiating, finally, the amount of money demanded was paid, and the border control officers closed their eyes to let them cross the border.

The group entered safely into the Algerian territory. After they had emptied their pockets at the border, another financial problem arose. Abdul and his friend would have to pay the smuggler stationed in Algeria to transport them to Morocco through the desert from the south to the north, then into the city of Oujda in Morocco, which had to cost them an excessive sum of 250 Euros each, unnegotiable fixed price.

Aliou had nothing left on him and had spent all his money at the border. The remaining money Abdul had was not enough to cover the costs for them to travel from Algeria to Morocco and also pay the sailors to cross the Mediterranean Sea.

Abdul was a man of his words who respected his engagements to honour the promises kept to Aliou when they were in Gao; he created a plan to allow Aliou to travel to Morocco for free.

'Don't worry Aliou, we came here together, we'll leave here together,' he reassured Aliou.

He left and went to see Martin, who was an intermediary smuggler, and told him that the amount of money he had on him could not cover the cost of transport for two people. Still, he promised that once they arrived at Oujda, Aliou's brother would double the cost of his transportation and in addition to the money that Abdul will advance him on the spot. Overall, he would have received twice the amount that he had asked, and also, he would ask Aliou's brother to add some money in addition to the expenses already paid as a goodwill gesture. He guaranteed that when they got into Morocco, the money would be paid to him, which Martin believe that he had nothing to lose but to win in this negotiation.

As a large interconnected smuggler's network, nothing could escape their sight. He didn't think of the consequences of letting Aliou travel without paying the transport. His desire to make more profits blindly dominated him. Martin went to negotiate with another smuggler called Mohamed, who knew the safest roads in the desert and the military checkpoints in the area. He was a well-known smuggler and very competent in the camouflages, not only of illegal immigrants, but he was also a professional drug trafficker. Mohamed was a criminal on the loose and locally known in his activities by the police of the two Maghreb countries. He agreed to take them at the double the price of the transportation and that Martin should also be on-board the vehicle to make it easier to get his money back when they reached their destination.

After several hours of insomnia, effort, and fatigue, finally, the time of departure arrived; Abdul and his illegal immigrant's counterparts were delighted to leave Tinzaoutine for Oujda in Morocco. They were a total of eleven people, among the group, there was a girl named Angel of Cameroonian origin. She was on her second attempt in the adventure after she had been arrested in Morocco and then sent back to her native country, and here she was again among them. But this time, she wanted to cross the Mediterranean Sea to get into Europe at all costs; she began to provide wise advice and encouragement to the group.

'I sold all my possessions in my country to look for a better life in Europe. I prostituted myself in the course of my journey to be in Europe; nothing will encourage me to return to my country, nothing but my death,' she said. A moment of silence, then she continued. 'I know the smugglers in Morocco and their connections in Spain. I was arrested once but not twice, this time, I know which feet to stand on.' She stopped there with a stern face. Other conversations continued one after another, and each of them explained their fortunate and unfortunate moments. The two hours passed quickly; they were still hidden under a shed just outside the city. They stood there impatiently, looking forward to the driver to show up. The time passed, Mohamed still didn't show himself. A few minutes later, he came back with a small black bag containing marijuana drug and a few counterfeit packs of cigarettes and hid it on the back of the vehicle. That plastic bag had to be brought into Morocco. All on-board, the merciless smugglers packed the immigrants like fish in a box of sardine and thrown behind the pick-up vehicle, an unbearable moment for them, not enough water to drink under the stifling heat of the desert all along in this painful journey but hoped to reach their destination safely.

During their long journey in the desert, voices were heard from the pick-up cabin: it was the senseless conversation of the smugglers Mohamed and Martin that Abdul listened attentively with his left ear. He understood that the black plastic Mohamed had in hand contained marijuana drug, and that should be delivered to another drug dealer who would be collecting them at the Moroccan border. When they reached few kilometres on the road, the vehicle that supposed to be driving them to the Moroccan border broke down, the engine failure was to blame, and there was no mechanic to help them to repair the vehicle. In the end, they abandoned the vehicle and continued the rest of their journey on foot under the direction controlled by Mohamed and Martin.

When they arrived at the border on the Algerian side, they found other Bedouin smugglers had already gathered some of their immigrants in tents, waiting for the right time to cross the border. Abdul and Aliou were detached from their group of immigrants and added to those ready to cross the border with their Malian passport. Abdul approached and leaned over Aliou, then whispered in his ear to conspire against the two smugglers and expose them to the Algerian police officers as Mohamed was well-known in the past as a notorious drug trafficker and was researched by the police. As they stood there planning their next move, Aliou gently stroke Abdul's shoulder and asked him to look at the Algerian border controllers whose eyes were unduly wicked nasty, flocked to the new arrivals who were mixed with the natives. And to those who came to meet with their friends and relatives shaking their hands, kissed and hugged tightly each other as a way to say hello. On the other side, travellers from the other side of the desert sat in the restaurants to recover their strength after a long and arduous journey. Martin was impatient to wait any longer at the border; he wanted to get back his money as quickly as possible and disappear from this place to avoid being recognised by a passer-by at the heavy presence of the police. He passed his phone to Abdul to make a quick call to Aliou's brother so that he could get his money back and the transport costs.

'Take my phone, call your friend's brother to come and join us here, so that he could pay me the transportation costs,' said Martin.

Abdul seized this opportunity and pretended as if there was a problem with the telephone network connection, then he advanced a little further. He approached a police officer and whispered to him that Mohamed is a drug trafficker and has used them to bring the marijuana drugs back to Morocco. He then walked away from the officer and went to join the group to locate Mohamed better.

'I cannot reach him on the phone,' said Abdul.

'What are you talking about?' replied Martin.

'It's out of the question to tell me that you are having a connection problem to speak to his brother. I need my money now, you must choose your death over my money,' Mohamed reacted angrily.

The officer being informed. Abdul forced the situation to escalate by refusing to pay what he owed to the smugglers and began arguing. Soon the argument turned into a fight, which drew the attention of the crowd around them. During this altercation, Martin, who felt a victim in this affair, lost his composure and threw himself to Abdul. To avoid staggering, Mohamed played the role of mediator in trying to calm Martin, who was utterly distraught by the screams emitted by Abdul. The police officer that Abdul spoke to, after their conversation he watched and followed Abdul's footsteps, as he approached the group who were fighting, he made a call for support on the radio, and his comrades rushed to join him.

Shortly after that, the police officers arrived at the scene that annihilated the tension. When Abdul saw the officers, a sudden relief descended upon him; he then took advantage of their presence to unmask the two smugglers publicly; he shouted out their names.

'Mohamed and Martin have drugs inside the black plastic and hid it in their rucksacks! They also have weapons on them,' he continued shouting louder.

'They are drug dealers; they also sell drugs to tourists, and they have guns!' Abdul burst out.

'What are you talking about?' said Mohamed; he tried to play the innocent in front of the police officers.

'Look in his black bag, there are drugs inside it and a gun!' insisted Abdul.

The officers surrounded the group and conducted a thorough search then found the plastic bag hidden inside a rucksack carried on Mohamed's back.

A brutal kick, Mohamed was on the ground with both hands and feet tied behind him like a cow ready to be slaughtered in Muslim countries, the marijuana drug bag was seized, and both were taken to the police station. Being an eyewitness, Abdul could not go unnoticed; he was, in turn, arrested and questioned by the police for further explanation of the facts.

For the first time, Abdul had managed and succeeded well in playing his part in deceiving the smugglers, which had facilitated them to continue their journey without paying anything to the smugglers.

After four hours of an intensive interview between the checkpoint and the interview room, Abdul took advantage of recovering his strength and got prepared for his next difficult journey. At nightfall, Abdul approached Angel, who knew very well these places as she had been there before and asked her for help.

'Aliou, come here,' said Abdul. 'I have to introduce you to Angel; she is our sister, overall she is everything for us in this adventure.' After he had introduced Angel to Aliou, he kept a moment of silence; then, he resumed. 'The money that remains will not be enough to feed us for two weeks, let alone pay the boat sailors for the crossing of the Mediterranean Sea. We need to find something to do to earn some more money,' explained Abdul.

'Have you ever seen a frog climbing a tree? Even if you put it on a branch of a tree, it will fall on the ground; I am tired and fed up with all these situations,' Aliou replied angrily.

Angel spoke. 'There is no question that you will return to your country empty-handed, after having gone through all these miseries, and now you have arrived at the gate of Europe.' A moment of silence, then she argued. 'The Cameroonians don't like shame. When I was repatriated for the first time to Cameroon, upon my arrival, I was greeted and welcomed by mockeries from my friends; my parents did not even talk to me because, for them, it was a sign of weakness and curse. I had lost everything, my hope, my money, and my dignity. As a result of this shameful situation, I had to run away again to find myself next to you today for another attempt to get into Europe,' explained Angel.

This little life experience, but full of emotion, encouraged Aliou to carry on until the end.

When they had reached on the Moroccan side, they met with another problem at the border. The immigrants found out it was closed due to political tensions between the two countries, Algeria and Morocco; only the smugglers could pass with the cooperation of the corrupt border control agents. Ali was another petrol smuggler, using his donkeys to transport the petrol in small barrels through alleyways, barriers, and ditches dug by the Algerian authorities to destroy the flow of traffickers at their border. Angel went and spoke to Ali. She then explained her willingness to cross the border. Immediately, he accepted, but on one condition that Angel gave herself to him for free and added some money on top of his desire. Angel promised him that as soon as they crossed the other end into the Moroccan territory, she would offer him pleasure and pay the money requested.

Ali gave them three donkeys and clothes to disguise themselves like Berbers and waited for the next convoy, which should pass at any time. They would camouflage themselves among the traffickers under the command of Ali.

'You can cross, but you cannot come back,' warned Ali.

They waited overnight and left with other smugglers; then, they entered into the Moroccan territory. When they arrived at their destination, the trio took advantage of the influx of petrol buyers and disappeared from the place without Ali realising that they have gone and took the direction of Oujda.

Oujda was a promising place for Angel; she could make money easily through prostitution, while Abdul and Aliou would have nothing but the saliva in their mouths. Two weeks of peaceful life, Abdul emptied his pocket and found himself without money; then, he decided to throw himself on all that can move to get what to eat. He continued unsuccessfully searching for any jobs for two weeks. The two wretches went to look for temporary shelter at the student's accommodation at the University Campus of Oujda, where they stayed in the hope of finding opportunities to grab so that they could make money before continuing their journey to Europe.

One of their shelters was the University of Oujda. It turned out that many illegal immigrants used this university campus as a hiding place, feeding themselves with the help of a non-governmental organization (NGO). Sometimes with meagre income from begging, and they had to work hard to earn little and other miscellaneous business risking their lives. They could spend the night quietly without fear under the cooperation of the sub-Saharan students who protected them against any attempt from the police to arrest them. In return, some of those students would receive a small amount of money from the illegal immigrants who would be forced to do a risky job in the black market with low pay.

At the student accommodation room, Abdul shared the meal with Diallo and two of his friends, all students from Guinea. They discussed everything in a general context as if they were in their family; they roared with laughter and even talked about businesses and politics in their own country. Abdul took advantage to seek for an extended stay.

'I was on the way to continue my journey to Europe, God has guided my footsteps to you, I put my everything in a cup of water and give it to you,' said Abdul.

Diallo, as a student, could not offer him anything but to let him spend the night in his room. Also, share the little food he had on the table because Diallo himself depended on a small amount of money that his parents sent him from his country Guinea. But considering Abdul's situation, he agreed to guide and help him but not for long.

'You can stay and sleep in my room whenever you want. If you have an important thing to do outside, such as collecting money from the western union, I will handle that to prevent you from being arrested by the police, that's all I can offer you at the moment,' said Diallo.

Abdul saw Morocco as the gateway to a better life in Europe and Oujda as the blessed land. If he could leave Morocco without being arrested and expelled and left to die in the Mauritanian desert at the mercy of the vultures, he would be grateful. Suddenly, an echo crossed his mind.

How long can I stay in this situation, and how long will this game of hiding like cat and mouse end? Oh no, probably until I get enough money to escape this mess, he murmured.

Abdul was neither crazy nor smart; he had faith in his destiny, he knew very well and was certain that his destiny and his death are linked together and that sooner or later, his dreams will be fulfilled. He was determined more than ever in the past to leave Oujda to a Moroccan town called Nador located near the Spanish enclave of Melilla, together with seven other illegal immigrants.

They left Oujda and arrived in Nador late at night. The town was in dead silence and quiet, except the dedicated night owls who were still hanging around the city. The security forces roamed in search of illegal immigrants. They continued to crisscross the streets like enraged dogs with one objective of arresting and repatriating any illegal black human body walking or hiding around the city. Abdul and his group of friends crossed the town quietly, using alleyways to reach the height of the forest of Gourougou mountain ten kilometres from Nador, near to the fences that separated Morocco to Spain. Behind the barbed wire fence was Melilla with a beautiful view lighting that gave them an impression and even more desire to reach these places at all costs. They were not alone who wanted to stay in the jungle for the opportunity to climb these fences, which measured from an enormous height.

Other illegal immigrants had stayed for so long in this forest overhung by the debris of fortune, hoping to cross the border.

The jungle resembled an abandoned war zone: Tarpaulins, plastic sheets hanging from the branches of trees, which served as tents and dormitories. The illegals immigrant's inhabitants they found at these places were very poorly dressed, malnourish, and exposed to the raids from the police forces and lived under the law of the strongest of the mafias that reigned between these encampments. Abdul took the lead to introduce the group to the leader of the jungle. As they stood gazing to the crowd in the hope of finding the leader, he turned to his left and saw young men consulting among themselves; he thought the man who stood outside the circle surely was the leader. He made a move and introduced the group to him. They were welcome to be part of the community and helped each other for their survival. Outside of their well-organised community life, it was also a battlefield between them and the Moroccan security forces. The leader of the group called commando had been living in the jungle for at least eight months and had escaped many attempts to arrest him by the Moroccan security officers who were well informed about him. He was the one behind many shoplifting in the nearby towns of Nador and Beni Enzar and sold the food back to his friends in the jungle and share the rest with those empty-handed who in turned begged or dig through the garbage in search of food to compensate him. As he explained the situation to the new arrival group, he pointed his finger at Abdul, who had represented his group and said.

'Life here is hell but giving up is out of the question. Either we find a way over the Melilla fences, or we will stay here if that's God's will as all of us had experienced horrors on our journeys through the Sahara and borders. We would never give up just because of six metres of barbed wire, no matter what the Moroccan police do to us, no matter how bad the wounds we have or we will receive while attempting to jump off the barbed wire fences; we will try till the end. Tell the rest of your group that you are welcome among us in the jungle'.

The commando's ankles revealed how many times he had tried. Every attempt leaves its scars, and his legs and hands are full of them. He then let his second-in-line introduce himself. Diawara was a Malian origin; he had lived in this place for more than six months and had never had a chance to jump the barbed wire fences. He was nicknamed 'loose tongue' because of the many languages he spoke indiscreetly, including the Arabic language, he said to them.

'My brothers, you came here at a difficult time, jumping these fences have become food to taste but not to swallow it because in here, we don't eat well. Furthermore, you have to be super lucky to jump off from this six-metre-high of barbed wire fences.' He heard noises on the other end of the street; it was the police patrol, he kept quiet and then resumed.

'I want to go home, no matter what. I'm tired of being hunted like a criminal. Look at the neighbourhood, very few black

Africans are visible on the street.' He kept silent for a while and wiped tears in his eyes, then continued.

'Our African leaders do not like us, the Arabs do not like us, and neither do the whites, what should we do?' he broke down in tears and sobbed like a child.

Still, Diawara was well known by the local people in the neighbourhood. Previously, he had served as an interpreter in case of arrest to help the local authority in identifying and separating the Malian passport holder from the illegal immigrants who obtained it through the black market. He used his language skills to ask them relevant questionnaires in Bambara, a language well-spoken in the Republic of Mali. Still, no one had ever told the authorities that he was a candidate for Europe who lived illegally in their territory without a single document. At the same time, he was being cared for and fed by the inhabitants of this district.

Abdul comforted him and said. 'The wild animals are here because they were born in this forest; the flock of sheep and the herd of cattle are here because the shepherds brought them, and the shepherds are here to look after them. Have you seen those birds over there, they are here because they like it and you and me and others immigrants are here because we have been forced to be here, we had fled hunger, wars, and persecution, so die for it.'

Given the magnitude of the situation, Abdul and four other illegal immigrants withdrew themselves from the forest and found a rented room in a deteriorated building. They used their Malian passports to rent a room from an old landlady who had bequeathed it to her late husband, as the time was getting harder for her to survive the hardship, she was then obliged to take in lodgers. With a simple contribution, Abdul and his group obtained money for one week's rent, which they rounded for seven days of attempting to climb the fences, and they should begin that same night of trying their luck on the fences. They enjoyed being separated from other occupants in the jungle, although they had the same objectives but not the equal chances of getting into Europe. Abdul and his friends had their room on the ground floor with a window facing the street. They lived there from day one to the rest of the week and had told the landlady that they spent their daytime looking for a local business to invest, which she believed and wished them good luck.

The preparations to storm and climb the barbed wire fences were well planned and carried on the right way; they were all sat in the room; each of them performed their prayer in their way. The Christians cut two planks of wood and tied it together to create a cross that they used during their prayers to chase away the misfortune and asked Jesus to come to their rescue so that they could climb the fences and enter into Spain safely. The Muslims on the other side sat on cardboard transformed into a prayer mat invoking God (Allah) to facilitate their crossing. Meanwhile, the non-believers, wore their heavy protections of charms and amulets called 'gris-gris' to their hips, in which they believed would protect them against the evil and brought them luck and thought that the spirits of the forest would protect them.

After an hour of meditation and prayers, Diawara brought out the cassava tubers and potatoes, he then called for help; they came and peeled them quickly and cut it into small pieces. They managed to catch a duck on the street and killed it, they plucked and cleaned it. The group shared the cooking tasks. Abdul went and brought some sticks from a huge bundle of firewood. He broke them in little pieces across the sole of his foot and began to build a fire, blowing it with his breath, and began preparing pottage. Soon after they had finished cooking, they shared the meal among themselves to calm down their hunger while waiting for the nightfall to try their luck on the fences. Age was respected, but achievement in education was revered as Abdul was the most educated among the immigrants in the jungle. So, he was designated to be the coordinator of their attempt to storm the fences. He took the oath to climb Melilla's fences in front of his warrior friends, ready to die to enter Europe than going back to their countries.

'You are going to show the group your skills tonight if we managed to get into Spain. You will become our liberator and saviour, and your name would be engraved in our hearts forever,' said Diop, a Senegalese who had repeatedly tried unsuccessfully to enter into Europe and was arrested in the past, then returned to his country of origin. However, he had managed to re-use the same journey to return to the jungle. In these situations, nothing could discourage them for the departure of that night, Abdul was not afraid of the challenge and liked to try his luck, but he did not want to be a leader of climbing or storming fences as he had never done so before. The time approached quicker than they expected, and each one communicated to themselves on how they had reached the jungle, and some of them had gone through more perilous journeys than others.

Pierre, an Ivorian of origin, was deceived by a smuggler, searched, and robbed by the prostitutes on his way. He spoke while holding in hand a blank paper sheet and a blue pen and asked his friends.

'Give me your numbers. If I ever get through these fences, I'll call you, but if I don't call you, that means I'm dead, rest in peace upon my soul.' He went and sat at the corner.

Attacking the fences depressed Abdul, but there were some things he liked about it: the value of being clever and the meticulousness. However, he hated the treachery, the deceit, and the way a friend becomes an enemy, and stabbed you in the back even though he had practised few of these dishonesties acts for survival in the past, but he had regretted of doing it.

In the streets of Nador, the police officers were not sleeping, and their eyes were still open like one of the hawks. Very vigilant, they patrolled all around the mountain and the main passages that lead to the fences. So, it was therefore not easy to circumvent them whereas, these agents could not even speak a few rudimentary words of Bambara language that allowed them to engage with these people in the event of an arrest, as many of these illegal immigrants had at least one Malian passport that authorised them to move freely from town to town without the slightest concern of being stopped by the police. However, they should have a better understanding of the language spoken in Bamako, to engage in conversation with any immigrant holding a Malian passport for reassurance of his country of origin so that they could avoid the diplomatic tension between the two countries.

During the time of departure, they were all standing. Pierre opened a bottle of alcohol and made them drink one by one and then urged each to smoke cannabis to raise their courage. It was a long time since Abdul had neither drunk nor smoked, but in this situation, he smoked and took a drop of alcohol. After two glasses, he felt something strange abandoning him, then felt

128

dizzy, he tried to stand straight. His thought went back on the wise advice of his late father, his ban on drinking alcohol and having sex before marriage. He felt very vulnerable to all danger; his guardian protector had abandoned him and had been replaced by misfortune.

The door closed behind them. Abdul stood in front of the group heading towards the fences of Melilla. They crossed in the darkness the forest of Gourougou perched on the mountain that overlooks the Spanish enclave of Melilla. A twenty minutes' walk, they were followed by other immigrant candidates who were also awaiting their favourable moment to try. The safety of Melilla's border fence was reinforced in such a way that even the flies could not escape, under the watchful eyes of guards patrolling day and night. During the night, they were equipped with sensitive cameras that could detect and see any movement carried out along the fences and were even more daunting than those in the day.

Abdul was worried about the frightening night that could cause him being arrested by these merciless border control officers. He whispered a few words to Aliou. The immigrants all over the place rushed to him; each of them wanted to listen to that whisper, they came from all sides and became dense. They advanced slowly but surely, like a snake looking for prey.

The presence of the guards was felt on the other side of the fences. 'It is the guards,' they said among themselves. But no one was too sure as voices were echoed. They argued for a while and fell into silence again. The footway had now become a narrow line in the heart of the jungle. The more they advanced, the more Abdul lost hope because of a lack of perfect coordination, and each wanted to try the chance to climb first or die trying. As soon the group diverted the path indicated by another candidate, all the groups followed them like soldiers who had lost the war on the battlefield. The heels of their shoes echoed as they stamped on the dead leaves and dried branches from the trees, their heartbeats too fast for fear about what might happen, and their clothes had become too heavy and irritating. Those who had their backpacks got rid of them; the cold sweat trickled down their faces that disturbed their gaze. They held wooden sticks to help them to separate the shrubs to find where to put their feet to maintain their balance. Somebody in the group gave a warning that suddenly interrupted their thoughts. Abdul ignored it, and the entire group did too. As soon they came closer to the fences, Abdul realised that it would be better for him to try his chance like many others. So, they hurried and joined other immigrants' groups already crowded down the hill. A second warning was given by someone else, but this time, it was Diawara who shouted.

'Attention! Attention! The military is near,' said Diawara.

Abdul stressed out and wanted to go back to the jungle but could not recognise his way. Instead, he decided to follow them and try his very first chance. The wind calmed down; the sound of their feet sent back a loud echo. A small movement around, they were ready to flee the place. As the effect of alcohol left Abdul, the cold wind of the night horrified him. Shortly after, they arrived at the level of the fences; everyone rushed to climb to reach the Spanish side fence, which caused noises on the ground; the stones that were leaking in the void prevailed an imminent fall behind them.

The Spanish guards were alerted by the movement of the attacks at the barbed wire fences, the alarm was triggered on both sides, and the group failed their first attempt. A loud sound of boots was heard behind them, Abdul looked around then saw the Moroccan security forces, he gave a signal to the group and all the immigrants dispersed, those who were stuck on the fences were arrested, and Abdul narrowly escaped.

After two weeks of misery, nothing changed from Abdul's lifestyle in the jungle. His goal was far to be reached but leave it to God to decide what would be good for him and waited for his lucky day. In the meantime, two of his companions had been able to jump the barbed wire fences to reach the other end of the Spanish territory, and he could hear them screaming for joy.

After he had spent six months in their hideout, Abdul became impatient and began visiting the jungle several times a day, leaving behind his other roommates; he continued doing that as a routine until he met with another group on their way to swim. Abdul was persuaded by the group to try once for all his chance to cross the Strait of Gibraltar as the distance was only a few kilometres and that they could swim within fifty minutes from Tangier to Ceuta. Their idea gradually influences him; he then joined them and tried to get into Ceuta. They went all the way to

Tangier to fulfil their dream. As they approached the sea, the group of seven were spotted by the coast guards who stood on the other side, whispering loudly. It looked like they were talking at the top of their voices, planning to arrest them. Everybody in the group was talking. 'Let's go and arrest them.' It was like a street gang from a distance. Their voices were deep rumblings carried by the wind. Everyone looked in the direction of the sounds, then fled the area, leaving behind a cloud of dust. Abdul went back exhausted from the previous experience and found his roommates worried about him, he told them nothing but smiled, then went to bed and drifted into sleep.

At midday, Abdul and three other candidates, including Aliou, were resting to resume their daily activities of the night. A piece of good news awoke them. They found out that three of their friends were able to breach the barbed-wire border fences that separated the Spanish enclave of Melilla to the Moroccan territory and that they would spend some time in a temporary immigration holding centre for registration. Shortly after that, they would be housed by the Spanish authorities, fed, and receive free medical care. After all that happened, they would be granted freedom to join the mainland of Europe. Exhausted by thought and emotion, Abdul decided to separate from the group and tried his luck with four other immigrants.

'We should change our tactics and develop a plan when there are enough people on the fences. We'll stay here, as soon as they come back, then that would be the time we should go,' said Abdul.

Heavy rain fell on the city as it had never fallen before, the streets were flooded. The rumbling of the thunderstorm stirred the trees violently. The immigrants in their encampment were sad under this ceaseless rain. They sat in a circle, warming themselves from a log fire and begged the rain to stop. Gradually it became lighter and less frequent; then, Abdul stood up.

'Hey guys, come and have a look. It's a fortunate moment for us to leave now and try under this rain. The guards might be sleeping at the moment,' he said.

They left and attacked the barbed-wire fences, but this time, seven of them were able to cross the first barbed-wire fences. Then for the second fence, the dogs who were already on guard barked at them, under the panic, Abdul tried to climb the fence at the highest point, he felt a little unsteady on his hands and feet. He became breathless then he lost his balance, he fell aggressively on his back, his body paralysed as a result of the shock and laid under the pouring rain. He blacked out for a while; his mind drifted away at that moment. It was less than a hallucination, but more than a dream, he saw his late father and mother staring at him in the jungle. They walked endlessly towards him, holding each other's hand, always getting closer but never reaching him. He knew that when they came within touching distance, he would try to raise his hand to reach for them, but he kept saying. 'Not yet, not yet,' as they walked, smiled, and swayed away slightly from him. He was tempted to follow them, but something at the back of his mind told him that if he followed, he would never reach them, so he waited and watched, then smiled back at them from time to time. He was now out of consciousness and slept until he was jerked awake to find that he was lying under the pouring rain exhausted. He was then arrested and subjected to a lengthy and brutal interrogation in pain to confess of telling them everything about the others, their plans, and also their smugglers.

During these circumstances, when torture takes control of a body, any questions asked, it's a pain that will answer to protect Abdul from all disturbing and false promises such as letting him enter Spain, his liberation, reward him with money and so on.

To secure his release, he denounced the first name that came into his mind, then he said. 'Martin,' he gave them all the information requested about him. It was based on this denunciation that Abdul obtained his release and then returned to the Moroccan side by the Spanish Civil Guards and handed him over and placed at the disposal of the Moroccan police who, in turn, tortured him by using truncheons. They targeted mainly his arms and his legs so that the wounded limbs would never get the strength again to climb the barrier for the rest of his life, and if by chance he survived his injuries as he had received deep wounds to his legs and arms. Shortly after that, they restored his freedom. Few of his companions had managed to breach the border fence, and he could hear their screams of joy in Ceuta inside Spain. Later that day, Abdul managed to get back in the jungle. All his other friends shouted with joy because Abdul's troubles were at last ended in peace, he was not killed or sent to the desert to be eaten by the vultures. Abdul felt ill, and then he began to shiver, Diawara and other friends brought him to the fireplace, they spread cardboards on the floor and built a fire. But his condition got worse and worse, that worried his group of friends. As he sat down on the cardboard, warming up his body, his friends stood around him, praying that he got well soon and experienced the joys of being healthy again. Peter came back from the city, carrying some medications and a bottle of alcohol. 'I brought some medications for you, but please do not ask how I got it,' said Peter.

Abdul took the medicines and laid on his back. Peter opened the bottle of alcohol and poured on his deepened and infected wounds. He screamed in agony as the alcohol seared through his wounded legs and arms, but a few hours later, the medicines relieved the pain. After a few days of treatments, the agony was gone entirely, replaced by sudden strength and energy. After a week of rest, Abdul felt himself again and gradually became stronger more than ever before, he left his hideout and went back to the jungle. He found out the Moroccan security forces had conducted searches in the mountains and around the cities of Tangiers and Nador and some popular areas in which the clandestine immigrants were living. They had arrested many of his friends who were trying to climb the fences, among them, his friend Aliou was part of those hunted down, handcuffed and were thrown in the back of the truck then drove to Tizni province awaiting to be expelled from the country and left to die in the desert. They had also destroyed everything they could find in the jungle, the cardboard boxes the immigrants used as beds were torn to pieces, as well as all little food they found in nearby dumpsters, ripped packs of noodles, and a few mouldy potatoes. He looks at the remains of a straw-filled cloth sack, which used to be the leader commando's mattress was now sliced and emptied in the bushes nearby. Abdul felt sorry for what had happened to his friends and now worried about his future as nothing was going well for him, and all his hope had turned upside down. Abdul walked slowly back to his hideout; his head lowered so as not to stick out of the bushes. He did not want to be seen by the Moroccan police; they had been mercilessly hunting down the remaining of the illegal immigrants. Abdul then met with two of his friends who had escaped in jumping from the truck handcuffed, they were seriously injured as a result of their arrests and explained to him what had happened but never mentioned Aliou's name being with them. Abdul then realised the severity of the situation and the danger of being arrested as the police officers would never stop hunting them, and soon, they would be able to find his hideout no matter how well he kept hiding.

A few steps away to his rented room, a firm, deep voice whispered behind a pickup truck. Suddenly, someone shouted, 'Stop! Stop! Don't move, and if you do, you will die.' He stopped, and he raised his hand in the air. The two officers approached him. 'Identify yourself, Negro,' said the officers. Abdul lost his voice a constant panic in his eyes, his pupils juggling in every direction he trembled like a bird that had lost its feathers in the open air. The police officers began to search his pocket. Fortunately, Abdul had on him the Malian passport.

To verify the authenticity of the document, they carried out the identification test to find his country of origin; until then, he presumed to be Malian. In his childhood, Abdul had received a good command of more languages, in which he spoke the Fulani, Mandingo that was somewhat similar to Bambara language, the Sussu, and a few Guerze, which helped him answer any questions in Bambara language commonly spoken in the Republic of Mali. Then the officers asked him some questions in that language. He answered them without making any mistake.

'*Iletokhobedi*?' in Bambara language (What is your name?) asked the police officer.

'*N'detokhobhet Abdul*!' (My name is Abdul!) Abdul replied in good Bambara language.

The officers handed him his passport, then he disappeared from the place and went to his room. After five hours of waiting without news from his friend, Aliou, Abdul decided to have a rest and wait for his remaining friends who would soon arrive if they were not among those arrested. Shortly after that, Diawara came to check if no one had escaped and intended to enter the room so that he could search their belongings and take any valuable he could find inside. He then knocked on the door, no response, he broke the door and forced himself in and found Abdul lying on the floor exhausted from the long walk.

'My friend, all other immigrants were arrested, I narrowly escaped, thank God for saving me, I fell into a pit at the right time,' he said, Abdul then stood up.

Diawara pointed his finger to his injuries and then reported the sad news of Aliou's arrest and that he would be taken back into the desert at the mercy of the vultures. Abdul lost his balance and banged his head on the wall, then fell on his backside and lost consciousness and laid down helpless. Instead of coming to his rescue, Diawara took advantage to strip off the belongings of those arrested in the hope of finding any valuable objects, including money in their bags.

After twenty minutes of a thorough search, he found an enormous amount of money totalling around six hundred euros, which he collected from different bags. Suddenly, Abdul regained consciousness and saw Diawara taking out the money from a rucksack of a member of the group of immigrants arrested. He turned his eyes around the room and discovered that all their belongings had been moved and emptied on the floor. He stood up and straightened himself; then asked Diawara of what he was doing, Diawara replied calmly.

'My friend, it's time to leave here, the police will storm this house at any time soon.'

'Where are you going with that money?' Abdul yelled at him.

Abdul threw himself on him, and they began to wrestle. Diawara had not enough strength to resist Abdul, his injuries were still fresh, and he pushed Abdul against his body with the little strength he had. Then he let Abdul take back the six hundred euros, which he had already kept in his pocket. Shortly after that fight, Abdul found himself alone with that amount of money, having no choice, he decided to try to cross by boat as he had heard that many of his friends had used that journey to get into Greece. Now with six hundred euro in his pocket, he would negotiate with a good smuggler to take him across the Mediterranean Sea without fear of losing his life or being arrested by the coast guards.

Abdul went out and closed the door and walked towards Nador's town centre. He walked quietly in fear of being arrested. After a short walk, Abdul found himself at an open-air market, he passed through and followed down the road, he arrived at the bus station called Jamia el-Arabia. He felt tired then smuggled anonymously among the people in the bustling, noisy, and crowded station, where everyone was busy doing their activities. Cheerful profanities flew through the air, Abdul felt a bit lost and could hardly understand any Arabic accents. At the end of the bus station, he saw a group of an individual arguing in broken French language. Abdul thought that this was an excellent occasion to be involved in the discussion to find out if they were also illegal immigrants who wanted to get into Europe. He approached and heard them planning to steal a boat when the nightfall.

Abdul stopped halfway and thought that tonight would be the time to steal a boat and cross the sea to get into Europe. A minute later, he joined the group and introduced himself as a mechanical engineer who could repair any faulty engine and wanted to try his chance to get into Europe. A perfect match for the group, now they were waiting for other candidates to complete the number required by the leader named Jamal. They had to wait all day, which left Abdul with waiting anxiously around the bus station with a group of individuals planning to find the quickest and largest boat to steal in daylight, which was riskier than at night. Still, he was too close to take risks to cross the sea with them by boat. Shortly after, other people came to join them.

The group made the tour of the docks and the harbour, and the security was operating perfectly. They spotted several places where they could stomp past the control points. They managed their way around to the sandy beach and saw a nice-looking boat that would well suit their group's purpose, but it probably might not have enough fuel. With the situation in their hands, the group split up in two; one group went to find some people to complete the required number while Abdul and Jack stayed on the beach, keeping their eyes on the boat. Jack left Abdul and went to a stall and brought two ice creams and two newspapers and said to Abdul.

'The beach is a good place to hide among the holidaymakers, isn't it?' said Jack.

'Yes, of course, but for how long before the cloud hid the sun and the holidaymakers will return to their hotels and leave us all alone here, then we will be left with no choices but to leave before the police check on us,' replied Abdul.

To avoid being spotted, they pretended reading the newspapers they held upright in their hands and covered their faces, they removed their shirts. They used it as a pillow to support their heads as they laid on the sand so that they could better glance at the boat and to see if anything happened, and the police had to intervene well before they reached the place where they sat. There would be plenty of time to leave the beach and vanish into the streets.

At nightfall, the leader returned to find them on the beach, patiently waiting for him to arrive. They spotted another two fishermen boats that had just arrived in the harbour, bigger than the previous one. The trio stood up on the quay and watched the crew getting off, then they tied up the ropes through the cleat and refuelled the boat before they left for their homes. They waited about thirty-five minutes to make sure that they were well away; they then walked slowly to the edge of the harbour and jumped into the boat. The leader took the role of captain. He found the wheel chained up and called Abdul to check on the chain, who then found that the chain was locked electronically. Abdul sat on the cabin floor, out of sight, and spent around twenty minutes, sorting it out in the dark. Finally, he succeeded in time. The sky had resumed its dark colour, and the moon shone like a car headlight in the middle of nowhere.

The captain thanked him and raised the anchor, then sprang back on to the quay and untied the ropes. He returned to the cabin, then started the engine, the engine coughed, and died. He called Abdul again to come to rescue them. Within a few minutes he tried again, this time the engine roared to life, he then began to manoeuvre the boat out of the mooring. They left the quayside and went to another place where other immigrants were parked, waiting for them to arrive in the darkness. Upon their arrival in the deep water, they switched off the boat and waited for other immigrants who used the canoe to reach them.

When all of them were on-board in the deep sea, Abdul felt a stiff breeze and hoped it was not a sign that the weather was about to break. The sea was surprisingly rough, and the stout boat lifted high on the waves. The captain panicked and began to check on the map reference he had found in the boat to make sure that they are heading in the right direction and engaged the wheel-clamp. The cabin windshields were splashed by water; it was hard to tell whether it was the rain or the sea. As they moved in deep waters, the captain tried to switch on the radio to make contact, but it was too soon to make contact as they were still in Moroccan waters.

The waves increased in size as they progressed, the boat rose up with each wave; then balanced unsteadily for a second at the top before plunging sickeningly down into the next trough. Abdul joined the captain in the cabin while the other immigrants screamed for their life. It was getting late in the night; they could see nothing at all. Abdul stared out the cabin windows; he felt faintly seasick. As they are getting far, the captain tried to convince the immigrants on-board to calm down, and coast guards on patrol would soon rescue them. A moment later, a bigger wave taller than the others lifted the vessel, then it fell back into the sea violently. They heard a big crack; they could not tell whether the crack was a thunderclap or the noise of the timbers of the boat breaking up. Suddenly, the water entered on the prow and washed over the deck, then in the cabin where Abdul and the captain stood. They went to look for life jackets; there were only a few lefts, which were not enough to cover all the immigrants on-board. The engine broke down, a total panic among the crew members; there was no way the boat could be controlled and where it was heading.

Packed like fish in the boat screaming for their lives, they had no idea where they were in the middle of the night on the cold sea. They might almost be back in Morocco or near the coast of Malaga; the captain sent Abdul to repair the engine as he had declared himself as a mechanical engineer to travel for free, now it was payback time. He hadn't had a clue on how a motorbike engine operates, let alone a boat engine. Nevertheless, he took the torch and lit it, then headed towards the back of the boat, praying for the storm to end. He pulled the starter, but nothing happened. He checked the oil level; it was absolutely fine; he tried several times then gave up. Suddenly, the boat rolled onto its side, Abdul fell and banged his head. He laid confused on the floor in the dark, thinking that the boat would flip at any time now. He stood up and went to join the captain and told him that the engine had run out of fuel, and there was no way it could be repaired at that time. While explaining the situation, another mountainous wave broke. Still, this one was too much for the vessel's timbers, the waves lifted the boat and hit the trough with a solid impact, the terrifying sound of the hull broke the silence of the night like an explosion of a dropped bomb and the cracked glasses in the windows shattered into pieces.

They realised that there was no way this boat could take them where they wanted to go, and there was no other boat nearby that they could call for support to save them. All crew members grasped anything they could on the boat to prevent them from being washed into the sea as the boat was about sinking below the surface of the waves. Abdul realised that the back of the vessel had disappeared, and all immigrants on-board were moving upwards to the cabin, and the waves were moving in one direction, carrying the vessel with them. New waves lifted the boat for the last time and threw it violently down like a plane that had lost its control in the middle of the air and heading to the ground. Abdul thought that this was the end of his life. The boat turned into pieces, the immigrants on-board found themselves in the water, those who could swim managed to grab and hold of any remains of the boat woods that were still floating on the water. In the desperation to survive, Abdul saw flashing lights, revealing a beach. As he swam to get to that point, the sea lifted the remaining debris from the ruined boat and knocked him on the face, but with his strong hands, Abdul managed to move them away as he swam so that he could clearly see which direction he was heading. As Abdul swam faster, he saw the waves were breaking right up to the cliff, and it would not take longer than expected to arrive onto the dry land. He knew that if he left the wooden hull of the boat, he held in his hand for the beach, the waves behind him would kill him. But if he could reach the beach in between waves, he might survive.

This is a race to survival, and I must win this course, he murmured.

With his long legs and arms, Abdul found himself in difficulty when he was still a few yards from reaching the beach. He switched on a different swimming position and was too exhausted. In the end, he had to roll over onto his back and float. The waves carried him a few yards away; then threw him as they gently broke down on the shore. He drowned and swallowed a considerable quantity of water, few immigrants who had already managed to reach the beach, slipped back into the water and swam to catch his arms and pulled him in the correct lifesaving position to the shore. Abdul found himself exhausted and breathless in the Moroccan seaside, he laid on his side helplessly while others who could not swim were left to die in the frozen Mediterranean Sea.

As the darkness of the night gave way to the daylight, the rising sun had begun to brighten the beach. Abdul felt insecure to stay lying among the other surviving immigrants, for fear that he could be easily found and sent back to his country. A sudden rage possessed him; he would not be arrested! He screamed his hatred at the storm, boat, and sea. He was on his feet and ran away from the beach with no sense of direction but knowing he would not stop until he reached the town. Abdul was so weak that his legs could hardly carry him, and he felt like a drunken elephant running with the limbs of an antelope.

Going back home would mean going to my grave and is more dangerous than moving forward to reach Europe, he murmured as he was running alongside the beach fainting like a drunker who had lost its memories. He left and resumed his way back to Oujda to look for work.

On his way to Oujda, Abdul met an oil smuggler called Khalil, who operates in defined areas along the international borders. Khalil was looking for merchants to help ease off his oil in the black market. After they had exchanged a few words, Abdul confided his fear and desire and detailed to him his entire unfortunate and dangerous journey. For Abdul, Khalil was not an Arabic descendant as he believed Arabs were generally wicked; they have no remorse or pity towards sub-Sahara Africans as he had experienced in the past and would never forget about it.

'Were you born in this country?' asked Abdul.

'Yes, of course, I was born here, my father, my mother, were all born here,' Khalil replied.

As the conversation deepened, Abdul gained more of his confidence. Then he began to explain the situation in which he had thrown himself in, and what had happened to him during his journey and his intentions to reach Europe at all cost. Khalil reassured Abdul that he was going to do his best to help him find his way out of the country, but he would have to get an amount of 1,500 Euros so that he could reach Spain by road, which was very secure and safe. And for that, he would have to pass through the Ceuta border by car to get into Spain. Their conversations fed Abdul with hope to reach Europe and thought that he was very close to the end of his ordeal, then he murmured.

One day, I will fulfil my European dream and get my freedom like a bird in the sky.

At the beginning of his life journey, the idea of going to Europe was not at all on his agenda. Still, as time went by, his thought gradually changed through the political integration of the Western countries that had chosen democracy over dictatorship and allowed every citizen to have a right of living a decent life and respect their freedom of expressions. Now he had decided to take life positively. If he had envied of going back to Oujda, that meant there were new channels developed to bring him into Europe. For Abdul, all the difficulties he faced on his journey depended on his lack of financial capacities, and that he should have money first before he thought of leaving Morocco to Europe. The experience gained on crossing the desert, the borders, the attack on the barbed wire fences at the Spanish enclaves, and the sea crossing left him nothing but bad memories. And all those unfortunate journeys were still vivid in his mind. He tried to find a job so that he could accumulate the amount of money asked to take him into Spain.

Through Khalil, Abdul found himself involved in an extensive mafia network of money laundering, documents falsification, and recruitment of high-class prostitutes for wealthy tourists. Thus, a well-structured network that had branches installed almost in all large cities of the kingdom whose headquarter was based in Casablanca in the Moroccan capital. He worked tirelessly for two months with a positive performance, where he received a salary of 3817.10 Dirhams equivalent to 350 Euros for a risky job, which could jail him for many years if arrested. Still, he saw the risk as normal for an illegal immigrant who had no right to any employment. To avoid being noticed on his success in the business. Abdul decided to abandon his job without informing Khalil and his boss Kashif to prevent a possible problem, or to engage in altercations with them, after all, it was a criminal job where you could win or die at any time.

After Abdul had stopped working for the organisation, an idea crossed the network leader Kashif's mind to find and kill Abdul as soon as possible. As an underground and complex business, no member of the group had a right to abandon without the authorisation of the network leader unless the member involved was behind bars or in the police custody. Abdul went and sought shelter at Diallo's room at the campus for fear that he could be found and killed by Kashif and his gangs. Meanwhile, he stayed there until he would find his way to get out of the country.

At the end of three months of hard work and endless prostitution, Abdul's friend called Angel, the one he had met during his journey through the desert, was fortunate to have a substantial amount of money. She had earned it in a one-off meeting with a Moroccan businessman in his sumptuous villa for an intimacy session; she drugged the man, which caused him to sleep deeply. Angel availed herself of this opportunity to rob him of all that she could find on the spot (money and jewellery), and she disappeared from the place and went to see Abdul in his hiding shelter at the campus.

'Fortune, fortune,' Angel shouted for joy.

She had at least something to present to the good smugglers. She decided to show Abdul the physical appearance of a good smuggler since he could not distinguish them. So, he made himself available to Angel; then they went in search of what she called a 'good smuggler' as in the past she had failed in her first attempt to reach Europe and was scammed by a smuggler who turns out to be an illegal immigrant and had used her money to travel to Europe. Given the fact that she had the bad experiences in her previous journey, Abdul confided his hopes in her, and they went on their way.

'How do you identify a good smuggler?' Abdul asked.

'Oh, my dear friend, suffering is a piece of advice,' her voice interrupted, and then she went on: 'I had met smugglers and rapists in the past. When it comes to the intermediate smugglers, they are small smugglers who often tried their luck through immigrants like us to get money and take advantage of going to Europe too. However, good smugglers are those who could show you a lot of money in foreign currency and stolen blank passports as proof of their availabilities and capabilities.' Her voice was interrupted for a moment, and then she continued. 'The evidence is that James, whom I know is a good smuggler, belongs to a well-organised network which has branches from the Moroccan border to inside the Spanish territory. Beyond all that, he also has his own business, which he runs twenty-four hours and seven days a week. I received all the information from a reliable source.'

Convinced, they decided to go and meet James, who is a good smuggler of Spanish origin and had his business connections in Spain. After an hour of the journey, they arrived at James's villa.

'I believe you've met so many smugglers, good and dishonest ones, haven't you?' asked James.

'Yes, with great regret and sadness,' replied Angel.

James was very expensive, but with 1500 Euros, they could find themselves in Spain within a day through a safe route. However, he won't negotiate with anyone; in addition to that, he did all his business discreetly. Besides those businesses, he kept at home a sophisticated photo camera that he used to take passport photos and many other things that allowed them to have an excellent travel document.

Griiiii, griiiii, griiiii was James's phone that vibrated; a call came from Spain. After a few conversations in the Spanish language, he shook his head and said to them.

'You are going to leave Morocco within two days, prepare the 2500 Euros for the documents plus 500 Euros for the cost of transportation, which will be paid separately. One more thing, you should keep it between us, I want full discretion,' he said with an outstretched eyebrow.

Angel had her money ready on her, Abdul whispered to her ear that he also had his money in full and ready. Since then, the two friends remain unseparated during the two days. They waited impatiently for their departure day and the arrival of those famous sophisticated cloned passports registered with a real social security number to be used deceptively at the border control on the Morocco-Spanish border as if they were legitimate travel documents made in Spain.

After two days had passed, they decided to feed their eyes with curiosity and then went to meet with James to honour their long-awaited rendezvous.

'The work is done!' said James.

'We are overwhelmed with joy, let us tell you that you have saved lives, I am speechless as we do not have words to express our gratitude to you than thanking you for this great job,' Abdul said.

James showed them the travel documents and all the information to be memorised before the departure day so that they could avoid any suspicion. The two could not imagine how well and sophisticated these two travel documents were made and identical to the original. The passports were ingeniously made to the extent that no one could spot the difference unless you knew very well the secret signs that show the travel documents are not genuine.

'Don't worry too much; it's a counterfeit made in the image of the original, which the owners hold in Spain.' He sighed and then continued. 'We will proceed to baptise you with new names, from now on, you will be named from the identities found in these passports.'

Abdul took the name Gaspard Aguillera and Angel took the name Georgina Aguillera, and they are a married couple and live at the same address since they got married two years ago. The condition imposed by James was that they had to memorise by heart the address of the document owners in Spain and some basic words in the Spanish language in the event of being asked of any basic questions at the Spanish border. As they are already in Morocco, they won't have any problem as they spoke the French language, they would be fine. The two friends became speechless, their mouth felt dry, and their voices were barely a whisper.

Meanwhile, they decided to leave Oujda by a car early in the morning to arrive at the north of the Moroccan city of Tetouan in the afternoon and then at the border of Ceuta, another Spanish enclave. From there, the journey would last only about twenty minutes before arriving in the Spanish territory.

The car engine switched off, the taxi driver who is meant to drive them to Spain was also involved in the smuggling network. He got off and headed to James's to complete the negotiation of their transport to Ceuta. After five minutes of conversation, they came to meet the passengers.

James smiled for the first time that morning and said. 'The driver will tell you that crossing is hard work, long hours, nervousness and frustration, but yes, it's exciting.' He looked at his mobile. 'Now, I want you to meet a very experienced member of the network,' he said to them and turned to the driver. 'Let me introduce you to them,' he said to the driver.

'Is that Mr and Mrs Aguillera?' asked the driver.

'Yes, we are!' Abdul replied in a more hesitant tone.

'I am in charge of driving you to Ceuta in Spain, through a slightly less dangerous route,' he said in French with a Spanish accent.

'Don't be nervous when you get to the border control, the agents who would be at the control point are very intelligent, they would just look at you to find out who you are, it's just a warning,' James added

'Please bear in mind after you leave here, we've never met, and our paths never crossed,' said James.

The driver started the engine, and it roared to life; he then drove off the car at high speed under the mid-day sun that was still heating the tar. For the second time in his life, Abdul had entered the country illegally and left illegally in a safe manner but at a price that had almost cost his life.

After travelling about 585 kilometres from Oujda to Ceuta, they finally arrived at the border checkpoint between Morocco and Spain. The driver was very attentive to the customs officers who guarded these borders and spotted that some Spanish guards from the 'civil guard' were systematically checking cars using detection devices, whereas, others allowed passengers to pass through a normal control. The driver spoke: 'Crossing this border at this time is a chance, especially when you have this kind of passport, but do not worry, pray to God.' He glanced left and right from his car's window then continued. 'Here, there are lots of people that crossed through these borders each day. The customs at this place won't be able to control all Spanish passports effectively as they should be in normal borders, they will rather be more interested in searching some cars in the hope of catching smugglers.'

The border was chaotic; people were frustrated, the cars honked due to the long queue and to the slowness as they were barely moving. They all wanted to enter at the same time. The driver was a regular visitor to this place and a professional smuggler; he could easily recognise the faces of wicked agents and those who allowed passengers to pass more quickly. Two minutes of waiting in the queue, the driver switched off the car engine and got off. He then went to look at the border if the time was right for them to continue the road. Otherwise, he would return, as there was a place specially designated for drivers who have forgotten their car documents to reverse back. Lucky day for Abdul and Angel, the time was favourable, and the passage was not risky. At the checkpoint, passengers in a vehicle would have to get out of the car and walked through to the passport control in the building next to the border as the driver has to go through a car checkpoint and will meet the passengers on the other side of the Spanish border.

'It's a moment of relief; you can get off and stand in the queue. I'll be waiting for you on the other side at the exit of the border, don't forget to have smiles on your faces,' the driver said to them.

At six o'clock in the evening, the post-control was already crowded; the two couples got off from the taxi and went to stand in the queue on the Moroccan side. They waited for thirty minutes before obtaining the exit stamp from the Moroccan territory, then they crossed the border on foot. A few minutes' walk, they reached the Spanish checkpoint. They showed their passports with smiles on their faces and spoke a few Spanish words learned during their journey.

'*Buenas tardes*,' Abdul told the agent.

'*Buenas tardes su pasaporte, por favor*,' the agent asked them to present their passports.

They handed the passports to the border agent after they had checked them, then the passports were returned to them. The agent said. '*Bienvenida.*'

'*Gracias*,' they replied.

They boarded the taxi, which drove them to Ceuta, three kilometres away from the border.

Soon after they had arrived at the indicated place, the driver dropped them off and then used a telephone box to inform James that they have arrived safely in Spain. Abdul could not believe that he was finally in Europe, he screamed with joy as he knelt, stretched his arms up, the palms of his hands widely opened and thanked God for giving him the chance to put his feet in the European land. To be reassured that they had arrived in Spain, James himself communicated with Abdul and Angel, telling them to leave Spain as soon as possible to avoid being arrested with the fake travel documents that did not belong to them. He told them an old African proverb.

'When they wash your back, you should be able to wash your stomach.'

James wanted to defend the viability of his business and at the same time, save his head. He also needed customers to make money through satisfied customers.

'The documents that you have in your hand are a treasure. If you used them properly and discreetly, they would help you, and would open many doors for you, such as getting a job in the black market and so on. But if the opposite happened, then it would become a burden of misfortune, especially if you tried to use them in Spain,' advised James.

Abdul knew that he could no longer use this document. And they had to destroy them as soon as possible for the reasons that concerned him: He doesn't understand the Spanish language; he was not used to a European life; and he was afraid of being arrested then expelled to his country of origin.

'These documents would be useful only to travel in the European Union countries such as France if we know how to get there,' said Abdul.

'It's straightforward Abdul, please use your brain. We will avoid getting into the police hand by paying our transport to Paris,' Angel replied.

They found themselves completely lost in the streets of Spain and out of touch with the rest of the world. The language barrier caused them enormous difficulties, and they did not have a place to go and had no money on them to pay for their transport to Paris. Having no solution, Abdul turned to Angel and asked her what to do? As the habit was her second nature, Angel decided to go into prostitution to find the cost of transport and provide them with food to eat.

The European El Dorado

Abdul had waited long enough for this moment to happen, and the journey had taken him weeks, months, and years to plan it. Finally, he had crossed the Spanish border and entered safely into Europe to secure a better life. As a result, Abdul was left exhausted by thoughts and emotions to find his way in a foreign country he had never known in the past after he had survived the gruelling journey from travelling thousands of miles from home. Trekked through some of the world's roughest and most dangerous territory in search of a better life in Europe, as he stood looking around him, he discovered that it was not quite the idyll he had envisioned.

The European countries he thought were the land of milk and honey was far from being a reality. After a long night of hardship in the brothel, Angel found the transport costs that could allow them to travel to Paris, the French capital.

Paris had become Abdul's song; he memorised it in his head and sang the word 'Paris' throughout the day. He couldn't wait to get there, in the capital city of France, visiting the famous Eiffel Tower and the different museums in the capital. He had already noted the plan in his diary. To avoid systematic control during their journey to Paris, they decided to use the road trip. They entered into negotiations with Imran, who was a taxi driver of Moroccan origin and Spanish nationality; he regularly travelled between France and Spain at least twice a week at a very affordable price.

After many hours of driving through Spain to France, they finally arrived at their destination. The car stopped in a crowded place at the train station called Gare du Nord Paris in the French capital. Abdul stared surprisingly at people as they were going about their daily activities; he could not believe that he was already in France, precisely in Paris.

'Are we in Paris?' he asked the driver.

'Yes, we have arrived in Paris,' the driver replied.

'What a nice journey,' Abdul said to Angel.

Abdul sighed with relief after entering safely into France, and he said. 'We have finally arrived in the promised land,' the two illegal immigrants burst into laughter with enormous joy in their heart. They paid the driver and began exploring the city, but their friendship did not last long before they separated, and each took the path of their destiny.

Being undocumented in France was like being left without dignity. And seeking asylum could take months or even years before the authority reached a decision to allow them to stay or leave the French territory during which they would remain without the right to work and access to free medical treatment. Working without authorisation was the only option for these immigrants. Once they crossed the border, their thought would be to find jobs and make money so that they could feed their families that stayed in their countries. Still, such an idea was not the case for the prostitutes who do not need to claim asylum or applied for the work permit to engage in their activities. Angel was professional in her activities as a sex worker. She knew how to make money without making the slightest effort. But she also wanted to have her documents so that one day she would freely travel back to her own country with dignity and without being expelled by force, chained, and thrown out to face her enemies, family, and friends in her country.

After an extended period of the sex trade, she found out that she was pregnant, with an unknown father. This situation arranged her a little bit; she claimed asylum. She was accepted in a reception centre for asylum seekers where she had received accommodation, free health care, and free meals. She gave up her prostitution job because her body was no longer attractive; she remained in the centre, waiting for the decision on her asylum case from the French authority.

At the Gare du Nord station in Paris, around six o'clock in the evening. A man who wore a navy suit with a solid white shirt entertained his interlocutors inside a cafeteria at the square, telling all he knew about African politics and the news from his native country Guinea.

On his way, Abdul heard a voice over his shoulder that seemed familiar to him and resembled one of his friends, Paul. After a few steps ahead, he turned back and stared at the speaker through the windows, but he was unable to see him clearly, so Abdul took a few steps towards the entrance, he stopped as he had not had the means to buy a cup of coffee, then he hesitated to enter. Shortly after that, he made a move and went to look at the window again, but the interlocutor was seated backwards opposite to the windows that prevented him from seeing the speaker's face. To avoid being seen looking at the windows, he decided to get in and walked to the counter. He pretended to buy a drink. He turned his head to the place where the chat was held; he found out that the speaker was indeed his close childhood friend Paul, the one with whom he was involved with during the political rally and were both arrested in Conakry and sent to prison. Abdul approached a little more to reassure himself and glanced at him; then, he asked people who were seated on the tables, how he could get to Champs-Èlysées?

'Good evening, do you know how to get to Champs-Èlysées, please?' he asked nervously.

The four friends interrupted their conversations. Paul pulled his phone out of his pocket and slightly rose his head up. They stared at each other for a while.

'There you are,' said Abdul.

They hugged each other tightly and talked briefly. After a long emotional hug, Paul introduced him to his friends, who were seated around the table.

'My friends, I present my dear childhood friend, with whom I suffered a lot in my country,' said Paul.

He joined them on the table with the cheapest beer possible and a half-emptied glass of wine on each side of the table. Abdul sat and faced the street; he stared amusingly at the passers-by as if he was looking for someone or something he had lost. A pretty white woman seated opposite, she was smoking her cigarette with a glass of wine on her side, visibly of red, and Abdul could not miss any of her gestures in the hope of earning a smile from her.

Suddenly, all his friend's eyes turned to Abdul, who could not cease to glance at the beauty of this woman.

'Abdul, you'll never know if she will agree to talk to you unless you approach her. I assure you that you can seduce her if she's willing to listen to you, then the matter will be resolved. On your first date, you convince her to marry you, then the residence permit will automatically fall into your hands, and you will breathe finally,' said Paul to his friend Abdul.

It was the obsession of undocumented immigrants living in France. For Paul, it was a sad reality. 'No work, no identification paper, no family, it is an ordeal life that many of us live from day to day here in France,' explained Paul.

Whenever Abdul tried to ask Paul how he managed to travel to Paris, Paul always interrupted him to avoid his friends who were seated beside him found out what had happened to them before he fled their country. Meanwhile, he left his friends and went to show Abdul his flat, a small studio located in the Paris suburbs, which he shared with his wife.

Soon after they had arrived at Paul's flat, they opened a debate; each one was curious to know the journey the other had taken. Given the fact that he had left Paul in prison at the time of his escape and had found Paul in Paris long before him, was magical and astonishment that he would never forget for the rest of his life.

'My friend, Paul, tell me more about your journey. Tell me everything that happened to you. Please do not leave anything out,' said Abdul curiously.

'Oh my friend, it's a tough and long story to tell, but before we start, I would like you to have a rest first, then I shall explain to you tomorrow because right now you've got a lot of fatigue,' replied Paul.

To feed his curiosity, Abdul woke up early and waited for Paul's wife to leave for work and went to wake Paul up, who was drifted into a deep sleep.

'What's going on, Abdul? You're up so early,' he asked.

'No, nothing special, I just wanted to hear the story about your journey,' replied Abdul.

At seven o'clock in the morning, Paul decided to give all the details of his journey to Abdul. After breakfast was hastily eaten, Paul sat before Abdul and began to narrate his journey back in the day after he was released from prison in his native country. Paul decided to embark on a gruelling journey in the search for a better life, as he had no future in the country. No job for the young graduates unless their parents were employed in the administration, and they had to have a strong connection with government officials. As the recruitment was not based on merit but on who recommended you and Paul did not have such a recommendation, let alone a family member who he could rely on to help him find a job.

One day, Paul went to the harbour of Conakry just at the time of disembarkation of goods from a ship, he came in contact with two risk-takers who were accustomed travellers by ship, and they wanted to sneak around the dock to get into the ship without being seen. One of them had an accomplice among the dockers. Paul quickly introduced himself to prove his presence and imposed himself in the group. Among them, there was an expelled from Europe named Fodey.

'Fodey was on his second attempt to take the shipping route; his first attempt was terrible; he embarked without knowing the destination of the ship. Nevertheless, he agreed to continue the journey. He went to find a good hideout and stayed there after five days of journeys, the food he had on him was finished, and so, he decided to wait until midnight then sneaked into the kitchen to find food. He continued his habits every night until the day the head chef found out that there were vegetables and fruit that were missing in the kitchen lockers. An emergency meeting was called, all crew members on-board of the ship gathered, and each pointed the finger at other. One day, the workers decided to change the place where they kept their food. After three days, Fodey came out of his hiding place without knowing that the cupboard was changed in the kitchen. He went as usual in the same way, much to his surprise, the kitchen was empty even water to drink was moved to another place. He began to search everywhere for the kitchen, on his return, he lost his way, a crew member saw him and brought him to the captain, who had then asked what to do with him.

'The decision fell in favour of throwing him into the sea. The captain took him by the collar and then brought him by force to a corner of the ship and asked him to jump. A chance smiled at him on that occasion, the captain's wife pleaded in his favour, he was handcuffed and then locked up in a room. When they arrived in Portugal, the wife of the captain convinced her husband to let him try his luck. After a long conversation, the latter accepted and gave him back his freedom. Fodey spent hours hiding in the harbour so that he could find his way out. Four hours later, he sneaked around and went out of the harbour, but didn't go far. His shabby coats and dirty shirt exposed him to all passers-by. Later that day, he met two police officers on patrol who asked him for his identification documents, he was at a loss, and the Portuguese language was a big problem for him to understand. To what they were saying as for him, they were talking through their nose and the mouth. He was arrested and then expelled to his native country.' Fodey explained his unfortunate journey to Paul, then wiped his tears and went on.

'This time, it's my last chance to take the ship, I will get to my destination in Europe,' said Fodey with determination.

He was very young but full of experience, and his story motivated Paul to try his luck. Paul joined the group; then approached Fodey, who had a good knowledge of the ship's various hiding places. He went to find out the ship destination along with the exact departure time and the duration of the journey. After the details were given to him, he began to think of a plan to embark without being seen by the crew members.

After he had received all relevant information regarding the risks and benefits from Fodey, he waited in the dock until the ship had started to move. He ran behind the ship and jumped to reach the rope, he fell into the water, while holding the rope in hand without letting it go then climbed up to reach the top of the ship. Upon his arrival at the height of the ship, there was no place to hide. He took the risk to climb the large chimney and then entered inside and fell vertically. He found a small door that he used to watch for any movements and listen for any footsteps or noise so that he could be ready to run for his life if anyone attempted to catch him.

After a week of travelling, his troubles developed, he began to question himself.

Why have we still not yet arrived at the destination? Paul murmured.

After two weeks of a perilous journey, they finally reached France. The biggest problem arose, how to get out of the ship without being seen as he was wearing shabby coats and dirty shirts, and nothing differentiated him from a coal miner because of the chimney he had used to enter inside the ship. He waited overnight and sneaked out, then went on to the streets. He walked to a bus stop where two young women were seated impatiently, waiting for a bus to arrive. He approached slowly behind and pulled the coat from one of the girls then ran away. He then managed to find a public toilet to clean himself and wore the jacket. As he walked down the street, he saw two gentlemen passers-by from the other side of the road, then went to ask them for help.

'Good evening, sir. I'm looking for a place provided for the homeless or the poor people; please help me. I am hungry,' he asked.

One of them answered him in Portuguese and began to make advances on him and tried to flirt as if he wanted to tease Paul, believing that Paul was a cross-dresser because of the clothes he wore and the smell of the ladies perfume that followed him everywhere he went. Paul had no idea that in Europe, some men cross-dressed as women, and sometimes, they use female perfumes. He was confused and then moved away from them for security reasons. After a few hours of walking around without a positive outcome, he found himself alone on the street and spent the night outside in the cold. The next day, early in the morning, he met a young Malian who was returning from work, selling his peanuts and grilled corn in the Parisian suburbs streets, who pitied his circumstance then took him home. After a short stay, he led Paul to the mosque, not far from where he lived. Later that day, he introduced him to the man who leads the prayers in the mosque called 'Imam.' The latter took good care of him, and offered him shower, clothes and then lodges him for a week while trying to find his community so that he could connect them.

Paul did not feel comfortable in his skin as he was tired of his trip but was more than ever determined to achieve his European dream. He began to go out to make friends, meeting people around and caught up with them. One day, luck smiled on him, a young Ivorian man approached him and guided his footsteps. As for this young man, helping someone in desperate situations, especially an African, was a duty. Since that day, they had become friends and had never separated.

This young Ivorian man whom he called brother, as he had never called him by his name, was the boyfriend of a friend of Jacqueline, Paul's wife. One day. Jacqueline's car tyre had a puncture and park on the roadside, and she was waiting for the assistance services. Paul approached her and helped to replace her car's tyre. Jacqueline looked straight to his eyes and stared at him for a very long time, then thanked him. She immediately realised that this man was either a homeless or illegal immigrant, as she could see directly through his accent, the way he acted, and he was looking miserable. Since then, the two had become inseparable friends and the beginning of their romance. During their dating time, Paul told her almost everything about his life, his current situation in France, his journey to Europe.

Jacqueline was a very sincere, humble, and generous lady. She loved to be told the truth. Whatever the personal situation, she would always find the lucidity to support him; she gave him all that he needed as an illegal immigrant living in France. They walked together, and she showed him the meaning of real European life, although the fear of being arrested and sent back home was still there, they took the risk to not worry about it. She showed him the areas to avoid so that he won't fall into the net of police control, then helped him to familiarise himself with popular places and even taught him to drink coffee in public places. Months passed quickly, and Paul began to make friends, he saw all the good things that Jacqueline was doing for him, whereas, he couldn't give her anything in return, except for the small amount of money he earned when working in the black market as labour. It was sometimes even more difficult for him to get these jobs in the buildings and farms.

A few months later, Paul decided to break up their relationship, for a simple reason that he was not able to offer her so much in return, heart-breaking for Jacqueline. Initially, she refused to accept, but shortly after, she began to understand him and put herself in his shoes. After three weeks of separation, Paul could not stand a minute without thinking about Jacqueline. Then he decided to win her back again, knowing all her activities, including getting in and out. He went to buy flowers then went to see Jacqueline at her apartment. He formulated his will and intentions to resume their relationships. He reassured her that he would never do this nonsense behaviour again and begged her to take him back. She took her time before she decided whether they could restart a new life together. After two days of deep thought, she agreed to give him one last chance, and then they continued their life in harmony and peace. Meanwhile, Paul still had not gotten a job, he was walking around doing all sorts of dirty work to make some money, which was a bit hard for him, but he clung to it until his situation would change one day.

Time passed, the concerns multiplied, Jacqueline suggested to Paul two options to stay and live legally in France. But for that to happen, they had to get married so that he could get his legal status quickly, but this option was not convincing him, and the second option was to claim asylum, a very long procedure of waiting with an uncertain result. Nevertheless, Paul considered the second option to seek asylum. At that time in France, asylum seekers were able to obtain accommodation if they didn't have a family in France to host them. If they do, they will receive a minimum amount payable to them during the investigation of their asylum claim.

Paul was afraid that his asylum claim would be refused, and then he would be expelled to his country with no other solution, so he decided to try his luck and engaged in the asylum process. His asylum was temporarily accepted, pending investigation of his case. Immediately, he received housing, food, and free medical care. The two lovers continued to meet daily, the distance was separating them, but they still loved each other. They were on the phone almost all the time until the day that his asylum was refused for lack of evidence; it was a hard time for Paul. He interrupted the contact of all his acquaintances, including his beloved Jacqueline, which left him in the dark for two months without seeing each other.

After several missed calls from Jacqueline, she decided to go and inquire about his situation, so that she could meet with him. Two days later, she called and left a voicemail to get in touch with her, still unanswered, then she went to visit him during her work leave. Much to her surprise, she found Paul in a terrible state, difficult to recognise. Paul, whom she had known before, had lost half of his body weight. Her visit gave Paul some relief; then, she decided not to leave him alone in this situation because he needed someone to help him. At nightfall, Paul collapsed into tears; his thought went back to his country, to his family. Furthermore, he was afraid that something had happened to them; he was tired of hiding all the time in his life, illegal situation, and racism towards the asylum seekers were growing at an uncontrollable level. He saw himself in a small world surrounded by heartless people who thought only of their own interests and who care less about the feelings of others.

The love that Jacqueline had for Paul was enormous; all she wanted in her life was to see Paul happy and smile again. But this could not be done if he remained in the hands of the social services from which she contemplated a plan to take him home and live with him in her new apartment located at Saint-Denis in Paris. In the vicinity where they lived, there were many other undocumented immigrants without a right to stay in France. Some waited so long to be regularised. Those who had just arrived were looking for a job to take on without any worries to be arrested by the police.

Paul was introduced to his neighbours, among which the Cameroonians, Congolese, Guineans, Malians, Ivoirians and other survivors from the Maghreb, were all immigrants in the quest for survival. Still, this introduction to his new neighbour did not convince him as everyone was jealous of the success of the others. Nevertheless, he found a picking and packing job in fruits and vegetable farm while waiting for his situation to be resolved. Sometimes when he had nothing to do, he spent his time in the coffee shop with friends to kill off the immigration stress. He thought, however, to avoid being arrested as he was working illegally in the country, he had to find a solution about it and act now.

The only possible solution for him to have a long-stay visa was to get married or have a child with Jacqueline. Finally, he changed his mind and chose the first option that was proposed by Jacqueline at the beginning of their romance because they loved each other very much. In addition to that, they lived together. So, they decided that they could advance their project in a few months. Jacqueline introduced him to her family for their part of blessings. However, the family was very pleased with their union and were delighted with their marriage proposal. Paul now is part of her family and now knows her parents. But Jacqueline's parents, for some reason, did not realise that it was too difficult or even impossible to be a foreigner in the French territory. At that very moment, it was the race against the clock to get married and regularise his situation as quickly as possible. She went to the town hall for an inquiry without informing them of their marriage so that she could avoid encountering difficulties as a result of Paul's situation because they had been living together for six months and could testify the seriousness of their relationship. Then they got married the following month. Paul finished explaining his journey story to his friend, Abdul.

After long hours of listening to Paul's side of the story, and the sad part of Fodey's journey, Abdul raised grave concerns about how their country's government had discharged its duty of care of its own people who had a legitimate right to have jobs and live peacefully and happily in a country they love. Abdul nodded his head and hugged Paul tightly, then shook his long-time friend's hand. He congratulated him on his courage and efforts. Paul saw in itself pride of being in Europe. Although Paul had nothing in France but preferred this miserable life than going back home to be humiliated in his native country. Abdul told him a little about his journey story and presented him the document that had allowed him to enter to Spain and then to France, and now he wanted to try to get a job through his friend before claiming asylum. The time was hard to find a job in France, and above all, it was not easy for an immigrant coming from Africa to be shortlisted, whatever the immigrant's skill set. It would be a job refusal unless you were super lucky to be accepted to do dirty work, with enormous risks of being imprisoned and expelled from the country. Whereas Abdul had risked his life by taking dangerous routes on the hands of those smugglers for a single purpose to succeed in his life, but when he arrived in Europe, he had become a slave of his own will.

He remembered the journey in which he testified and saw a systematic rape. The moments when he found himself piled up with other candidates like a fish inside a box thrown behind the pickups trucks without air, water, bread, empty looks on the face, flat stomach, and violence, especially from their smugglers and found himself between life and death. Now the misery in their country of origin pursued them, and Europe no longer wanted them.

Spring had just arrived. Work had become rare jewellery to find; Abdul still could not secure the smallest job. Sometimes, he hardly managed to get the minimum food, clothing, and personal expenses through his friend Paul, who worked part-time between nine o'clock in the morning and six o'clock in the evening, three days a week at a clothing merchant boutique at Château Rouge in the suburbs of Paris. Paul fought the way he could so that he could find a place for his friend Abdul to work as he did not want to lose him again after all those years of being apart before they had met mysteriously by force of circumstances at the station of Gare du Nord.

Life in Paris was far from being a safe haven for Abdul, especially for being without a residence permit was not only running the risk of being arrested and then deported without challenging it through the immigration court but also being humiliated too. Even for those who succeeded in hiding and working in the black market, the difficulties remained considerable: from a constant fear of being arrested and taken back home, struggling to get medical care, feeding themselves with good food, to work in peace, and to have an accommodation to stay. Looking back to the deplorable situation that many of them lived through, Abdul did not want to stay the way of those undocumented immigrants he saw walking around in the Sunday markets selling SIM cards, pants, or rechargeable phone cards. So, he preferred to take the risk of trying his luck in the United Kingdom so that he would seek asylum for a better life as he thought that seeking asylum was not a privilege but a right. For those who wanted to manage to survive in life, nothing was impossible. So, for Abdul, it was out of a question of staying any longer in Paris, because Great Britain was the destination of the predilection of undocumented immigrants, so that nothing could keep him in Paris. He wanted to leave at all cost to reach the other end of the channel as he had heard in the past, and he believed that the English immigration system was a bit more tolerant towards immigrants than the rest of the European countries; he cared less and feared nothing. Abdul went to look for his fake passport and got prepared for the journey. He then took his way to the bus station of the Quai de Bercy in Paris; later, he went on board of the coach to minimise the risk of being arrested at the border between Pas de Calais in France and Dover in the United Kingdom. Upon their arrival, Abdul managed to enter the country once again without being arrested by the border control. He went and asked asylum on humanitarian grounds, knowing that if he had asked officers asylum at the border before entering the country, he would have been refused and sent back as he was still in the French territory. He then joined a growing number of migrants seeking asylum in the United Kingdom. Unlike other immigrants who may want to come to the United Kingdom to seek an improved standard of living, but those who sought asylum fearing for their lives of prosecution from their home countries. The Home Office grants asylum protection to those who could prove that they fled their countries based on a credible fear of persecution, such as race, religion, nationality, gender, political opinion, etc. And that for Abdul, his case was political persecution as being a member of political group and prisoner on the loose out of his country, Guinea. He was then sent to the Home Office in London for screenings. Shortly after he had asked for asylum, he was sent to the immigration detention as a routine procedure, where he stayed for months. At the same time, the government investigated his asylum claims of fear of persecution.

After he had spent a month in detention, he was finally called for an interview. Abdul was seated in the interview room; his body was flooded with black sweat, with a sad face. He had a constant panic in his eyes, his pupils juggled in all directions. The Home Office interview room aroused in him a fear. The officer began to ask him questions about his asylum application. Abdul tried to answer, but it was very difficult for him to describe his life in his country, bad memories stormed his mind, the journey through the desert to Europe created confusion and almost made him lose his mind. He thought only of his odyssey and could not remember what he had done before he got in the United Kingdom, what he was doing during his journey, and how he lived in the jungle. When the officer came to ask him a question about his trip to Spain, Abdul unpacked everything in a more disorderly way. Suddenly, his memories rose up without warning. He moved his head up and down as if there was music playing in his head. Shortly after that, he remembered everything and began to tell his crossing of the Sahara Desert, the engine failure and the breakdown in the middle of the desert, how he found the money needed to pursue his journey, Aliou's arrest in Gourougou and so on. The officer noticed that Abdul needed medical attention. He was then sent back to the detention centre pending his asylum case to be reviewed.

In detention, Abdul met Haseeb, an asylum seeker from Iraq who was fighting a deportation order and hoped to get the immigration court to recognise his recent marriage with a British woman named Christine and let him stay in the United Kingdom. As the conversation deepened, Abdul reminded him that it was not easy to leave their countries, their families, their communities, and their languages, to come into a country and claim asylum desperately without an understanding of what that country's asylum laws are. Still, all they knew was that if they did not come to Europe, their life would end.

'In the past, I thought of coming to Europe was perfect, but right now, I am not looking perfect, and nothing is going well for me since I came into Europe. I am nervous because I don't know anything about my future.' He tried to blame his unfortunate adventure on the media and politicians. He thought if the media had been able to describe the oppression and the terrifying ordeal that many people are subjected in their countries. Nothing could stop them from speaking to the public that Europe is far from being a safe haven for those desperate immigrants who died trying on the fences of Ceuta and in the sea to make their way into Europe so that many lives could have been saved. '*Oh, Europe, when the media deceived and refused to show us the reality and hardship that many Europeans lived and had affected most of their social activities. And here I am today, to discover this needle of lies and cover-up which does not stop pricking my brain and that of all those illegal immigrants present in the continent for making us believe in the existence of a European El Dorado*' he thought in soliloquised. During his stay in the detention centre, Abdul became acquainted with several other people of all nationalities. He had met some of them during his journey in the desert and the jungle. It was from them he learned that his friend Aliou and forty-eight people had drowned after their boat capsized during a storm in the middle of the Mediterranean Sea.

Touched by the sad news, Abdul withdrew from the group, then went and sat alone in the corner for a moment of reflection, his thought went back in days when they were struggling to survive in the desert and the jungle, he began to meditate.

'If Aliou knew that by wanting to realise his dreams was to discover the European El Dorado, he would never have wished to leave his family to realise that dream. Consequently, he had died as a result of chasing up that dream. He has gone forever, and he had stayed alone under that cold Mediterranean Sea's graveyard for illegal immigrants,' he whispered.

The next morning, as usual in the canteen during breakfast time, Abdul was called at the reception; he had a letter waiting for him. Knowing well the difference between the envelope colours, he went and glanced to see the nature of the envelope. He thought that: *if the envelope was white and small, that means he has an appointment either from his lawyer or from a doctor, whilst if it were a large brown colour, it would be a categorical refusal of his asylum application from the Home Office.* Abdul took in his hand the small brown coloured envelope and went to hide it under his mattress until everyone had gone to sleep so that he could easily read the contents of the letter.

Throughout the whole day, Abdul was anxious and nervous, soon after midnight, Abdul went into the room he shared with four other people; he was delighted to find good news written in the letter. The letter was from the National Asylum Support Service (NASS), they provide asylum seekers accommodations and weekly allowances while waiting for their asylum claim decision. The NASS granted his claim, and he would leave the centre to be relocated independently to another city. He remained calm in the room as if nothing had happened because, in the centre, they did not trust each other. His whole being thrilled with happiness, and he could not wait to leave to begin a new life outside the detention centre fences. The preparations were well underway, the individuals chosen to leave the centre should first start learning how to live within the community and then how to integrate into society. The day of their departure was scheduled in three days' time, during which all his friends came to wish him good luck and exchanged their contact numbers. The three days went by so fast; Abdul was transported to Manchester, a city situated in the northwest of Great Britain, with three other people who came from Somalia. Upon their arrival in the city. He was welcomed by an agency which led them to his new home and was taken in charge by NASS, where he had received his first weekly allowance of £35 and was required to check-in with immigration enforcement officials at Dallas court in Salford. While waiting for his asylum claim to be processed. Abdul was not allowed to work or get involved in any charity work.

Not having the right to work, Abdul went to an organisation called Refugee Action, which was in charge of helping asylum seekers and refugees in a difficult situation. He asked for help and guidance on how to enrol in an English language school. He met hundreds of strong young men and women who had fled their countries from famine, war, and the dictatorship from their heads of state to come and seek protection in the UK, a country that's supposed to protect them, instead had left them nothing but to fight for their stay in the country. The reception was filled with people to a breaking point, they were all sad and silent, and they seemed desperately in need to solve their problems. Each of them had their own immigration issues and was provided help, depending on their cases. But priorities were given to those who had their asylum claim closed. And they were waiting to be expelled from the country. Others had their support terminated and were in the process of appealing.

Meanwhile, the refugee action and other humanitarian charities had to find the best lawyers possible to defend their cases. But hardly any of them could count on a favourable decision after they had successfully made their appeals. Abdul hurried to leave the place as he had been through a several-year-long ordeal; he barely escaped slavery on his trek through the Sahara and had survived on the Mediterranean Sea. After all those years of the fight for survival, he now believed he had reached his destination. But what comes next was utterly uncertain.

Abdul's case has not been an easy one after he had waited a year for the outcome of his asylum claim; his housemate named Kareema from Eritrean had also waited for many years after he had made a fresh asylum claim. He let him know that the asylum system in this country was mental torture and an open prison that would deprive them of working. Abdul would never get peace of mind as long as he remained an asylum seeker and that he would live with a permanent fear of being arrested and sent back to his own country to face the danger he had left behind.

'Here, we are in Europe, and yet they claim it to be the mother of democracy and the so-call freedom,' Kareema said, a minute of silence and then continued.

'When we were subjected to physical torture in Africa, here in Europe, we are subjected to the mental torture, and this is the freedom and democracy of the western countries that many of us had envied.' After a pause, he said:

'My friend, since I arrived here in 2001, they have not yet given me the right to stay, and my asylum application is still opened, and yet here we were in 2004. So, I use my work permit to do hard and dangerous works at meagre wages. I wanted to help you. Still, considering your current situation, I am afraid I cannot do anything for you right now until you get permission to work or receive the final decision from the Home Office regarding your asylum application.'

Being satisfied with the advice given by Kareema, he was convinced that he would have to lead his battle to earn his stay in the country; then, he decided to change his lifestyle. He began looking for a friend with whom to share his ideas and tried hard to improve his English language to better integrate into English society. In September, he started to attend Oldham College, and then he went out regularly to socialise himself in the nightclubs. His meeting with Arnaud relieved him a bit; the latter helped him to find a member of his community who was named Francis through whom he used to obtain the news from his own country. At that point, Abdul's worries subsided because staying in the country without status or living in the absence of his community was like to refrain from going back home, attending a family wedding, or simply the desire to go and visit his Uncle Bobo. The year 2001, after the terrorist attack in the United States of America, had brought a lot of trouble in the world, Muslims were seen as terrorists, wicked people without human values. This stereotype affected him enormously and had prevented him from having a soulmate, but after many attempts, he finally met his first girlfriend. She was a conservative Englishwoman since she was born in a conservative family who disliked that their daughter dated other people of colour than their own. She was

164

called Chloe, with extraordinary beauty, and was the kind of woman a man would look at twice.

The weekends are generally off days; every worker should enjoy it. Abdul and his friend, Arnaud, decided to walk around the city centre in search of the first-come-first-serve lady in clubs and restaurants. The nightclub was filled to burst. Soon, Abdul stepped inside the club; his eyes pointed to those of Chloe. Arnaud understood that there was a chemistry between the two, but a problem would arise soon, since Abdul did not speak English fluently and his only main spoken language was French, it would be harder for him to convince her, besides that, he was Muslim by faith. As a good friend, Arnaud went to Abdul and showed his support and said to him:

'I know you like this girl, you have to invite her to dance with you, but be careful not to mention your status as an asylum seeker and if she asks your name, tell her that your name is Jean-Pierre, a French name. English girls love French men. They always believe that the French are romantic. Don't forget that name and then never mention that you are a Muslim,' he advised him.

A piece of advice that would produce success, Abdul won Chloe's heart. After three months of romance, Chloe decided to introduce Abdul, nicknamed Jean-Pierre, to her family. Still, before that day, Abdul invited her to a beautiful and quiet place and approached the subject of his status and told her his real name (Abdul), then his religion (Muslim) and his reason to seek asylum in Great Britain. Chloe lowered her head and rose it up. She shook her head like possessed by the devil; then she went crazy on him.

'Don't you dare or even try to approach me, you didn't tell me the truth at the beginning, so you lied to me all along, and now it's the time for you to tell me everything that you're hiding inside you. Please stay away from, before I do something which I shall regret,' she overreacted as a result of her shock, and she continued. 'Why didn't you tell me this before? You had lied to me, and you have betrayed my confidence,' she shouted on Abdul.

Abdul remained calm and said:

'I was afraid of being rejected by you, given the fact that I am a Muslim, and especially what had happened around the world with the crazy activities of those damned terrorists had created controversy in the western countries.'

Chloe still loved him; she had not sought to know the rest of his story. She fixed an appointment to go and visit her parents. On the day of their visit, Abdul wore the clothes which Chloe had bought for him and used a nice smelling perfume and presented himself as a gentleman before his girlfriend's parents.

'Dad, Mum, this is Abdul, the one I had told you about, he is very nice and treats me very well,' she said.

'But where is Jean-Pierre? Since you had told me that you were dating a Frenchman named Jean-Pierre,' asked her mother.

'Mum, it was him, Jean Pierre, but his real name is Abdul,' she explained with embarrassment.

'Oh, I see where you're coming from,' her mother replied.

Her father got angry; the contour of his mouth narrowed in the perpetual movement of suction to the rhythm of his breath.

'Abdul, what kind of job are you doing to survive?' asked the father.

'Well, at the moment, I am not working, but I'm going to school,' replied Abdul.

'Which country do you come from? As many black people living in Europe have their country of origin somewhere in Africa,' asked the father.

'I came from Guinea, Conakry, to be more precise,' Abdul replied.

'So, your parents live there?' continued the father.

'My father and my mother have passed away, but the rest of my family stayed and lived there,' Abdul replied hesitantly.

'Which church do you go to? As for myself, I am a religious person,' asked the father.

'Oh no, I'm a Muslim,' replied Abdul.

Her father blushes and abruptly pulled Chloe to the room. He had a horrible argument with her for dishonouring the family rule; then the mother re-joined them and let her know that Abdul had followed her simply because of her status and that he did not love her. Chloe came out of the room with her face reddened and went to the door and said. 'Let's go, Abdul, don't listen to them.' Her mother followed them a few footsteps ahead and then threw on him all sorts of insults and racially abused him.

'Never come here again, you, black monkey, you're an illegal immigrant, go back to your country,' she said to him while sobbing.

'Oh, mother, don't embarrass me, please,' Chloe interrupted.

'You are fifteen years late to tell me what to do in my life; this is 2004, you know that mother!'

Her mother coloured slightly reddened. 'Very well, Chloe,' she said mildly.

Abdul walked quickly, his face full of sweat and tears. He knew there was no future between him and Chloe. He was wholly discouraged from seeing Chloe's parents reacting this way and began in his turn to play with her feelings, knowing that she had seriously fallen in love with him. Abdul was very proud to have a beautiful girl at his feet and knew that he was wrong to play with her feelings. Whenever they quarrelled, Chloe could not resist; she always came back to him. He began to worry after every bad thing he had done to her so far, she continued to love him, and that continued to happen until the day he realised that she no longer felt anything for him apart from hatred. And from that moment, he regretted his bad behaviour towards her. Although he realised that Chloe was the only person who could understand him and that his immaturity led him to his failure.

A week passed without seeing her, so Abdul noticed that the love he had for Chloe was fading away slowly. He decided to turn the page and face reality. To calm his mind, he followed the behaviour of his friends by drinking excessive amounts of alcohol and smoking cigarettes. They believed that these habits would take away the anxiety caused by their asylum claim application and the refusal to give them the right to stay in the country. At the same time, it would make them forget the moment spent without achieving the European dreams that had pushed them to leave their respective countries to take the dangerous journey to reach Europe. Abdul reduced his ambitions and increased the night out and frequented different nightclubs. Suddenly, he found himself in a situation that allowed him to fill his pocket with money without making any effort.

On Saturday night, Abdul went to a nightclub. He observed people jostling to be served drinks at the counter, whenever a customer put his hand in their pocket to withdraw money; a few banknotes fell on the ground without realising it. For some, when trying to put back the changes in their pockets, their coins fell accidentally, as they were under the influence of alcohol and continued drinking while chatting.

'Here, people don't drink to satisfy their needs; they drink to destroy their brains,' said Arnaud.

Abdul went right up to the counter. He took out a few coins that he had kept in his pocket and asked to be served a drink. Pretending to pay for his drink, Abdul stretched his hand out to the bartender and then dropped the coins to the floor, then bent over to pick up his money and amassed any money dropped accidentally on the floor from customers. He then carried on gathering all along the line any money found on his way.

This night practice had become tactics for Abdul to fill his pockets without the slightest effort.

'Excuse me! Excuse me, can you please step aside and let me pass,' he told customers in the queue, waiting to be served their drinks.

Soon they moved aside, he bent over again and picked up all he could find on the floor, then stood up, put the money into his pocket and then sat down to breathe a bit, then resumed. After an hour of constant movement, he left that nightclub for another nightclub. He carried on doing the same routine until three o'clock in the morning, the time all nightclubs closed, then went back to his house to count the amount earned at night.

Early in the morning, his friend Arnaud received a letter from the Home Office. In the letter, it was written that his asylum application was refused and that he had no right to appeal and should leave the United Kingdom territory within a short time. Consequently, he lost his right to housing, his weekly allowances, and health care. Having no choice, he left his house and went to join Abdul, and shared the food that Abdul kept in his house while waiting to find a favourable solution to be legalised in the country.

Arnaud remained hidden in Abdul's room until the day he met Jeannette, a French national who worked at the library in Oldham's town. However, this library was the nucleus of several asylum seekers' meetings, a place of distraction because it was the only place that they spent their day learning new things and inquired about the news of their country of origin and also chats through the internet. Jeannette was in charge of registering all those newcomers in the city who had French as their first language and showed them the services available at the library.

To chase away the stress, Abdul and Arnaud set off for jogging. On their way, Arnaud found an object on the ground and picked it up. It was a purse that contained £85, which was a lump sum of money to find on the street by a failed asylum seeker. Inside the purse, there was a French identity card, driving license, and bank cards that belonged to Jeannette.

'What a lucky day for you, my friend?' said Abdul.

'Let's have a look at the content of the purse somewhere quiet,' said Arnaud.

The two-stop running and went to sit in a secluded corner and began to search piece by piece. It was a sign of relief for both, especially the money found, Arnaud decided to buy himself a ticket to re-join his community in London so that Abdul could manage the small weekly amount of money that (NASS) National Asylum Support Service provided him. After a few minutes of thinking, the two agreed to return the wallet to the owner at the library.

Arriving at the reception, Jeannette was not there; they asked after her.

'We want to talk to Jeannette, please,' they asked.

'She's not at her desk, but she will be back soon. Can I help you?' said the receptionist.

'No, we'll wait for her,' replied Arnaud.

A few minutes later, she came back with a sad face.

'Well, here she comes,' said the receptionist.

Jeannette was unhappy; she passed them and went to sit behind her desk. They thought she was not in a good mood.

'These two young men wanted to talk to you,' said her colleague.

Jeannette walked straight to the two seated on the chairs.

'Good morning, what can I do for you?' asked Jeannette.

'I came here to give you a big surprise,' said Arnaud jokingly.

'Oh, okay,' she answered anxiously.

'Actually, I picked up a wallet last night during my jogging, that belongs to you,' said Arnaud.

Arnaud pulled the wallet in the jacket he held in his hand, it was well wrapped in blue plastic and handed back to her, she kissed Arnaud on the cheek. Suddenly, all her whole body began to tremble.

'I am out of words to thank you. Can I have your name, please?' she asked.

'My name is Arnaud, and he is my friend Abdul,' replied Arnaud.

'Happy to meet you, and thank you for returning my wallet,' she said.

Jeannette didn't delay taking Arnaud's contact number and thanked them again. The next day in the evening at six o'clock, she invited them to a coffee bar to have a glass of wine with her. Since then, Arnaud's life had changed, and they were seeing each other until the day the immigration officers arrested him and began the procedure to expel him from the United Kingdom to his own country.

It was required by the Home Office that each asylum seeker check-in with immigration officials at least once a month to prove their presence in the United Kingdom territory. Abdul went to report himself to the immigration office at Dallas Court. On his way back, he decided to buy food at the nearby supermarket. He saw Francis running, choked by the march and asked him what was going on.

'Abdul! Abdul! Arnaud was arrested this morning by the police, he is currently in detention,' said Francis, trembling.

Abdul was confused and couldn't understand or believe what he was saying.

'What happened to him?' asked Abdul.

'They fell on him during a routine check. The police asked him to stop and then to identify himself. From that very moment, they found he had no right to stay in this country,' he said sighing. 'Then he was arrested and taken to the police station in Oldham pending to be transferred to the detention centre,' he explained sadly.

The matter had become serious; Abdul went to meet Jeannette and told her the whole problem. She rushed to the police station and then to the detention, through her lawyer, she was able to communicate with Arnaud and spoke a few words. Two days after his arrest, Arnaud was expelled from the country and found himself in the Democratic Republic of Congo (DRC), his country of origin. Jeannette loved Arnaud very much, Abdul saw that in her. He knew that if she had the possibility, Arnaud would never be expelled and left her alone in this country. As a French national, she had a solution to bring him back into this country through the family reunification act adopted by the Union European Law. She worked hard and paid her taxes to the British authority; therefore, she had the possibility through the law to bring back Arnaud if she desired to get married to him.

After three months of continuous work, Jeannette decided to join Arnaud in DRC. Upon her arrival, a decent wedding ceremony was organised, and they got legally married. After six months of their marriage, Arnaud re-joined his wife Jeannette in the town of Oldham, where they lived peacefully and had two beautiful children.

Two years had passed, Abdul still waiting for a decision on his asylum application, no follow-up, the concern intensified. He went to sit on the chair in front of his small screen that was prominently at the back corner of his living room. He watched TV programmes that showed the images of the asylum-seekers journeys to Europe, their dangerous routes, the shipwrecks, inspired him with both compassion and fatalism and felt sorry for all these victims. If immigrants took such risks, it was simply to have a better life, knowing the economic crisis that recently hit the world; it would be difficult to accommodate all of them. But this couldn't take away their hope of finding a better life on the European territory. He changed the BBC channel and captured SKY news, then France 24; it was the same story. They kept talking about it as if it was the only problem in the world. He then sank in deep thought.

Probably not many people appreciate us to be here, but surely, a few will understand the reasons for our presence in their country, murmured Abdul.

When we looked at the past, immigration has always been a phenomenon known around the world. The west should tend to accept these immigrants not as an obligation or a threat, but as an opportunity. Moreover, beyond demographics, these immigrants brought different skills and aptitude, which could be transmitted to those non-immigrants background friends and colleagues. They could also increase competition in particular labour markets, increasing the incentive for natives to acquire certain skills. Over time, Abdul had changed. He forgot the mistakes he had made and began to appreciate the marvel of life, but to be without a resident permit in Europe was a tough life in which he lost his hopes dramatically. For those who remained longer in the country and had received their work permit took advantage of it to find a job; others who had failed in their applications saw their supports terminated and did not have permission to work. Without any income or family, they received support from fellow asylum seekers they met in detention and the occasional kindness of strangers. They also depended on a friend of a friend to let them in their accommodation so they could sleep on their couch. These intolerable levels of hardship forced them to work illegally in the black market to achieve their needs and repatriate the rest of the money to feed their respective families back home.

On Monday morning, Abdul thought of finding something to do that could distract him; he then decided to visit a man called Alassane, who he met a long time ago at the Refugee Action. Alassane was a debtor, and he owed every refugee in the neighbourhood some money, from few pennies to quite a substantial amount and sent that money to his family back in Africa and hoped one day to find a job and pay back his debts. On the way, Abdul met his old English school friend called Johnny. As they stood talking, he saw Alassane and introduced him to Johnny, who in turn promised to help them find a job in a company that he had joined a few days ago and decided to meet up and discuss it later in Manchester city centre. Both were happy and laughed in a delighted way, then they left and walked to the city centre and waited for Johnny to arrive.

Meanwhile, Alassane whispered to Abdul that he was hungry and have not eaten since breakfast. Both headed to buy hamburgers and chips at the Burger King restaurant. Abdul and Alassane ate a sandwich and nibbled a few chips while waiting for Johnny to take them to his workplace that had just opened its doors. After long hours of waiting, they decided to visit the workplace indicated by Johnny. As they walked through the city centre in Piccadilly, a street trader tried to sell them a fake phone. The man followed them and insisted on the fact that they could buy the phone, as they walked along the street, Abdul decided to explain to him the reason why he didn't need it.

'Sir, we don't have money to buy your device, and we also need money, because we are looking for work to make money,' Abdul said.

The man answered them and said that he has a friend who had places to work in the black market. Abdul pulled Alassane aside to make him understand that these kinds of works are high risk, and besides that, they did not know who he was. He might be an undercover police officer or an immigration officer. Alassane did not want to hear that kind of words from Abdul and warned him not to get involved in his life as the only thing that matter to him right now was to find work.

'Listen to me, my friend Abdul, I have a wife and a child, so I don't have choices but to find a job, earn money, and send to feed them and also pay back my debts,' said Alassane.

Not wanting to let him go alone with a stranger, Abdul decided to join them to meet the employer. Upon their arrival, they were hired without providing any identification papers. On their first day at work, Abdul met with other employees who were subdivided into three groups: the seniors and the more experienced were in charge of packing boxes containing animals' foods on the wooden pallets based on the first floor. The less competent unloaded the products from the container also based on the first floor, and the newcomers, including Abdul, Alassane, and many others, completed all the physical works, included cleaning of all toilets located in the basement. The room where the products were mixed had not had any windows or ventilation systems, and the walls were constantly wet.

Twelve-hour shift to work without a break from morning to the night. Abdul made a joke. 'Here in Europe, we eat or not, and whether we live far or not, we work twelve hours without stop. And if you need a robot, come to us.' They were supposed to be paid a fair amount for the task they had completed. Instead, they received derisory sums without a clear explanation from their employer who often used illegal workers for their own advantage to carry out the high-risk tasks without considering their employees' health and safety at work.

Abdul and his co-workers were in a very precarious and vulnerable position, abused by their crooked bosses. They could not complain about their unfair treatment and bullying while there was a whole unfair exploitation system operating in the company, such as unfulfilled promises of a pay increase. Their working conditions were violating human dignity, insufficient or non-existent rewards to a given task. But they preferred to stay and work there than leaving the company to preserve their dignity by considering that they were the targeted individuals such as those who had not been granted a work or residence permit and the illegal immigrants and asylum seekers.

The end of the working week approached. All the employees gathered in the reception hall, Abdul and Alassane held their scorecard, each wanted to be paid in the first position. On the other side, a woman dozed off on the chair, her head resting on her bag. She had wounded her hand when she was unloading the products from the container, and she also expected her payment. Instead of receiving medical care, she had received a letter never to come back again to work for the company.

Suddenly, three blue minibuses parked in front of the workplace entrance. Surprisingly it was the immigration officers, a total panic for undocumented immigrants. Abdul left the queue and went to glance at the window. He saw the men in blue uniforms with the logo on top 'immigration officer,' they were heading to the company's building. He quietly left the reception without saying anything to anyone and went to take shelter in the toilet situated next to the emergency door. The reception door opened, an officer poked his head around the reception door to see what was going on and saw a packed group of illegal immigrants forming a long queue at the front of the reception desk. All eyes turned to this unexpected visit of the immigration officers in the company.

'Come and see; we have a visit from the police!' said the curious man.

Within minutes, all the payslips and clock cards disappeared, the dozing woman woke up, and all pressed to be in the middle of the group to avoid being the first to be interviewed by the immigration officers. Fear increased among those who had just claimed their asylum, and their cases were in the process of being examined.

The presence of the police officers was traumatising; they encircled almost all exits. They ignored to secure the small emergency door that faced long fences, which could not allow anyone to escape. They began to survey about seventy

174

employees working in conditions comparable to human trafficking. Moreover, their checks reveal numerous recruitments of undocumented immigrant workers and asylum seekers whose testimonies on their working conditions left speechless: a wage of between £ 2.66 and £ 3 per hour for an average of twelve hours a day. A salary, at least, two times fewer than the average wage paid per week at that time, not to mention the exceeding of statutory working hours. Under the loud noises of the officers and the murmuring of the employees, Abdul slowly opened the toilet door, which he served as a hiding place and threw himself on the emergency door and opened it abruptly. He found a long fence in front of him, then leapt high to reach the top of the wall. He climbed and fell back down on the other end of the street and ran away. Abdul bypassed streets to reach the train station near his workplace. To erase any track of pursuit, he infiltrated the street traders who were distributing newspapers and selling phone SIM cards along the pavement.

The Despair

Mid-November, winter had arrived; the cold air that tickled Abdul's dry skin made him sad. He, who had teased all women he met on his way during the past summer, was now confronted with a dilemma. He sometimes felt impatient to see the nightfall so that he would run behind those beautiful young ladies with tan summer skins who were jumping in Manchester public squares and nightclubs.

He remembered those sleepless nights, trying to drown his grief in discussions with customers in a cafeteria. That time where the activity of the night allowed him to forget life as a couple was far behind. The unforgivable moments where the beautiful women were won easily, this cold wind announced the arrival of winter. Abdul seated on the stool, wearing his sweater shivering with cold, the cafeteria emptied gradually as the cold became more accentuated, he found himself alone surrounded with a couple of lovers. He needed to be in a couple on that night. The street emptied little by little. Soon, he would remain alone sitting on the stool. Abdul decided to go to his poor room; the long night was waiting for him on his soft mattress. He began to listen to the song of Julio Iglesias, remembering Hadja, Chloe, and others. He remembered those sweet voices, those envious glances that melted him like butter, but what to do, the night would be very long while his friends in a couple enjoyed an excellent night's sleep.

'Oh, we single, winter is our dry season,' he murmured before he went to bed and drifted into sleep.

The next morning, Abdul left the house to go and collect his English-language certificate obtained from his college.

'Winter is finally here, and I have only one desire, and that is to have my residence permit,' he soliloquised.

On the way to his college, he received a phone call from his lawyer. He was frightened to answer it and began to worry but had no choice; he took the call.

'Can I talk to Mr Abdul?' asked the lawyer.

'Yes, it's me, Abdul, on the phone,' he replied.

'A decision had been taken on your asylum application, the British government denied you the right of asylum,' the lawyer said.

The phone slid from his hands and fell abruptly onto the ground. He quickly bent and picked it up to avoid losing the connection, and then continued to listen.

'What can I do now?' he asked his lawyer.

'Nothing at the moment, I will review your case before appealing to the court if that's possible.' Said the lawyer.

He was not entirely satisfied because the last word possibility put him in doubt. And soon, he would lose all his rights to all the support provided to him. In the hope of easing his worries and keeping himself out of trouble, Abdul began to rub shoulders with his community that was strongly represented in the city so that they could support him when his NASS support comes to an end.

Two days later, he received a letter to leave the house as his asylum application case was now closed; consequently, he had to leave Great Britain within three weeks. To avoid being arrested, Abdul decided to leave the house and tried to remain in the country without any means of subsistence.

Every evening, he met with his friends at Omar's flat, who had obtained his residence permit soon after he had entered the United Kingdom. His friends regarded him as a blessed man; each confided and told him almost everything about their daily lives in the country. Some even went so far and gave him their parents' contact numbers back home, to keep them informed in case of their arrest and detained by the immigration officials.

On Sunday afternoon, there was a football game on the TV, Abdul and his friends sat tirelessly on the sofas trying to overcome their fear of been refused asylum. Meanwhile, they began relating their own stories to lower their anger and chase away their stress. Suddenly, a discussion arose about immigration.

Barry asked a question. 'Why such an influx of immigrants in Europe? Why have we taken all these risks by devaluing our lives to come and live in misery?'

'Oh, my friend, that's a simple question to answer. We left our country because of what was going on there, if the politics and the stability were well controlled, I confess that no one would be facing with this difficult decision, as you know that most of the Europeans don't want us to be here. Our heads of state don't want our existence too, so in your opinion, what should we do?' replied Diallo.

'In that case, better to stay here suffering in poverty than to be humiliated in front of your enemies, friends, and family in your country,' added Baylor.

'There is a reason why we all had to leave our dear country,' said Abdul. A moment of silence, then he continued. 'I personally had not left my country for a simple pleasure of being in Europe at all costs, but for a reason of humanitarian protection and be happy to fulfil my dream.'

Sidiki nodded his head and pointed his finger to his friends.

'Listen, I left my family, my country, in the desire to succeed in life. I was unemployed after finishing my studies, the poverty had followed me everywhere I put my feet. For that reason, I had sold my soul to the devil to be in Europe. So, whatever the difficulties, I will stay here, looking for my better life and make my dream come true,' he said with determination.

They had all left their different countries of origin, respectively, because of poor governance, the slowdown in economic growth that resulted from the increase in unemployment. Africa is a continent rich in natural resources, and those resources are exploited and sold in full view and knowledge of the entire population. The money goes into the pockets of those corrupt heads of state in foreign countries. The lack of investment in different sectors such as agriculture, livestock, fisheries, crafts, small and medium-sized enterprises are no longer considered active due to a lack of adequate investment. The crisis had slowed down all social activities; the high rate of chronic illiteracy among young people had often led them into delinquency, poverty, and violence. Lack of democracy and the change to the constitution to cling for life to the power also contributed to arbitrary arrests, corruption, injustice, and fraud. All these factors had destroyed the development of Africa in general and particularly in Guinea. Consequently, the younger generation who had to pay the price.

Abdul had spent two days in vain, awaiting the decision of his lawyer, fear of losing his appeal tortured him inside bit by bit. Abdul went to the Refugee's Action for assistance, then made a call to his lawyer who was absent from his office. He left a message to call him back as he ran out of credit. The centre's closing time approached, the workers informed him to get prepared to leave the place, another anxiety arose, Abdul had neither transport nor anything to eat. A few minutes later, he found himself outside, empty-handed without credit in his phone to inform his friends about the situation in which he was involved and his whereabouts. Afterwards, he began to look for churches and mosques to find a place where he could put his head until the next morning.

These worship places and other organisations represented everything for asylum-seekers who had lost their right to social and housing assistance. So, these churches and mosques were their last hopes. They received a need for survival, such as eating, clothing, and sometimes housed them according to their most urgent cases.

Their desperation facing the unbearable conditions of survival was compounded with a severe disappointment and risks of getting involved in all sorts of crimes. Often, these failed asylum seekers were exposed to prostitution and violence on the street in which they were impotent witnesses. By looking at the condition of life that Abdul had left behind him, the journey he had already taken, and the welcome received on his arrival in Great Britain sponsored by the refusal of his asylum application. He made the bet that the game is not worth the candle. His determination to survive led him to find a church where he joined many failed asylum seekers who were comfortably eating a well-flavoured soup and warmed bread. They were sitting in a group whispering together all over the place. It looked like whispering, but in reality, they were really talking at the top of their voices. Despite the fatigue and the weariness, the nuns were at their side to support and provided everything they needed: water, food, and information about their rights. They had a kindness and warmth that put Abdul and his fellow asylums at ease. Each of them felt being in a family and started to relate the difficult conditions they faced in their daily lives, including racial abuse, physical and verbal aggression throughout the day. Although these conditions were treated differently, nevertheless, they spoke about it to lower their discontent.

'Oh my God, we have been hijacked by immigration. If the time could be changed, I would have stayed in my country and died for my right!' shouted Abdul.

After they had satiated their hunger, Abdul felt comfortable and confident. He began to remember the words often used by the international press regarding the human rights in western countries such as freedom, having a decent life, right to asylum, social cohesion and human dignity, so on. Suddenly, he raised his voice.

'It was normal to report on TV and to the radio, the brutal acts caused by some African leaders who abused their authority and clung to the power and oppressed their poor populations. But it was also not forbidden to disclose about the reality of hardship and psychological torture that many of us, as asylum seekers, suffered once we reach the European land mostly called by the destitute the European Eldorado,' he told the audience.

A sudden silence descended from the roof and swallowed the noises, and the discussions continued until the last click of the switcher, and the bulbs went off, then each turned back on their sides and slept. The next day, early in the morning, Abdul woke up before others and went to the canteen to be served first. Shortly after breakfast, he disappeared from the church and resumed his fight of the day.

Manchester Piccadilly was the highlighted place for these destitute young immigrants from many countries. A place where they exchanged ideas and acquired news from the journals, word of mouth, and through the internet about the current situation back in their countries. Also met newly granted people to remain in the country and congratulated them for the opportunities they had been offered to develop and contribute to what has made the United Kingdom a great nation. They discussed their lives' experiences as an immigrant in the United Kingdom and how they had integrated into the society which had helped them appreciate the gift of life. Indeed, their immigration stories were linked to so much loss and despair, pain, and anguish that had yet to heal since they had fled their countries many years ago and sought asylum. During those years, many of their families had died, and they could never see them again. Abdul spent his entire day hoping he could someday have a family around and felt the love that everyone seemed to feel.

After a fun day, Abdul decided to return to his temporary host church. Along the way, he met a young girl named Salimatu, who had recently applied for asylum in the country. As a result, she had every right of support, she had accommodation and received a weekly allowance, and she was better off than Abdul. After greeting her, Abdul discovered that she was prohibited from doing any work. She had neither diploma nor qualification and even the English language she barely spoke, which seemed to be her disadvantage. He asked her to do him a favour.

'Good evening, madam,' said Abdul.

'Correction, sir, I am a single lady. By the way, how are you?' replied Salimatu.

'Please, I need £4 to complete my transport fee, and also, I am hungry,' begged Abdul.

'I am sorry. I don't have anything on me. Otherwise, I would have helped you,' she said with a smiled on her face. 'I was about to go home, can you please accompany me, since it is late and dark?' she asked.

Abdul's face darkened and said.

'Okay, of course, madam, sorry I apologise, miss,' he said hesitantly.

He agreed to accompany her safely home. On their way, Abdul played the role of the lover and pampered her with insipid jokes that had the gift of making the biggest night owls sleep. During this long night walk, they arrived at their destination. She thanked him and offered a few coins that allowed Abdul to reach his temporary accommodation. Abdul thanked her and then went back on his way, promising to repay her as soon as his situation in the country changed.

A month later, Abdul thought of going back to see Salimatu and remembered the day they had met. It was recurring; he always wanted to go over and meet with her again. She had a particular sense of humour that caused him to laugh incredibly ever since they saw each other; it seemed he had fallen in love with her; he thought of her always. And yet, at first sight, she was the kind of woman a man would look at twice. She needed a man; there was no doubt of that. He wondered for a moment whether she might be what people called a teaser, but when love takes control, you lose your sense of thinking; he dismissed the idea of her being a teaser. Salimatu needed someone to smarten her up and give her courage and determination, Abdul needed a woman to keep him company and to love him and yet, he never made a move. Although he had loved women in the past, and he has never felt the way he thinks about Salimatu. Nevertheless, she was of pure African beauty that should be taken care, Salimatu was made for Abdul, but it took a month for him to realise that.

Meanwhile, he was reluctant and thought that she was too beautiful for him to have. Although his friends had told him to go and declare his love for her; Abdul did not know how to start teasing her, as he was a failed asylum seeker, unemployed, and homeless. Nevertheless, Abdul took the courage and went to meet her to tell stupidly that he liked her. Still, soon she approached him for the first time after they had met a month ago, his courage flew away without talking to each other.

She understood that Abdul wanted to say something important to her, so she helped him pronounced it. Then Abdul took the opportunity to say that he loved her more than anything and that it was not just an attraction but an admiration; he then made her understand his feelings. They stared at each other for a while without saying anything. Then he took her in his arms and kissed on the cheek, a moment full of emotion and feelings. That night, they talked about everything, and little by little, they became very close. She was looking for an honest and sincere man, and Abdul was looking for a faithful, friendly, and respectful woman. They found that they both had led a strange life, the same stories and similarities in the past. As a result, both decided to try to live together fearlessly, trustworthy, and total self-confidence. It was love at first sight for him; she was the woman he has been waiting for a long time.

'We all had and lived a similar life in the past: laughing, seeking asylum, misery, a moment of glory, painful journey, and lately the separation from our ex-partners, all that within two years,' he said.

It was a marvellous moment, full of tenderness and emotions; a strange destiny had brought them together in a moment of distress with the same journey of life. An incredible destiny, after all the misfortunes they had experienced in the past. Finally, his happy moment had arrived to spend with his love, the true love, the one that came from his heart.

Abdul was able to meet a soulmate with whom to share his life. He knew what he wanted since his asylum was closed pending an investigation, and his willingness to stay with Salimatu would increase his chances of success on his asylum application.

Salimatu whispered to Abdul that she wanted to have a child since her asylum application has not been decided yet, so it was time to get pregnant.

'We are going to get out of this ordeal situation. Once I am pregnant, the government would have no choice but to give me the residence permit. Therefore, you shall get yours through me too,' she said.

A proposal that would not see the day as Abdul had other ideas in mind and murmured. *Getting pregnant is an excellent strategy to survive in this time of dilemma and confusion. But I am not ready to have children in this country as I have been denied my asylum claim. I would not be able to support the baby while waiting for the Home Office to grant Salimatu's asylum claim.*

Abdul thought carefully before deciding as if her strategy did not work in their favour and her asylum claimed was refused. Abdul had to support her and the baby financially at a time when he could not afford to do so.

'We will think about this pregnancy a little later,' he told her.

According to Abdul, having a child would only benefit Salimatu and not him because his asylum situation was suspended and remained in the hand of the Home Office.

The following day, Abdul was heading to the Refugee Action Office, he received a call from his lawyer asking him to go to their office to finalise the paperwork of his appeal against the Home Office decision to refuse him asylum. The next day, he went to meet his lawyer and presented the evidence to validate the credibility of his appeal. Shortly after he handed the evidence, he resumed his way back. As he returned with the hope of success on his appeal, he was annihilated by an arbitrary and human clumsiness. After a simple identity check at London Station, he was arrested by the United Kingdom Border Agency. He was then transferred to Harmondsworth Detention Centre at London Heathrow Airport, where he was cluttered with four people in a room which meant to be for two in a dirty, rundown room. His dormitory was infected with cockroaches and insects; he used an unhygienic toilet and shower in an overcrowded area. Abdul stayed for more than six months in a centre designed for only the shortest possible stays, in which he had developed severe psychological consequences. Despite the proven impossibility of expelling him from the United Kingdom to his country, the Home Office did not obtain the document called 'Laissez-Passer' allowing Abdul to be deported legally out of the country because there was not an agreement signed between the United Kingdom and his country, Guinea.

During his lengthy and ruthless incarceration, Abdul succumbed to the nervous breakdown, completely lost his mind, and desperately tried to end his life in the room he occupied. After several attempts by the British authority to obtain a laissez-passer from the consular representative of his country, who could only issue this valuable document to re-admit Abdul to his country. If his nationality was officially established, his status as an irregular resident proved, and Abdul did not appeal for regularisation. He was later released at the end of his seventh month by order of the court and following his lawyer's persistent warnings about the grave psychological damage caused by his imprisonment.

Abdul felt confused and hopeless after leaving the abusive detention and the mental anguish behind him, he finally saw the light of day. Still, his freedom had not gone unnoticed because everything had changed for him. He was disoriented and did not know what to do in his life.

He was wary of others, especially the organisations founded to help people like him to find his way to rebuild a new life. The person who was supposed to guide Abdul approached and handed him a paper containing contacts of various charities and humanitarian aids. Through him, Abdul found himself by mistake in Newcastle, unable to return to Manchester, where his friends and his girlfriend Salimatu lived. He had no phone, no contact number to call and no money to buy food. With nowhere to go, he slept in building entrances all over the place, frequented the toilets for brushing his teeth, and spent the whole day walking between kebab restaurants in search of food thrown in the trash.

I am doing a dog's life; I feel rejected, humiliated in the street, he murmured.

All doors were closed to him in Newcastle. After a few weeks of hardship, he realised that he needed to find a way to leave the city, so he started looking for organisations to help him get to Manchester. He was welcomed by a charity that had hosted and fed him for three weeks, during which he recovered physically and mentally. They gave him clothes, shoes, and transport to join his community in Manchester.

During Abdul's absence, Salimatu's asylum claim and appeal were denied, NASS support suspended, she had to leave the country within three weeks but decided to stay in the country without any means of subsistence. She was unable to return home because her country of origin was considered very dangerous. Therefore, she chose to disappear than stay in the house provided by NASS (National Asylum Support Service) to avoid being arrested and then expelled to her own country. She had no choice but to resort to prostitution to survive by building relationships with men, only to have food to eat and shelter to protect herself. Shortly after, Salimatu became pregnant; the father of the unborn child was unknown. She found herself again in the street in extremely unsafe conditions. She began sleeping for a month at Manchester station before being rescued by a Good Samaritan who took her to a charity organisation that helped and provided her with the needs she wanted and made a fresh claim for her asylum. After her nine-month pregnancy, Salimatu gave birth to a baby girl and named the baby after her mother.

After a long night and distressful journey, Abdul arrived early in the morning at Manchester Station. He immediately went to Salimatu's house and found out that she was no longer lived there; another asylum seeker now occupied her room. Abdul left and went to downtown to spend time meeting one of his acquaintances. Suddenly, he saw from a distance his friend Celestin, who had recently been granted remain to live in the

United Kingdom after he had spent ten years waiting for a decision to be allowed to stay in the country. And finally, he got this precious document called indefinite leave to remain. He was comfortably seated around a table at Cafe Nero, in the heart of Piccadilly, with few of his asylum seekers friends celebrating their joy.

'Welcome, my dear Abdul, we missed you a lot, sit down, please,' said Celestin enthusiastically.

Abdul took his place and was introduced to the group. Celestin got up and went to buy him a cup of tea.

'Raise all the glasses to congratulate our friend who just got indefinite leave to remain in the United Kingdom,' said Omar.

At the end of the celebration, Celestin asked Abdul where he had been hiding all this time, leaving the town without telling anyone and even his girlfriend Salimatu. Abdul's face darkened, a constant panic, his eyes jiggled in all the directions. The place where he was sitting seemed small to him, Celestin continued to ask him questions, Abdul tried to answer, but he had a very little memory to describe what had happened to him. Each time, he remembered his period of incarceration to his release caused him a whirlwind in his head.

He thought more about the mental torture he had experienced when in detention and did not remember what he had done before his arrest. Suddenly, he unpacked everything in an anarchistic way; memories sprang up without warning and recounted his inhumane treatment inflicted by prison officers when he was detained at the Harmondsworth Detention Centre at London Heathrow Airport.

After he had finished talking about his ill-treatment, all his interlocutors began to whisper with fear and emotion. They were all astonished to hear about this injustice against an asylum seeker in a country where the fundamental human rights and freedoms seemed to be well respected and protected by law. So, they came together, hand in hand to support him. Others made themselves available to help him find a new lawyer and re-launched a new asylum application and took care to accommodate him until his situation was resolved.

The news of his detention and his release spread in the city like a bush fire. All asylum-seekers began to be wary of the local population and the police. The next day, Arnaud visited Abdul and gave him his share of support.

'Since I learned that you were in detention, I stayed all night without sleep, even my wife was worried,' said Arnaud, wiping his tears. Then he continued. 'I did not know at all you were arrested, but God does not sleep, these people treat us as if we were drug dealers or thugs. In fact, our presence in Europe is a burden of wood that weighs heavily on them, and they would do everything in their power to burn it so that it would be easy for them to get rid of us," said Arnaud.

'It is not our fault! We have fled hunger, war, oppression in our respective countries, supported by the colonial power, we are just victims of neo-colonialism,' added Abdul.

'Since I found myself outside the prison, I did not see Salimatu; it seemed to me that she is no longer lives in Manchester, something bad might had happened to her during my absence,' said Abdul.

'How did you know that?' asked Arnaud.

'When I arrived at the station, I went straight to see her, the person who occupied her room told me that she's no longer lived there,' Abdul replied.

'So, we have to find her,' said Arnaud.

'Of course, you know I still love her very much,' said Abdul.

'You know, my friend, the human heart is like a flower. When it runs out of the water, it will die, so we will do everything to reunite you again,' Arnaud reassured him.

Early in the morning, Abdul left to see his lawyer with additional information in support of his new asylum claim, he diverted his way and went to Omar's house to retrieve the pieces of evidence kept by his friend when he was incarcerated. Soon he had received the documents. He ran to his lawyer's office. On his way back, he saw from afar a young lady with a pram, he stood for a while and stared at her and then made his move. He hurried and went to see her.

'Excuse me, excuse me, Mrs! I would like to ask you a question, please?' he said with a trembling voice.

She heard a voice over her shoulder, then she stopped and turned her head back. Suddenly, their eyes fixed endlessly. Salimatu's beauty had remained unchanged, her beautiful face with tanned skin made her more radiant; her pretty cheeks emphasised her aquiline nose that pinches when Abdul called her the love of my life. Both looked at each other for a while without saying anything. Then Abdul held her hand and began to explain his incarceration. At that very moment, something strange was going to happen between the two that would change their future; they were so close after a very long absence of love and affection. It was a powerful moment full of emotion, tenderness, and feelings. They had already forgotten the world around them. They then decided to stay together forever because it was a strange destiny that reunited them again from thousands of miles away with the same journey of life.

'You left me on my own for a while. Then I got pregnant by accident and I had spent nine months of endurance during which you had disappeared when I needed you most,' she sobbed.

'Give me a minute. I shall explain what had happened to me please,' he asked while begging her to let him speak.

'Yes, go ahead. I'm listening,' said Salimatu.

Abdul saw that she still loved him. Otherwise, she would never give him a chance to talk to her. After explaining what had happened, she began to cry and begged for forgiveness for having accused him of all sorts of words. After the pleadings, Abdul decided to leave them at his friend Arnaud's house while finding a solution to their situations.

African solidarity has rarely found its place in Great Britain when it comes to supporting a member of their communities. Salimatu had lost her asylum claim and her social allowance. She had been abandoned without any support from her community. As a result, she had to sell her body for food, and that reminded Abdul of those women he met during his perilous journey to reach Europe. They sold their bodies to support themselves and their children whose fathers were unknown. They ended up in the hands of criminal smugglers who operated between the desert and the Mediterranean Sea, where they were eventually raped, then sold into slavery and to lawless and heartless employers who often exploited them rudely without any pay. There was nowhere to complain, prompting them to prostitute themselves in deplorable conditions.

Thus, Salimatu was not alone to experience this kind of life considered inhuman. Many other women had endured this endless debauchery that made them humiliated in the eyes of everyone because of the strengthened asylum policy set by Great Britain government, which aimed to target the asylum seekers. And that left Abdul and Salimatu with little hope of settling one day in the United Kingdom as they had suffered and continued to live in a similar situation.

'I came to Britain in 2002, and my dream was to live in a country that respects and values human rights,' Abdul said.

Since he had arrived in Britain and sought asylum, his dream has turned against his hope and left him nothing but disarray.

Abdul finally decided to take the matter in his hand and tried to find a job in the black market. An office cleaning company hired him as a housekeeper under the discreet complicity of a girl who also worked in the same company and covered him up so that no one could detect him. But the company went into recession, Abdul lost his job and began to look for another opportunity.

Three months of suffering and anxiety, Abdul received a letter from his lawyer telling him that he had to attend for his asylum appeal hearing in the immigration court. He felt happy and smiled for the first time since he had re-applied for asylum. On the day of the judgement, Abdul went with his lawyer; the immigration officer was not present at the hearing. The judge allowed ten minutes of waiting. After the immigration officer had failed to show up on time, the judge proceeded the hearing. Abdul overcame his fear and answered all the questions asked by the judge. When the judge's hearing was over, and the session was lifted, Abdul left the court of justice with a fourteen-day of waiting during which a decision would be taken to determine whether he has the right to asylum in the country.

A week passed, Abdul began counting the days and prepared to welcome whatever decision would be taken, as he was ready to return to his country. But since there was no repatriation agreement between his country and the United Kingdom to provide the Home Office with a laissez-passer to facilitate his deportation back into his country of origin. It would be tough for him to survive in precarious situations unless he found work in the black market to support himself. The days passed; Abdul was no longer sleeping; stress and anxiety were becoming an uncontrollable headache. He had almost lost his memory, walking into the house late at night like a sleepwalker. One day, early in the morning, Salimatu approached him to give her support in the event of an unfavourable decision from the judge, so that Abdul could avoid the risk of suicide because she had already experienced the same situation in the past. She knew how distressful it could be if he were refused asylum unless he had a strong faith.

Two days passed after the fourteen days deadline; no letter was sent by mail. Abdul called his lawyer, who confirmed not having received anything yet, but he reassured him that if however, he did not receive a response within a week, he would write to them asking why Abdul did not receive a decision.

The next day, Arnaud and his wife were going to town. They invited them to go together so that they could relax for a while because Abdul had spent more than two weeks without going out.

'Hurry up, Abdul, we are ready to go,' said Arnaud.

'We're coming,' replied Salimatu.

Tuc! Tuc! Tuc! 'Someone's knocking on the door!' shouted Salimatu.

Arnaud hastened to open the door and found the postman with his mails bag; he was holding one envelop in hand.

'Hello! Are you Abdul?' asked the postman.

'No,' said Arnaud.

'Abdul! Abdul! Abdul!' Arnaud called Abdul loudly.

Abdul rushed out of his room and came to the door. The postman asked him to identify himself and then signed for the letter. He turned his back; all eyes were fixed on him, then he went into his room and closed the door. After a few minutes, he cried out with joy and began to dance until the others joined him, and the party continued.

Abdul obtained his refugee status. His life has been transformed from the worst to the best. Unlike many asylum seekers when they are granted indefinite leave to remain in the country; they go straight to work regardless of training or qualification. But this was not the case for Abdul; he had challenges to overcome. He found a place to live, got married to Salimatu, and then adopted her daughter. After that, he decided to go back to school to learn new skills and gained experience. As a graduate from Gamal Abdel Nasser University in his country of origin, Guinea, Abdul's decision to pursue his master's degree encountered financial difficulties as he had to pay the tuition fees for his program.

Having no savings, he abandoned this pursuit and decided to go back to college and learn a Business Management that would serve him as a work tool in the future. He joined Manchester College, after two years of study; he obtained his first Certificate (HND Diploma) in Business Management that allowed him to apply for a place in any university. As a result, he applied to three universities, including Salford, Bolton, and Manchester Metropolitan Universities, where he received conditional acceptance letters based on their admission criteria.

Four months before the opening of the classes, he received another letter asking him to provide his primary and secondary school certificates, which was difficult for him to obtain, because Abdul had fled his country without any documents. Nevertheless, he sent the English level two certificates obtained from Oldham College.

He explained his situation to the student recruitment staff at Salford University. However, his conditional offer was denied even though he had obtained a Merit in his HND. Still, that was not enough for his admission. During his struggle to secure a place, he was offered admission and enrolled at London Metropolitan University through the entry clearance channel. A system put in place to give a chance to those who were not accepted into their first choice of university and may be accepted in other less demanding institutions.

His stay at the campus in London was marked by many financial difficulties that forced him to find a job in parallel with his studies. This enabled him to finish his studies and allowed him to visit his family living in Manchester and provided them with financial support.

After his brilliant studies, Abdul graduated in Business Administration (Hon), first class. Subsequently, he re-joined his family in Manchester and began looking for a job. The year 2007 was the beginning of the recession that had caused countless problems in households, no work, corporate bankruptcy, marital separations due to financial troubles, and unexpected displacements due to unemployment. Finding work was not up to everyone, and the immigrants were unlikely to find work, especially if you had no work experience.

The recruitment selection was based on the job seekers' sounding names, background, and accents. In some cases, and conversely during the telephone interview. If the name did not match to a familiar British name or the accent used are not convincing the employer regardless of how many certificates you got and how suitable you are for the post applied you would be rejected by bringing excuse such as:

'After long consideration, unfortunately, your job application for the position will not move forward due to more qualified candidates.' So, the individual would never get the job.

After exhausting his efforts to find work, Abdul eventually went to join his other unemployed friends. He registered at the jobcentre hoping to find work through services such as job-hunting programmes and external job vacancies. He claimed Jobseekers Allowance to support his family.

On Abdul's first official signing day, he left home earlier to be on time. He walked into the jobcentre with his friend Omar who had been receiving jobseeker allowance for more than six weeks and had failed to attend his two weeks signing day. And now he was on the verge of being sanction; they were both feeling suspicious of their surroundings and welfare policy, but optimistic they would, at the very least, find a supportive and compassionate environment. After being welcomed at the door by two security guards. They were ushered up to a vast open-plan room and seated next to each other. A work coach then went around the room and collected their work signing cards one-by-one. Abdul left Omar and went to check jobs advertised on the whiteboard, he came back with the name of few companies that were hiring and started filling in application forms. A minutes later, Omar's name was called to go to the desk No 3. Abdul slightly raised his head then saw Omar seated – he was in the middle of his work search review and was being interrogated. Two job coaches are standing over him, and one of them quizzed him about why he did not attend his two weeks signing day, Omar arms and legs began to tremble. Everyone could hear Omar desperately trying to explain his reasons for not attending the previous weeks. He stated that all his young children were really struggling with chickenpox. He also contracted a virus similar to the illness too. His work coach challenged him:

'Have you had chickenpox when you were a child, sir?'

'Yes,' Omar replied.

'You cannot have it again then sir! Unfortunately, we cannot accept that as a good reason.'

"I swear to God that I had the virus similar to chickenpox, and I was very ill!' said Omar.

'I think you mean shingles sir' said the work coach.

'Did you see a doctor?' asked the work coach.

'No.' Omar replied.

'Why you did not see your GP?' asked the work coach.

'I was so ill to the extent that I could not walk by myself,' answered Omar.

'Unfortunately, we can't accept that as a good reason, sir, we are going to have to sanction you,' said the work coach.

The work coach then shouted Omar's confidential details – name and full address – across the room to a colleague in the full view of those present in the open-plan room – his life became an open book from which his eligibility to welfare was determined. Abdul was furious as he thought and believed that local job centres functioned as a supportive and protective public office, but not to humiliate, shame and punish jobseekers.

In front of his very eyes, welfare was being administered in a degrading and humiliating way. Abdul saw unsympathetic and disbelieving work coaches' shaming Omar by questioning his credibility and subjecting him to unnecessarily public scrutiny.

Shortly after Omar was sanctioned and escorted outside the building, Abdul was called to attend the desk No 1. His work coach introduced himself and said. 'My name is Anna Gibson. I am your work coach and will help you find a job. Do you have a CV and work experience?'

'I am a recent graduate and unemployed without work experience, but I have an up to date CV. I really need a job to feed my family, that's the reason why I have claimed Jobseekers Allowance to pay our bills,' replied Abdul.

During their interaction, his jobcentre work coach gave him a company recruitment contact that was hiring workers. Abdul took the phone and called; he spoke to the receptionist who asked him for his details. While on the phone, she made it clear that the job advert gives 'native English speaker' as a requirement, but Abdul was bilingual and met all the other requirements, then she hangs off the phone. A few minutes later, he called back the same number, she kept hanging off the phone again and again, and she continued repeating the same thing over and over knowing that in the event of an interview, Abdul would be rejected as a non-native English speaker. Meanwhile, Abdul went back to see his work coach and explained what had happened to him. She was shocked because, for her, what Abdul said was unfounded, and the prejudice did not exist in the recruitment system in the country, therefore, hard to believe him. Abdul was not the only person to whom she had helped to find work; she gave the same recruitment company number to another job seeker who was native so that she could verify Abdul's allegation. To her surprise, the native with similar skills and experience was offered an interview and hired instead. Then, she realised that the selection was based on the colour of the skin and not on the qualification.

The work coach felt humiliated. Abdul frustrated, left the centre in a state of discontent and went home. While on his way, he realised that the minority, especially blacks with a university degree, are twice as likely to be unemployed as all other graduates. And job applicants with white-sounding names get called back more of the time than applicants with black-sounding names, even when they have identical resumes. Regardless of the prejudice, Abdul was still determined to find a job to support his family. The next day, he continued the same routine, although the work was rare to be found but hoped one day, he would be fortunate to find a job.

Abdul was not alone to be in this situation, so many other people lived in a worse condition than him. They all thought that once their immigration cases were settled and their degrees in their hands, then they would have a better future without thinking that only a few of them would succeed in having a better life after their graduation.

Abdul had never been disappointed by his host country like now since he was no longer an illegal immigrant in the country. His naturalisation to become a British Citizen could change his life if there were equal opportunities created for all and treated at the same level as the natives. Still, that was not happening.

Abdul's main goals in life were to have a job and take care of his family without being discriminated against his will, but God knows the best. As a result, Abdul found himself in disarray. Despair or marginalisation, total confusion, and said. 'God, what did I do to deserve this?' He had no chance to get what he wanted, so he continued to apply for a job without success. After having experienced so many disappointments in England, Abdul decided to leave behind his hope of a European dream that he had been vainly pursuing for ten years since he had fled persecution in his country and arrived on the continent. And now he wants to go back to his country of origin.

Return to Homeland

Ten years was a long time to be away from one's country. Abdul's wasted times and weary years of chasing up his dream were, at last, dragging him close to his motherland. Although he had a wife and stepdaughter in Britain, Abdul knew that he would have a lot of children back home if he was not in danger and had fled for his life as a result of his involvement in politics. In those ten years, he would have succeeded in every step of his life as he was graduated in one of the most prestigious universities in the country. And so, regretted every day of his exile. He met lots of good people in Britain who had been very kind to him, and he was grateful, but that did not alter his social living conditions and the fact that he wanted to go back home empty-handed. Abdul had lived ten years in European territory. He did not have money to send to his Uncle Bobo to build him a house where he would live, but he had what many people did not know to have: 'wisdom and knowledge of life.' He had discovered the 'Eldorado' that they dreamed a long time ago did not exist in Europe, and the word was made up and only used to embellish the image of western life. Thus, his decision to return to his country of origin would contribute to its development. He would also explain to the younger generation of what he went through during his journey to Europe. And what he had experienced when on exile in the continent. He would encourage them to be resourceful and confident about their ability to challenge the dictatorial regime that was hurting the country economically for many years. And that had left many of them to flee massively for a better life in Europe at any cost hoping that would lead them into the hive of the bees.

The time has come for young Africans to stand up together and make Africa a united and prosperous continent. Investing massively in education and leadership development to eradicate the poverty and dictatorship that drives them, whatever the cost of their lives, desperately leaving their countries to pursue and realise their dreams in Europe, which often resulted in disastrous consequences and loss of lives.

Every month, hundreds of young Africans took enormous risks and put their lives in danger. Some of them arrived disappointed, and others would never reach their destinations, they mostly died or captured by smugglers and sold in the slavery market during their dangerous journey, leaving their families in uncertainty.

Abdul was determined when he returned to his home country. He would act as an emissary to tell the entire population that if they chose the illegal method to enter Europe, then they would suffer an unexpected ordeal and would also meet criminal smugglers in search of vulnerable illegal immigrants. They would be sold to heartless employers, whom in turn, would exploit them without pay, prompting them to prostitute themselves in deplorable conditions. They need to know that achieving a dream and having a happy life is in the hands of those who have shown great courage and resilience to defend themselves from losing hope to overcome challenges while preserving their culture, their dignity and the value of their lives.

On Thursday morning, Abdul missed two crucial calls as he slept soundly, leaving his phone plugged into the dining room.

'If you cannot find a job at least, you can sleep to rid of stress,' he said, scratching the head.

'Abdul! Abdul! Wake up; it is eleven o'clock in the morning. All your friends are awake, and you're still in bed!' shouted Salimatu.

'Don't shout at me, honey, even if I get up early, what would I do?' he replied with a smile.

'I'm sick of your way of seeing things. Here's Europe, no one had invited you to come, if you're already here, you must get up and do like many others, which means you must go out empty-handed and come back with food in hand. I do not care where you will get it from, but you have to come back with something in your hand,' said Salimatu.

He stood up abruptly and went straight to where he had left his phone, which was still plugged into the socket on the wall. He switched on his cell phone and was alerted by beeps sound with messages and voice mail. He pressed the 'OK' button; he found two missed calls, and echoes crossed his mind.

Who could call me at this early hour in the morning without leaving a message instead of voicemail, maybe a friend who needs my service? Or probably someone who wanted to talk to me? He murmured.

He decided to call back the number. After several unsuccessful attempts, his credit ran out. Then he used Salimatu's phone to call back, this time, the receptionist of an employment agency answered the call and informed him that he had been shortlisted for an interview with the company manager. He lost his voice and swallowed his saliva, then shook his head. He had not given too much consideration to the shortlisting because, for him, it was merely an additional means of deception, as he had experienced the recruitment process in the past. Shortly after that call, he went to find Salimatu and explained the content of their conversation. She encouraged him to attend the interview and reassured him that he was going to get the job.

'I know you're a confident and thoughtful man, you sometimes take things the wrong way, and that's not good, try to think positive as this job is definitely yours. You can rest assured that you are going to get an offer,' she said with a smile.

In the evening, Abdul received a surprise visit from his friend Arnaud, informing him that he had negotiated a vacant position at his workplace and that he had sent all his information to the recruiting office in his company. They promised him that they would call him shortly for an interview, Abdul nodded his head and informed him that he had effectively received a call and had secured an interview and thanked him for his efforts to help him find a job.

'Actually, my friend, I had received a call from a receptionist in the morning. I even got an interview appointment with the boss tomorrow at ten o'clock in the morning,' Abdul confirmed.

'I was about to call you tonight to keep you informed of the news. Salimatu and I had agreed to try my luck again,' he added.

'This was the reason for our visit tonight. Also, make sure that you had received the call from the recruiting agent and to support you. I know it's difficult for you right now but have these ten pounds for tomorrow's interview transport and get ready for the interview!' Arnaud brought him support. Abdul was filled with joy for his friend's help and all his advice and motivation; he thanked Almighty God for being surrounded by good Samaritans. Abdul rushed and went into the bed to get up early in the morning but remained awake all along that night. He was more worried about what would happen during his interview day and if he was selected for the job, how could he reorganise his life and that of his family.

The next day, Abdul went to the interview. After an hour and a half of the interview, he passed his assessment. Abdul returned home with a smiling, almost happy face. He had a renewable six-month contract, which was better than nothing. But he wanted a permanent contract so that he could benefit all the rights a permanent worker could get, such as a right to twenty-five days of holiday, entitlement to a pension, right to paternity leave, and sickness.

He worked in the company and respected all the conditions imposed by his managers. He worked tirelessly and endlessly to earn the trust of his colleagues. In the space of five months, Abdul had increased the hierarchy, and this was frowned upon by some of the employees he had found in the company and sparked a controversy over his success around the offices. A black man and an immigrant taking a tireless pace in a company until reaching the leadership position had left his peers speechless and upset.

His colleagues began to distance themselves and developed a circle of enemies around him. They uttered slanders against him and started calling him with all sorts of names in the canteen, in the corridors, and the company's car park. Seeing all this hatred against him, Abdul felt uncomfortable but tried not to think about it, because for him, only hard work would demonstrate the intrinsic value of a good worker. If he did not work well, he would neither be appreciated nor promoted. The racial slur mounted as the crisis continued within the growing number of his enemies in the company. He used his technocratic skill to play them false and left a blank on their face. He made them believe that their path was clear to discourage him from working hard.

As a last resort, Abdul launched a complaint to the general manager and took his case to an employment tribunal after being racially abused by two colleagues. In the run-up to the hearing, many more of his colleagues stop talking to Abdul and his line manager puts him on probation.

After five months of working for the company, Abdul was summoned to the office by his manager for review and feedback and to discuss the termination of his contract at the end of the month, which did not surprise him at all, as he was expecting it anyway, and also, he wanted to leave.

'What I liked about you is your determination, your courage, and your honesty. You gave your heart and soul to help this company moving forward. So, on behalf of the company, I thank you very much,' said the manager. A minute of silence, then he continued.

'At the end of your contract, the company will give you a month's free salary as a goodwill gesture,' said the manager.

Abdul was pleased with his manager's compliment, even though his manager had an idea in his mind but had not shown it to him. He was very grateful for the chances he had given to him, and the bonus of a month's free salary was a blessing.

After the meeting, Abdul returned home very tired; he met Salimatu in their daughter's room, then whispered in her ear to follow him to the living-room.

'Honey, I want to inform you that my contract would end after this month and that I will have no chance of renewing it. I had a meeting with my manager, who notified it to me,' he said.

Two weeks passed, Salimatu began to distance herself from Abdul. Since she knew he would be unemployed soon, she changed her commitment to their marriage. She left home when she wanted and returned late at night. She also repeatedly ignored the safety of their daughter.

Each time when she found that Abdul was about to ask her for intimacy, she always made excuses to avoid him. The worst of it was when they went to visit one of their sick friends in the hospital. On the way, she complained of a stomach-ache. Abdul decided to take her to a clinic for consultation before continuing to the hospital.

'I suggest that we see a general practitioner at the clinic for a consultation,' said Abdul.

'No. It's okay. I would be fine; it's just my period pain,' replied Salimatu.

Abdul understood that this was the pain caused by her period menstruation and suggested that she could return home to prepare herself accordingly.

'Do you have your hygienic cotton on you?' he asked.

'No! I did not expect it to happen today. Normally, it should come two or three days later,' she said.

'Anyway, I am going home, and you can continue to the hospital and pass my regards to your friend,' she said.

Abdul continued his way to the hospital, and Salimatu turned her back and went on her way. After twenty minutes of the journey, Abdul arrived at the hospital then entered quickly, he met with his friend and had few conversations, he spent ten minutes at the patient's bedside. He then resumed his way back home.

When he arrived, he discovered that Salimatu had not come home yet. He tried to reach her on her mobile phone once, twice and three times, she refused to answer the calls. With increasing anxiety, he decided to go and get their daughter, whom they had left at their neighbour's house until they returned from the hospital. He came home with her, and Salimatu still had not arrived yet. He tried to call her again, no answer, their daughter began crying and asked for her mother. Abdul's heart was filled with fear and discontentment and could not cope anymore. Then he decided to call the hospitals for inquiry if anything serious had happened to her. After checking, she was not among the patients admitted to the hospitals that day; then, he contacted the police to inform them of her disappearance. After an hour and a half, Salimatu came back furious and banged on the door then waited for Abdul to come to the door. When he opened the door; she hit him with a hard object on his head. Abdul lost his balance and fell unconsciously on the floor. She continued beating him and threatened to kill him like she was possessed despite the crying of her daughter and repeatedly asking her to stop abusing Abdul because he had informed the police of her disappearance. A few minutes later, Abdul regained consciousness and realised the damage she had done to him. But instead, he tried to calm her anger down, fearing that he might aggravate an already bad situation.

The relationship continued to deteriorate between the couple. To save their marriage, Abdul refused to recognise that

Salimatu was having an affair with someone outside his circle of friends. Instead, he tried to find a compromise to live together for the sake of their daughter.

Since then, Salimatu was no longer in love with Abdul; the reasons for their leaving together had faded from her memory. She repeatedly asked him to leave the house and find elsewhere to live.

'Do you really want me to leave the house?' asked Abdul.

'Of course, I want you, Abdul, to leave right now!' she replied proudly.

Abdul had nothing to be ashamed of but preserving his dignity, so he decided to leave the house thinking that one day, when the time would be right, then they would get back together again for the sake of their daughter.

He thought genuinely and wondered how it had happened and why it occurred to him. He did not doubt that his love for Salimatu no longer existed, as he had once believed to hold the key to her passion, the understanding of her feelings, the ability to comprehend, not only her words but also her unspoken gestures. He was always there to forgive her unreasonable behaviour and accepted her mistakes and all the indecent assaults she committed against him.

He loved her unconditionally and shared happy and unhappy moments; he tried to overcome their problems and find a solution. He fought for their happiness, but that happiness was far from being reached.

Abdul's life had become more difficult and complicated since he had separated with Salimatu; he seemed to be lost in the void and did not know what to do. Salimatu had banned him from approaching his stepdaughter, whom he adored very much. He often used his friends to get information about her. After several attempts to reconcile them through his community and friends, Salimatu had always refused to participate and had maintained her position of not wanting to reunite with Abdul. And if by chance, he approached them, she would not hesitate to call the police against him and said. 'living in poverty, she did not want to get involved in that situation anymore.' She had made her decision, and she did no longer want him in her life. The social allowance was going well in her favour as a single mother, and she would rely on that benefit to survive. She whispered the famous English slogan. 'Time is money.' So, she had nothing to lose but to win because her daughter was her source of income, her treasure. As she thought, having a child was a capital gain for those who decided to live alone to satisfy their desire while ignoring the feelings of their children's helpless father to see their kids.

Salimatu knew that if she lived alone with her daughter, her social allowance would double, and that would be added to the amount of child support that Abdul would have to pay each month. Given these advantages, it would not be necessary to live with a man who could not give her a penny. At the same time, the benefits system was put in place to support an unemployed single mother. She then took advantage of the welfare system set up by the government, endorsed by the law which protected her and forced Abdul to pay her daughter's maintenance without, however, establishing a system that could facilitate him to see his daughter without paying the court and lawyer's fees to access to the child.

Salimatu closed their marriage chapter and embarked on a new relationship with a man called Herman who was involved in all sorts of business, she assumed her responsibility and helped him find customers and all the money obtained was kept by Salimatu. At the end of each sale, they shared the interest.

In Salimatu's life, what mattered was to get rich quicker to relieve the hardship her parents experienced in their daily lives in Africa. So, nothing would prevent her from making money and at any cost. In the afternoon, Abdul was heading to his friend's house. He saw a heavily pregnant Salimatu coming towards him. Their eyes fixed for a while; then she turned her gaze away, pretending not to see him and looked down. However, Abdul, armed with courage and approached her.

'Hello, beauty!' he bowed.

'Hello!' she answered bitterly.

Without letting Abdul continue talking, she began to blame him for their relationship break-up. Abdul lowered his head and pointed his eyes on her belly and asked the question.

'Since when did you get pregnant?'

'Don't you know I live with a man in my house?' she replied.

'I know that, and how is our daughter?' he asked.

'Oh, I left her with her father!' she said.

She concluded from Abdul's voice that he was vexed and disappointed with her and ended their conversation. She thought that she had destroyed his mood and forgotten that Abdul may be unhappy about her actions but not beaten. When she arrived home, her hands filled with gifts that she had bought for her lover's birthday occasion. She found her daughter sitting on the floor crying on her own, the house was half emptied and a note saying that:

'Sorry Salimatu, Herman is no longer living in this house.'

She checked her room and found out that her man, with whom she boasted of living, had stolen everything she had saved and left a little girl in danger at home. Astonished, she stood for a while. Suddenly, terrible anguish struck her heart. She felt a dreadful ache as if something was being torn inside her and she was dying. She began screaming loudly then, collapsed to the floor. The neighbours heard her voice then ran to her rescue. They found her unconscious as a distorted corpse. Salimatu was taken to the hospital to make sure that the unborn baby was not in danger. After two days of recovering in the hospital, she returned home and left the rest to the police to continue their investigation.

She slept very little that night. The bitterness in her heart was now mixed with regret, as she laid on her bed next to her daughter, she thought about the abuse she had inflicted on Abdul and felt sorry about it. Her regret made her unease and decided to meet Arnaud the next day and explained her sorrows. Still, Arnaud and the rest of his community were already becoming highly critical of such a woman who betrayed her husband, and they were not unduly perturbed when they found her lover had robbed her.

The following day of the investigation, the police contacted Abdul and questioned him about the robbery that took place in Salimatu's house. Unaware of the situation, he denied any involvement. At that moment, he realised the danger that their daughter was involved in and the risk that Salimatu had taken to get rich quickly. After the interrogation with the police, Abdul returned home exhausted by thought, emotion, and anger, he went to bed and drifted into sleep.

Abdul could not bear the life he was leading, and all the bitterness he had encountered on his way, he was abandoned without a family. He felt a deep sense of loneliness and nostalgia but was trying not to worry as time did not allow him to handle the problems correctly; and to what he had experienced in the past with Salimatu. Suddenly, Abdul felt dominated by the freshness of nature and sunk into the waves of nostalgia. His thoughts turned to his country, to the gruelling journey in the desert, to his poverty-stricken family and the poor friends he had met on his quest to find a better life in Europe. He had never forgotten his friend Paul, who, carelessly, waited at the end of classes to meet and walked around the university campus of Gamal Abdel Nasser in Conakry. He remembered back in days when they played innocence, and yet, he was in love with his female classmate, and Paul had his girlfriend at Donka High School, where they visited every afternoon before going home. He dared to declare his love for fear of being rejected by his classmate but claimed her with all his seriousness, and each of them knew the beloved of others. They had a brilliant childhood dream, both dreamed of becoming president and prime minister after their studies. They thought only about a better future for their country and its people and that men and women were making their country so proud to such an extent that the whole world had to bow.

For the two young dreamers, Guinea was the most beautiful and the best in the world. Suddenly, everything changed for them, and each one had taken the path of his destiny. Paul found himself indignant in France, and Abdul faced with the most precarious situation offered by his daily life, unbearable psychological torture that left him nothing but struggles to survive. He remembered the good time spent in his village sitting under the giant trees next to his father during an appointment ceremony. The griots of the village sang and played with their guitar, the most beautiful melody that rejuvenated them with joy.

After deepening his thoughts, he came back to himself and saw clearly the difference in lifestyle between his beautiful country and the western world. He concluded that a man could not be happy in exile as he does in his home country.

Abdul was still young; he could go back to his country and start a new life again and succeed in realising his dreams. However, the young generations in his country still living in precarious situations with no hope; they had been abandoned to grow in poverty by all the dictatorial regimes that had succeeded in power since his country had gained its independence. He was tired of seeing his country's socio-political and economic situation deteriorating and had not improved ever since. Moreover, these factors were the fundamental cause that drove the wave of young people to take their destiny into their hands.

Abdul had seen and experienced the gruelling journey with less hope and tremendous courage that many people desperate to realise their dream had attempted at all costs to reach the European continent. Others used the makeshift boats to risk their lives and drowned in their death-defying journey as they tried to make their way into European shores, despite the ongoing human tragedy. It always surprised him when the African leaders turned their blind eyes on the loss of lives of these young future leaders of their countries made him sink under a load of despair. He thought about it and said:

'If all the actions were taken and the resources made available to the youths, many lives would be saved and if these youths were also capable of taking great risks in finding their happiness and a better life elsewhere. We should ask ourselves why they would not give themselves to death to demand the socio-political and economic change that could guarantee them the security and a better life in their respective countries. That will demonstrate an effect less risky than being courageous to confront the Mediterranean Sea, the criminal smugglers, and the border guards in the destination countries to die or send back where they come from. The lucky ones will find themselves in the detention centres or wander in the streets without qualification where they could not read or write in the countries in which they will land.'

In 2009, Guinea was in the transition period. The country had emerged from dictatorship imposed by the military junta, and a transparent election was expected to take place for the first time after fifty-one years of independence.

The population was still living in poverty; the country needed good governance to revive the stability policy and reformed its economy for the well-being of its people and fought corruption, building and developing schools, and health infrastructures. Create jobs for youth and exploiting natural resources to contribute to the socio-political, economic growth, and development of the country.

On Sunday evening, at the community centre, where all refugees and asylum seekers gather to brings a stronger sense of connection within the community, Abdul announced his intention to return to his homeland to serve as an example and to contribute his part for the development of his native country Guinea.

'We belong to our country when things are good, and life is sweet. But when there is a famine, oppression, atrocities committed and bad governance, we will seek refuge in a country where we can find safety and protection, and that does not mean we are condemned for life in exile. When the time is right, we had to return and face the challenges as the country needs us. We had run away from our country, despite the gruelling journey to make it into Europe. We can use the same courage to face our destiny and become optimistic that one day, we will make changes to our beloved country.'

An emotional message that touched the hearts of everyone present at the meeting, after he had spent ten years in misery, without respect and human dignity. It was time to turn his back on the past and looking to the future. He thought that he could not get a better future in England but in his home country, because Guinea could not be developed without its own people and that it was the right time for them to begin preparing for their bright future. Besides, going back to his country was also a proud recovery. He then said:

'I cannot get what I want in this country and achieve my dream here as I do in my country, regardless of my social rank at least, I would have a decent place in society without prejudice.'

According to the media, his country had just embraced the path of democracy, and the fruits of this democracy would soon start to fill the baskets of the starving population.

The emotion reigned for a few hours amongst his community members. At the end of the meeting, they decided to organise a farewell party for Abdul at his friend Arnaud's house.

On the day of the party, heavy rains were pouring down incessantly. Gradually, the rains became lighter and less frequent. Abdul ran out of the house and went to make a surprise visit to Salimatu and his daughter for the very last time. He bought a bunch of flowers and a packet of chocolate for his daughter. After a short conversation with them, he slipped away from the place and headed to the party. The community anxiously waited for him; after a few minutes had passed, the concerns began to grow among the guests. Suddenly, Abdul appeared in front of the door; a handclap resounded in the room, and then silence descended from the roof and swallowed the noise. The gathering of his community and warmth reception they offered him was a very touching and unforgettable moment that would remain in Abdul's head for many years to come.

'My brothers and sisters, this moment of joy will be engraved in my heart forever. I am more than happy to see you all gathered in this room to support me in my decision and my conscience to return home. There are no words I can express my gratitude to you, and I do not know how to thank you all,' he said sobbing.

'We had left our country in search of a better life, and if we cannot find it, then we should go back to Guinea where we belong with dignity, at least, that's our country,' he paused for a moment then continued.

'We have nothing to lose but winning because many of us have studied with a degree that will be useful as a tool for the development of our dear nation,' he paused then continued.

'Anyone can say that he works to make himself happy, but nobody can say that we, immigrants present in these great western countries such as Great Britain, will benefit a general privilege over natives in this country,' he added.

During his speech, Abdul stood on one foot and rubbed his cheek on the left side. He stared at the ground. He said that his decision to return to his country would bring significant value to the working capital because his native Guinea needs more qualified employees like him. He had benefited from high academic qualification and experiences that could contribute to the development of his country and said: 'By examining the global industrialisation in the developed countries, Guinea is in a phase of economic growth that's increasingly complex and diversified. The country needs us, the skilled Guinean diaspora living all over the world, to bring our expertise and techniques to the smooth running of its industries, which would form the basis of Guinea's sustainable development.' He went and sat down.

The guests passed one after the other wishing him good luck and hailed his decision as to the best that had never been made by a Guinean immigrant living in Great Britain. Some congratulated him for having such a good idea that inspired them to follow his footsteps to join their family under the giant baobab trees of the old continent.

Index

B

Balafon
Name of Guinean musical instrument., 18, 33
Berber
A member of the indigenous people of North Africa, among whom are the nomadic Tuareg, 122
Bhōnoh
Name of hyena in Fulani, 15, 16
Boubou
A long flowing garment worn by men women, 14

C

cowrie
a marine mollusc which has a glossy, brightly patterned domed shell with a long, narrow opening, 13, 106

D

Dhuhr
Noon prayer, 25, 60, 79
Djembe
Name of Guinean musical instrument, 18
Djinn
An intelligent spirit of lower rank than the angels, able to appear in human and animal forms and can possess humans, 19, 20, 21
Dundunba
Name of Guinean traditional dance, 18
Name of Guinean traditional dance.. *See* Dundunba

F

Fajr
Dawn prayer, 25

Fetish priest

A person who serves as a mediator between the spirit and the living and worships their gods in enclosed places, called a fetish shrine, 13, 39

Flute

Name of Guinean musical instrument., 18, 33

Fonio

Are millets with small grains and has the appearance of shrunken couscous., 21

G

griots

An African tribal storyteller and musician, 14, 18, 22, 23, 24, 32, 33, 205

H

Harmattan

A cool dry and dusty wind that blows from the Sahara Desert over West Africa into the Gulf of Guinea, 18, 57

I

Imam

Person who leads prayers in a mosque, 22, 23, 154

K

Kalimba

Name of Guinean musical instrument., 18

Karamoko

Name of knowledgeable person, an avid learner and reader of Qur'an., 34

Kenkelibah

is a shrub species often found in tiger bush and on hills in West Africa. It is used traditionally for making tea and is believed to be an aid to weight loss and have detoxifying properties., 17

Kinkelibah

is a shrub species often found in tiger bush and on hills in West Africa. It is used traditionally for making tea and is believed to be an aid to weight loss and have detoxifying properties., 36

Kola

Tree bearing large brown nuts, 27, 28, 29, 32, 34, 105, 106

Kora

Name of Guinean musical instrument., 18

M

Madrassah

A school where people go to learn about the religion of Islam, 26

Makuru

Name of Guinean traditional dance, 18

Marabout

A Muslim religious leader and teacher in West Africa, 69, 70, 71, 92, 93, 102, 104, 106

Q

Qur'an

Islam holy book, 23, 34, 35, 40, 54, 56, 57, 61, 70, 104, 105

S

Salaam Alaykum

a greeting in Arabic that means "Peace be upon you, 27, 30, 31

Salam Alaykum

a greeting in Arabic that means "Peace be upon you", 105

Shekeret

Name of Guinean musical instrument., 18

T

Tambourine

Name of Guinean musical instrument, 33

Tuareg

A member of a nomadic Berber people of the Sahara living mainly in Algeria, Mali, Niger, and western Libya., 104, 105

Tumbucesse
Name of Guinean traditional dance, 18

W

Wa Alaykum
a greeting in Arabic that means "Peace be upon you, 30, 105
Waa Salaam
a greeting in Arabic that means "Peace be upon you", 105

Y

Yankady
Name of Guinean traditional dance, 18